# EYES UNVEILED

## UNVEILED SERIES
### BOOK ONE

## CRYSTAL WALTON

IMPACT EDITIONS LLC

Published by Impact Editions, LLC

This is a work of fiction. Names, characters, places, and incidents are a product of the author's imagination. Locales and public names are sometimes used for atmospheric purposes. Any resemblance to actual people, living or dead, or to businesses, companies, events, institutions, or locales is completely coincidental.

Cover Design © 2020 Blue Water Books

Author Photo by Charity Mack

Eyes Unveiled / Crystal Walton.

LCCN 2014921993 (pbk.) | ISBN 978-0-9862882-1-0 (pbk.) ISBN 978-0-9862882-0-3 (eBook)

❀ Created with Vellum

# PROLOGUE

TWO MONTHS. Riley could hold out for that long. He had to.

His heel scraped down the edge of their back deck as he brought his guitar to his chest. Breathing in, he begged the strings to outplay the memory of his latest fight with Dad.

Not tonight. The harder he played, the deeper the words jabbed until they shredded his hope of becoming a recording artist down to an unrecognizable dream.

Riley shoved his guitar aside and craned his neck to the sky. The back door squeaked open behind him. His youngest sister, Jasmine, plopped onto the deck with her strawberry-embroidered shorts pressed against his cargo ones.

He looked ahead to keep from smiling. One more second of a stare down with that pudgy face, and he would've caved.

Undaunted, she crossed her arms. "Why you and Dad always gotta fight?"

His brow creased. "Wish I had the answer to that, kiddo."

"Don't wish. *Do*."

Apparently, he wasn't the only dreamer in the family. He rustled the top of her hair. "Not everything's that easy."

Shadows streaked across the wood from the window above them. Probably Mom, cleaning an already-spotless kitchen. Staying busy was the only thing that seemed to keep her sane when Dad ran off to some bar for hours on end like this.

"Rose?" Dad's slurred voice pummeled through the walls. Something crashed onto the kitchen floor, followed by a string of swears. "What'd I say about leaving mugs on the edge of the counter like that?"

The tendons on Riley's neck throbbed. "Jazz, go to your tree house."

"But—"

"Now."

Once she cleared the top of the ladder, he scooted against the bricks beneath the window.

"Do you always have to do this, Jonathan?" Mom's weary tone struck Riley's gut with the painful reminder that he wasn't the only casualty in this war zone.

"Do what?" A kitchen chair scratched over the floor. "Give that boy music lessons? 'Cause I think someone 'round here should be thanking me for all I teach him."

"*That boy* is your only son. And he doesn't need a music teacher. He needs a father." Mom turned on the faucet. "A sober one."

"What he needs is someone to show him how the real world works." Dad grunted. "Boy's still a kid caught up in a fantasy, thinking a few local shows makes him big-time. If he'd give up his delusions, maybe he could actually get somewhere."

The guitar strings sawed into Riley's fingers.

"A college freshman hardly makes him a child. You had his same drive when you were his age. And you know he has the talent. If you could just support him—"

Dad slammed the table. "Dern it, Rose. Why do you always gotta nag?" His voice rumbled right in front of the sink. "You think you know best? Were you the one pitching to agents night and day, watching them devour your pride?" He flung a rag at the window. "Talent isn't enough."

*Riley* wasn't enough. The insinuation rung in every word.

Dad's ranting slurred into a harsh snicker. "Or maybe you just want a household full of disappointments. Is that it?"

"Jonathan, please." Mom's soft voice quavered.

Riley lunged to his feet. Dad could attack him if he wanted, but Mom didn't deserve his berating. He stormed through the back door, anger fueling adrenaline.

The glare straining to focus on him turned into a

cutting sneer. "Like I said. Just a clueless kid. All passion, no control." He stumbled forward, caught the back of the chair before he tripped, and nodded at the guitar. "Get ready, Rose. I think your son, here, is about to prove he's got what it takes." He waved his arm in a half-bow, prompting him to perform.

Riley released the guitar. "I'm done trying to prove myself."

Dad stayed bent over and shook his head. "Still haven't learned a thing I've taught you, have you?"

"That I'm a disappointment? Yeah, Dad. I got that loud and clear." Riley steered him to the dining room. "How about we call it a night before you add to your regrets."

"Regrets?" He shoved Riley and tottered into the counter. "Don't act like you know *a thing* about regrets. About my life."

Riley's jaw pulled taut. "*Our* life, Dad. The one you're ruining for our family."

A wobbled attempt at straightening brought him to eye level with Riley again. "You already ruined it in Nashville."

The jab caught Riley low in the gut. He'd tried for months to block out the mistake he'd made. Would he ever stop blaming him for having to move back home?

Chest heaving, Riley grabbed the bottom of his dad's shirt, seconds away from decking him.

Dad wheezed a Bourbon-scented laugh into his face. "Look at you. Can't even control your own emotions.

You think you'll last a day in the music industry? Take it from me, boy. They'll eat you alive."

Mom rushed forward with the dishrag balled in her fingers, tears streaming. "Please."

Riley let go. He wouldn't fight him. Not like this.

His middle sister inched around the doorway in her nightgown. "Mom?"

Riley's stare darted from her back to Dad. "Go to your room, Mel." The last thing she needed was to see another man in her life lose control. Nashville had scarred her enough.

Mom nodded. "Go on, now."

Scowling, Melody returned down the dark hallway.

Dad hunched against the wall with his hands on his knees. A soundless laugh shook his rib cage as he looked up at Mom. "Do you see this? The reckless boy, trying to be the parent." He slapped his leg and almost lost his balance.

Riley dug his fingers into his palms. "You're a lousy drunk." He strode for the back door and the cool air he needed before his blood hammered through his veins.

"And you're a lousy son," Dad yelled.

Riley stopped. A decade worth of words coiled around that single confession. His shoulders fell and trapped his voice under the wreckage. Pressing a hand to the door, he inhaled, then raised his chin. "There's an easy fix for that." Without turning, he yanked his guitar from the wall and jerked the door open. "I'm done being your son."

Outside, wind rushed off the river onto his over-heated skin. The night closed in on him. The crickets, the water lapping the shore, the creaks in the wood. Every noise raged louder than it should've—all joining the imprint of Dad's harsh words crashing against the music that never left his mind.

He wanted it to stop. All of it. Pulse pounding, Riley smashed the guitar against the edge of the deck. With broken shards of their shared dream strewn across the lawn, he waited for even the music to fade for good.

"Riley?" Jasmine poked her head out of her tree house at the same time Mom flung open the back door.

The ache in Mom's eyes bled into the fear in Jasmine's and propelled Riley off the deck—away from hurting anyone else.

He thrust his Civic into drive and didn't slow until he reached the woods. It was peaceful there. Safe. Parked by the lake, he trekked down the trail he'd come to for escape more times than he wanted to admit.

Shadows deepened. The canopy of leaves was supposed to block everything from reaching him, but the image of his smashed guitar pierced deeper into his side each time pine needles crunched under his feet.

His stride turned into a jog. He pushed harder. Through the underbrush and overgrown branches. Across the gully into a cave. But even there, he couldn't outrun himself. Hands on his thighs, he strained for breath and some measure of control.

"I can't keep doing this." He dropped to his knees and

clenched the back of his hair. "I'm done." Done with Dad. With music. He faced the dark heavens. "You hear me? I'm done." The cost of hope was too high.

A whispered breeze sang through the trees.

He'd never be able to explain what followed, but there was no denying the assurance ushering in with the wind. It reached inside to the unspoken place holding every dream he was terrified to believe in. And somehow, he knew.

Hope wasn't done with him yet.

## 1

# SUSPENDED

*THREE YEARS Later*

FIVE YEARS' worth of reminders filled my academic advisor's office with the weight of a promise I had to keep. I couldn't give up. Not now.

Mr. Oakly shot forward at his desk and scooted paper stacks aside until I had nothing left to hide behind. "Miss Matthews, what would you like to do with your life?"

A sliver of Oregon's skyline flickered through the blinds, just as out of reach as a suitable answer.

I stared at my Reed College tee and twisted the hair band around my wrist. "I don't know."

The tremor in my voice hung between us. Raw. Exposed.

Mr. Oakly tossed a crumpled piece of paper into his

wastebasket, where he evidently thought my confession belonged. "You're in your junior year of college, Miss Matthews. I would suggest now is the time to figure that out."

The guy's comb-over could outstretch his sensitivity any day of the week.

He had to know I was trying. I'd taken career assessment tests, changed majors three times. There was no map, no blueprint. And somewhere on that stark canvas, I was supposed to see where my life fit? It wasn't as easy as he made it sound.

I yanked the band from my arm and twisted my hair up into a half-bun-half-ponytail mess that sprang long strands down my neck seconds later.

Slumped back in his padded chair, Mr. Oakly took his time scrutinizing my latest degree plan—all five scratched-through pages of it. The bottom sheet rubbed against his bulging stomach every time he wheezed through his nose.

He drummed his fingertips over his keyboard. "Your grades are impressive," he finally said. "But we expect more from you the closer you near graduation. Especially if you want to keep such a prominent scholarship."

*More.* The word slithered down my spine into the sweat gluing my hamstrings to the chair. Was he waiting for a response? Because my mouth seemed to be functioning as well as my eyelids were. I'd worked my tail off to stay on the dean's list. There was nothing *more* to give.

I stretched my hair tie to its limit, forced it another

time around the tangled knot on my head, and kept my mouth clamped shut.

"Your father was one savvy businessman. He left quite the impression with his internship supervisor." He moved his keyboard back and leaned on his desk again. "Similar to the other Beasley recipients, he had a certain... prestige about him. Something I'm afraid you still seem to be lacking. And if you don't find it soon, you can count on forfeiting your scholarship to someone more qualified."

I gripped the armrests. Losing that scholarship would jeopardize all I'd fought for. "Please, I can't afford school without it. My dad—"

"Scholarships aren't based on heredity, Miss Matthews. Reward is about performance. Same as in the job market, you have to prove your merit." He straightened his bowtie while glancing at a shelf laden with plaques and photos of prize students. "Which is exactly why securing an internship and receiving a noteworthy performance review during your junior year is an eligibility requirement for the Beasley award."

As if I hadn't been stressed enough over that already.

Mr. Oakly shimmied his glasses onto his square face and shuffled through a handful of papers. "I'll make you a deal. I'll give you a list of possible internship placements to start with." He held a page in the air. "And you simply take your pick."

Simply? We weren't talking about some part-time job to get me through a summer. We were talking about my life, my identity—things I couldn't find on an arbitrary directory limited to the size of a loose-leaf sheet of paper.

I reined in a sigh the way I always did when my thoughts started down a rabbit hole that only led to disappointment. Now wasn't the time to start chasing Dad's ideals again. As much as I loved him for being a dreamer, there was no romanticizing the way life worked.

I tucked my dad's voice deep inside, rose, and reached for the list of prospects.

Mr. Oakly held on and stared over his thick-rimmed glasses. "You have until the end of the semester to submit your review for evaluation."

What were the chances one of his navy-blue suspenders would snap and slap that smirk off his face? I wanted to jerk the list from his hands, but my intended snatch ended with my arm drooping to my side.

"And Miss Matthews?" he called once I reached the door. "Keep in mind there are other candidates competing for those Beasley funds." His gaze slanted past me to the waiting area, where a petite Asian girl peeked up from a binder pressed to her stomach.

I recognized her from my accounting class last year. Miriam Somebody. It was probably better that I didn't know her. Competitions were easier if you kept your heart off the battlefield. I'd learned that much.

With at least thirty paces distancing me from the office, I loosened my grip around the list and smoothed out the wrinkles. The overhead lights glared over the black ink bulleted down the page. Printer companies, computer services, accounting firms. Could one of these internships be enough?

The double doors ushered me outside Eliot Hall without any answers.

My brother materialized out of nowhere. "How'd it go?"

"Jeez, Austin, you have me under surveillance or something?"

He scanned side to side and lowered his sunglasses. "Can't reveal all my secrets."

I nudged him down the walkway. "I'm not sure a computer graphics major qualifies you to be an MI6 operative."

"Hey, never underestimate a big brother's covert skills."

Covert? More like overprotective.

"Listen, I appreciate you driving me up and staying the night, but I'm all moved in now. I'm good. Really. You've got a long trek back to Cali."

Already a step ahead of me, he motioned toward Mom's Malibu parked at the curb.

My stomach tightened. Okay, maybe I wasn't as good as I thought.

A few feet away, squeals erupted from roommates reuniting after being apart for the eternity we all knew as summer break. As thrilled as I was to be back with my friends, too, having to say goodbye to Austin suddenly caught me in the gut.

The walkway ended too soon. I dawdled in front of him with my hands in my pockets.

He reclined against the passenger door. "You didn't tell me how your meeting went."

Why couldn't he have missed that part? I blew an unruly strand of hair out of my face. "Nothing better than getting an ultimatum your first day back."

His jaw clenched. "What?"

Bad choice of words. "Relax, 007. It's more of an incentive to keep me on my mission."

"So, now you're MI6 too?"

"More so than you." I flashed him the best Bond pose I could.

Pathetic.

He straightened, probably buying it as much as I did. "Em, you need to take a little pressure off yourself."

Easy for him to say. A senior at the University of California, internship down, job offer nearly in place. His pressures were already behind him.

He ruffled my hair. "Try enjoying your college experience. Make memories with your friends. Date." A pack of freshman boys strutted by the girls on the sidewalk with their hormones whirling faster than their footballs. "Second thought, maybe you should skip the whole dating part."

Like that would be a problem. "Dating is the last

EYES UNVEILED | 15

thing you need to worry about. I'm too sensible for fairy tales."

His mouth pulled sideways. "You sure you're the same sister I went to high school with?"

I shoved him against the car. "Yeah, the one who learned her lesson."

Love always abandoned. Besides, I had a career to focus on... as long as I didn't blow it.

The thought churned in my stomach as it had in Mr. Oakly's office.

"You all right?"

"Fine." Everything would be fine. I let out a slow breath and stretched my neck from side to side. "Thanks again for being here. But, seriously, you really should get back. Mom needs you, and you've got your internship evaluation this week to prep for."

Ankles crossed, he rested his arm across the car door rim. "Piece of cake."

"You aren't nervous?"

"Nah." He spun his key ring around his finger. "I'm pretty sure it's in the bag." His grin expanded with each syllable. "Clearly, now that they've seen how talented I am, how could they not offer me a full-time job?"

My eyes circled up to the sky and back down. "Clearly." I'd never admit he was probably right. He'd always been too smart for his own good.

Austin pushed off the car and tapped my chin. "Aw, don't be jealous 'cause I'm older."

I swiped his hand away. "Barely."

"And smarter," he said, ignoring my objection.

"Ha." I crisscrossed my arms over my gray tee. "Haughtier is more like it."

He backed up two steps and cast one overhauling glance up and down my arrogant pose. "Clearly," he said in a perfect echo of my earlier remark.

I pursed my lips, refusing to return his smile.

Useless.

Austin's focus flitted from me to inside the Malibu. "You know, you should've brought Dad's guitar with you. We could've squeezed it in the back seat."

I almost choked on nothing. "Are you kidding? I'm not Dad."

"No one said you were. That doesn't mean you can't have a part of him."

"Not the artist part." He changed lives through those guitar strings. I was lucky not to botch changing keys. "I'm more comfortable with my own guitar. Half the time, it's just the two of us fighting for sanity."

"Still haven't won that battle, huh?"

I thrust a commendable punch straight into his gut.

He doubled over, more from laughter than pain. Figured.

Bracing his knees, he positioned his face directly in front of mine.

I pushed him back and wrinkled my nose. "That garlic breath warrants at least three feet of personal space, thank you very much."

As if he'd listen. All joking set aside, he lugged me

into his classic bear hug and rested his chin on my head. "Sometimes vulnerability's worth the risk, Em. I know there's a lot of pressure on you, but trust me. You're stronger than you think you are."

Was I? After battling so long, I wasn't sure anymore. I grabbed hold of Austin's T-shirt and his assurance, wishing I didn't have to let go of either, but his ornery-driven reflexes didn't give the sentiment a chance to percolate.

He rubbed his fingers through the top of my hair until the level of static electricity competed with his self-amused snorting.

I kicked him around the front of the car. "Be safe."

"Always am."

I waved from the sidewalk until the old Chevy rounded the corner past the school's entrance. Like an old friend, a breeze rolled up the walkway and blew an it's-going-to-be-okay sigh across my face. Maybe it was —with a little determination. Headphones in place, I exhaled. Under Oregon's gorgeous skies, anything was easy to believe.

The campus already vibrated with energy. An array of blankets peppered the lawns with students. Suitcases and dollies rumbled over the sidewalks leading to the dorms.

There was no denying it was the beginning of a new year. No telling where it would lead. But at least for one tiny moment, it didn't matter. With my head lifted to the sky and the rest of the world shut out, it was just me, my music, and my private dance with the afternoon's sun-soaked breeze.

Until I opened my eyes again.

Shoulder to shoulder with someone passing in the opposite direction, I froze. Blue eyes held mine, searching with depths of loss and dreams as if he understood the exact tug-of-war Austin and I had just talked about. His eyes held something vulnerable inside them. Something that didn't let go until he passed and freed me to breathe again.

Gravel churned beneath my sneakers as I spun around, but it was too late. He'd already disappeared into the sea of faces streaming along the fast-paced current of move-in day.

In the middle of it all, I stood suspended—desperate for Austin to be wrong about vulnerability, terrified he wasn't.

## 2

# UNRAVELED

THREE WEEKS WAS MORE than enough time to forget about some random encounter with a stranger. It didn't matter how blue his eyes were, such a brief connection shouldn't have left me feeling like I was fifteen instead of twenty-one.

*"You sure you're the same sister I went to high school with?"* Almost a thousand miles away, and Austin still managed to weasel his obnoxious voice into my thoughts.

I tossed a highlighter into the crease of my textbook and snagged my list of internships and my cell.

With the mortgage back home in arrears, the only thing I needed to focus on was rebuilding the security we'd lost. It would break Dad's heart if he saw Mom struggling the way she was. Even more so if I ended up like her. I couldn't let that happen. For both our sakes, I had to get the right internship.

I nearly tapped a hole into my desk with my pen cap while waiting for someone to pick up. "May I speak with..." I ran my finger across the page. "Mr. Johnson, please?"

"He's in a meeting," a woman with an overly nasal voice said. "If this is regarding the internship position, it's been filled."

"Already?"

"I'm afraid so. Just earlier today actually." A second line beeped in the background. "Good luck to you," she said in a rush to exchange one call for another.

Evidently, luck wasn't on my side. I added a fifth bold pen stroke to the page. How could they be filling up this quickly? I lurched back in my chair. My textbook bumped into a picture frame preserving my eleventh birthday behind a thin sheet of glass.

What I would've given to be in Dad's lap again, drawing from the courage his music had always provided. I grabbed my own guitar from the corner instead, and right there—in the middle of unsettled beginnings—I lost myself in a song he'd played for me for as long as I could remember.

Tears welled above my lashes.

"Little help, here, Em," my roommate called from the living room.

I flinched so hard, I almost dropped the guitar. I scrambled to dry my eyes, never more grateful for an interruption. My runaway emotions were getting the better of me, and the year had barely even started. I needed to get a grip fast.

In the living room, Jaycee balanced three overflowing shopping bags in the air while propping open the front door with her foot. The sunglasses holding back her auburn bob slid down her forehead. Even in a simple pair of capris and a Kelly-green baby tee, the girl looked like she'd just walked off a runway.

I had to smile. She truly was the best distraction. I grabbed the door for her and peeked inside two bags full of frames, lamps, and throw pillows. "Go a little overboard?"

"Oh, c'mon. Two years we've been waiting to get an apartment, and *this* is what they give us?" She flicked a glance at the threadbare couch in the corner as she hauled her bags over to the scuffed-up coffee table.

"Don't you have a fiancé somewhere who's supposed to help you carry all this stuff?"

She curled her lips to one side. "Who do you think is bringing up the rest?"

"The rest? What'd you do, buy out the entire IKEA home décor department?"

Trevor filed in behind Jaycee with a train of bags extending down his arms. "Like you have to ask." He dropped the evidence of her shopping spree onto the couch and hugged me to his side. His burly arm nearly squashed me in half. "And guess who gets to help her put it all up." His goofy grin was seconds away from being even more obnoxious than his fluorescent orange sneakers.

I reached for his sunglasses to block the glare, but he sidestepped around me in his famous basketball move, whisked Jaycee into his arms, and slid his sunglasses to the bottom of his nose. His brows bobbed into the chunks of blond hair poking through the back of a ball cap pressed to his forehead. "Sure you don't want to cancel on the others tonight?"

"Not a chance." Flashing a too-cute-to-turn-down smile, she pecked him on the lips and sauntered toward the bedroom. "Meet you out front in five minutes," she called behind her. "I'm just going to change first."

Trevor winked at me. "Think I can get a full game in before she's ready?"

"Like you have to ask," I mimicked on my way down the hall.

In our room, I flopped onto my half-made bed and watched Jaycee put herself together as though preparing for a dinner party. I couldn't blame her for not fearing the mirror. Her reflection held the promise of a future she was tailor made for. Of course she'd like what she saw.

A heave of exasperation rebounded off the top of her suitcase and jarred me from my thoughts. "I know those DKNYs are in here somewhere."

I tried not to laugh. If she dug any deeper, she'd fall in. "Where you guys going tonight?"

"Nuts and Jolts."

"Jae, I don't think you need to wear heels to go to the local café."

Elbow-deep in an entire suitcase dedicated to her shoe collection, she barely batted a lash. "Okay, first of all, any occasion is a good excuse to wear cute shoes. And second of all, we might go out to the city afterward." She pinned the sides of her hair behind her ears and spun around with two sling-back pumps dangling on her fingers. "Mission accomplished."

"Prepared as usual."

"You know me." Jaycee sat down and pressed her shoulder against mine. "So, you wanna tell me what you're thinking about?"

Like always, there was no point trying to hide anything from my best friend. I moved to my chair and picked at the corner of my internship list. "I was thinking about being back. It's our junior year, and—I don't know—I feel like I'm running out of time."

"Out of time for what?"

"Figuring everything out." The whitewashed wall above Jaycee's bed glared at me with the same emptiness I felt any time I tried to make more out of life than there was. I grabbed my pillow and buried it under my arms. "I feel like I'm searching for something that doesn't exist. Do you think I'm crazy? Wait—don't answer that."

Too late. Her laughter said enough. She bit her lip to reel it in. "Just focus on enjoying where you are right now." She squeezed my hand on her way up. "Things have a way of working themselves out when we give them time."

Sometimes I swore she and Austin shared the same calendar of daily maxims.

At her dresser, Jaycee held several pairs of earrings to her ears until she found the perfect match. "You're coming with the rest of us to Nuts and Jolts, right?"

The corners of a visibly loaded smile peeked above the top of her jewelry box. I knew that look. Whatever she was thinking, it couldn't be good.

"I should stay in." I tapped my laptop. "Gotta make some headway on this portfolio."

Flexing her palms against her dresser, she lifted onto her toes and stared down the economics book on my desk. "Don't be so stubborn. You can afford to spare a Friday night away from studying. It'll be good for you."

The obstinate ring in her tone outplayed the steady rainfall beating onto the windowsill with the perfect accompaniment for an evening at home. I doubted I had the option.

I curled the pages of my book toward the binding. "Who's going?"

"Just a handful of us. Trevor, Ashlea, Becky, A. J.—"

"A. J.?" My chair shot upright, knocking my words and me forward. "As in, A. J. Bowers?"

"Yeah. You've met him?"

"Don't need to. The girls in my aerobics class gave me a good enough idea." They hadn't stopped gushing over the new transfer student. All six feet of him. Sculptured, no less. If they thought he was that good-looking, chances were, he did too. I knew the type well. Interchangeable faces. Same disappointment. Same reminder of the way love had left me flat on my face.

Jaycee clipped her bangs back with a tiny barrette. "He might surprise you."

Right. I picked the lint off my shirt and stole a minute to iron out the edge in my voice. "When did you start hanging out with him?"

She kept her focus glued to her work in front of the mirror. "Trevor met him over the summer. Been playing pickup games with him ever since." Each brushstroke glided through her sleek hair. "You know Trev—never meets a stranger."

Yeah, just like I knew when she was trying to downplay.

"A. J.'s a really nice guy," she added. "I think you're going to like him."

And there it was. "Jae..."

She slipped around the corner of her dresser. "Relax. I'm not saying you have to marry the guy."

"Oh, well, that's a shame. You know how eager I am to get married." I slanted her a pointed glance.

"Hey, you'll change your mind once you meet the right guy, but forget about all that for now. Just get to know him. You never know where it'll lead."

Except I did.

In perfect synchronization, Jaycee's grin grew in direct proportion with my scowl. She hunched over my desk without recanting her optimism. "You could use a night out with your friends, Em. It'll be fun. Please?"

She made it impossible not to give in. "Fine. For you."

Jaycee tapped her fingertips together with enough excitement for us both as she headed to the bathroom for one of her warp-speed makeup rejuvenation sessions.

Shaking my head, I scooted back far enough to give my clothes a quick appraisal. Something gave me the distinct feeling she wouldn't approve of the T-shirt I'd dug out of my drawer after a quick post-aerobics shower.

"Oh, and Em?" she called from down the hall. "You probably want to change."

Classic.

I sifted through a row of hangers, grabbed a scoop neck shirt worthy of her fashion endorsement, then rummaged through her elaborate jewelry collection for a pair of complementing earrings, and met her at the door.

The earlier rainfall must've already wandered past the campus border. An iridescent layer of steam was the only evidence left of the shower's momentary collision with the overheated asphalt. Too bad it couldn't evaporate my unease with it. I crossed my arms to hide the neon warning sign still blinking inside me.

"Fun, remember?" Jaycee whispered as we walked toward the group waiting for us at the curb.

Becky's double French braids and pink-framed glasses made her appear even younger than usual. Of course, standing next to Trevor didn't help. Even in a clunky pair of heels, she barely reached the top of his torso.

She looped her arm around Ashlea's, clanking their bracelets together. Ashlea's long red curls spread over her poised shoulders as she swayed in place. I followed her gaping stare toward the only person in the circle I didn't know and toward the source of my earlier—now justified—apprehension about the evening.

A. J. had the kind of physique that could turn an off-white, long-sleeved T-shirt and tattered jeans with a worn leather belt into an Abercrombie & Fitch ad. Complete with rich brown eyes matching the bits of gelled hair poking out from under a baseball cap flipped backward. And those dimples. Why not tattoo "Campus Charmer" on his forehead?

There could've been a small chance he leaned more toward the sports fanatic type I expected from a friend of Trevor's. He certainly had the build of a basketball player. Even the cotton shirt hanging over his defined upper body seemed to take notice of his visible athleticism.

The second he met my gaze, I twisted toward Jaycee with fleeting hope that no one had noticed my initial perusal. Yeah, right. The telling look on Jaycee's face sent heat rushing to my cheeks faster than the steam rising from the asphalt.

"Should we all try to squeeze into one car?" Ashlea spun in a half-circle while taking a headcount.

"I'll drive." A debonair smile danced above A. J.'s closely shaven jawline.

Jaycee rolled onto the balls of her feet. "Em, why don't you ride with A. J.? The rest of us can fit in Trev's car. We'll meet you two there. You know the way, right, A. J.?"

Her convenient speed talking eliminated any opportunity for me to object.

"I've been there a couple of times." A. J. wrangled his keys from his pocket and faced me. "I can run to get my car and be back in two minutes to pick you up."

Jaycee's already-beaming expression stretched far enough to leave permanent wrinkles behind.

"I don't mind walking," I said before she could answer for me. If I kept moving, maybe the uneasiness spiraling in my stomach would dissipate.

Wouldn't be that lucky.

An awkward silence lingered the moment Trevor's Outlander gunned away from the curb. *Thanks a lot, Jae.*

"Do you go to Nuts and Jolts often?" A. J. asked as we walked.

"Not really. I'm not a big coffee drinker, but the shop's atmosphere is cool, especially on Friday nights."

"Nothing beats live music." He kept his face forward, but the shadow of a furtive grin fell on me. "My car is that Acura ZDX over there." From the edge of the parking lot, he pointed out a shiny black sports car parked between a Corolla with its muffler held on by

Duct Tape and a Ford pickup speckled with enough rust spots to make Mater from *Cars* blush.

Was I supposed to be impressed? *Sorry, but flaunting Mommy and Daddy's wealth won't score any points with me.*

He held my door open, his warm eyes offering the same unassuming gesture. Maybe he wasn't trying to bait me with snobbery after all. I sank onto the tan leather seat and tried to decide what to make of A. J. Bowers.

He angled toward me right as he turned the key in the ignition, about to say something. Bass pulsated through the speakers. He reached for the controls, accidentally turned up the volume before turning it off altogether, and laughed. "How's that for smooth? Sorry. I don't usually have other people in the car with me."

His brief flicker of embarrassment disappeared in seconds, along with the college entrance behind us. He looked like he didn't have a nervous bone in his body. With his Ray Bans on, chic profile, and carefree expression, he'd probably stick his hand out the window and wave-ride the wind any minute.

"So," he said, "what kind of music do you listen to?"

Nothing like first-time-small-talk sessions.

"Honestly? I listen to almost every genre. I was sort of born into loving music."

"Do you play any instruments?"

Staring at my lap, I ran my fingers up and down my seat belt. "I play the guitar a little, but I'm not very good."

"I bet you're better than you're admitting." His luxury car's smooth suspension had nothing on his voice.

"What makes you so sure?"

"I've seen you around campus. Off by yourself, playing where no one can hear you."

My jaw dropped halfway open. Had people on campus actually been watching me? I thought I'd tucked myself in corners where no one would notice.

"The way you glow when you play, you have to be enjoying it. So, it can't be *that* bad, can it?"

Heat swept up my neck. I wasn't sure which mortified me more—the fact that those moments secluded on campus hadn't been as private as I thought or that this guy, whom I hardly knew, felt incredibly comfortable telling me he'd been a part of the audience.

"Wait a sec." My shoulders arched. "You just asked me if I played, but you already knew." *Start talking, buddy.*

"Trevor warned me you were a little shy about it. I wanted to see how open you'd be with me." He stole another glimpse across the car under the stoplight. "You blush easily. I'll have to remember that."

The charm trailing his words fueled my growing debate over which type of guy he was. *Ladies' Man, up one point.*

"With all your time spent watching girls you don't know across campus and trying to make them blush, do you ever actually study for classes, or is the whole academic scene kind of overrated for you?"

He laughed. "Just because I've noticed one girl on campus doesn't mean I've noticed any others."

*Right. And Ladies' Man takes the lead.*

Light from a crosswalk sign flashed in sync with his blinker's steady ticking. "Sports medicine," he said a few ticks later.

"Excuse me?"

"That's what I do with most of my time. It's a tough major. Worth it, though. I'm a decent athlete but not good enough to play pro ball. At least as a personal trainer, I'll still get to be around the action."

*Sports Fanatic, match point.* He wasn't making my debate any easier.

"How about you?"

The pavement passed outside my window in one continuous fill-in-the-blank line. "The only thing I was sure about when I completed my application was that I didn't want to come to college undeclared. Too chicken. I've changed my major three times already. Finally decided business would be the best stepping-stone into the job market."

Or hoped, anyway. The idea of barely getting by on some dead-end job like Mom was? No way. There had to be something with more promise.

"I doubt the job market's going to be a problem," he said. "Not for someone like you. Trust me. A business degree will be one more great asset you've got going for you."

Personal trainer, huh? Maybe he could tack on being a life coach too.

A sharp left-hand turn led us into the café's lot and through rows of makeshift parking spaces. Each time the car bounced over a dip in the uneven gravel, my mouth opened a little wider. It hadn't been nearly this crowded the other times I'd been here.

A. J. rolled up to the front door to let me out. He flipped in his side-view mirrors, reversed into a gap between the dumpster and the curb, and slid out of the car window.

Show-off. No wonder he and Trevor had hit it off so well.

"You a stuntman on the side?"

He pointed at his license plate as he jogged toward me.

NVRHLDBK. I sounded it out and shook my head. "You really never hold back, do you?"

He hopped over the curb and edged in until I bent backward in search of something to keep me standing. "You only live once, Emma." He grabbed the door handle behind me, whisked it open, and motioned for me to enter.

Straightening my shoulders, I forced my diaphragm to expel the air trapped inside it and speed walked through the door.

The warmth of the small coffee shop fanned me with inviting aromas of roasted coffee beans and homemade pastries.

Jaycee waved from a table tucked in the middle of the room just past a three-tiered bookshelf piled with an eclectic assortment of books and board games. She'd left two empty seats next to each other for A. J. and me. How convenient.

My gaze locked horns with hers until someone passed directly in front of me and broke my line of sight.

I couldn't mistake those eyes.

Mere seconds. The moment couldn't have lasted longer. Yet, I would've sworn it extended long enough for the entire café to empty except us. Then he was gone. Again.

My Converse sneakers flexed in half as I lifted on my toes and craned my neck to follow the trail of his silhouette weaving away from me toward the stage.

*He* was tonight's performer?

A. J. pressed his arm into mine. "I'd find you a step stool, but it's kind of crowded in here."

I dropped back on my heels. He saw that? Great.

He nudged me forward. "Musicians tend to have a celebrity complex, anyway. Doubt he'd want to share your natural spotlight."

Oh, brother. I fled toward the girls at our table, needing to counter the testosterone fumes taking over the coffee fragrance.

"Hey, guys, we saved you some seats." Jaycee patted the wooden chair next to her and batted her lashes with an exaggerated reminder of my agreement to enjoy the evening.

I draped my sweater over the back of the chair and faked a passable smile.

Trevor greeted A. J. with one of those universal guy handshakes.

"Who is this dude? A local star or something?" A. J.'s question followed a sweeping appraisal around the noisy room.

Trevor squinted to read one of the flyers taped to the cobblestone wall across from our table. "Riley Preston, according to the posters. You guys better get your orders in now. Looks like he's got quite the crowd going on."

"I can see that." A. J. extended his arm. "Shall we?"

Halfway up to the front counter, I caught another glimpse of Mystery Eyes busy arranging a stool and guitar stand on top of the wooden stage in the corner. *So, Mystery Guy has a name. And. Is. A. Musician. Perfect. As if he didn't have a hold over my thoughts already. Now he has to go after my heart? I knew I should've stayed home and studied.*

"What can I get for you two?"

As casually as possible, I pivoted toward the counter, where a short, middle-aged woman wearing a black apron and matching visor waited to take our orders.

A. J. withdrew his billfold. "I'll have a medium house roast. Regular, please." He moved to the side and nudged me forward with the slightest touch against my back.

The woman's attention shifted to me. "And for you, sweetheart?"

"Um…" I clutched the counter and tilted back on my heels. Between the barista hovering over the register and

A. J. unfolding his wallet, I probably had thirty seconds to finagle a way out of him buying my drink.

"A. J., why don't you go ahead and pay for yours. It's going to take me a few minutes to decide what I want."

He turned away from the barista. "You sure?"

"Yeah, absolutely." Okay, so that wasn't true, but lying had to be better than giving him the impression we were on a date. If A. J. was going to be hanging out with us from now on, the last thing I wanted was to risk things ending up being awkward between us.

After hesitating at first, A. J. paid for his coffee and made his way through the maze of people to our table.

Coffee beans churned in the automatic grinder, my nerves not far behind. "I'll have a small—actually, make that a *large* chai tea." It had the potential of being a very long night.

The barista twisted from the back to the front counter and set my drink next to the register before I unburied my wallet from my purse. "That'll be $3.79, dear."

Someone set a five-dollar bill in front of me. "May I?"

Each beep from the oven timer behind us ratcheted my pulse higher. Slowly, I lifted my head toward a voice I didn't recognize to find the eyes I knew by heart.

## 3

## CENTER STAGE

I couldn't answer him. Not with that half smile tying my vocal cords in knots.

Riley propped an elbow on the counter. "I'll take that as a yes."

*Blink. Say something.* What in the world was Riley Preston doing paying for my drink?

"It's rare you see a non-coffee drinking college student." His voice was rich and dangerously mesmerizing. "That's impressive."

*Words, Em. You can do it.* "I... I never really cared much for the taste of coffee. Tea has less caffeine, but it still helps. I'm a tea kind of girl."

*Really? I'm a tea kind of girl?* I buried my chin in my shoulder and reached for my earring to block his view of my now-burning cheeks.

Riley circled around, flashed a soft, playful grin, and

handed me my cup. "Well, 'I'm a tea kind of girl,' I hope you enjoy the night."

Good thing the stage was on the other side of the room—away from the ridiculous smile I couldn't coax my jaw into releasing. My piping hot tea branded a mug-shaped imprint into my hand until the pain finally jolted me back to reality.

Apparently, I wasn't the only one wondering if that had really just happened. Jaycee blinked from the table as though transmitting her question through Morse code.

I slipped into my seat, wound my tea bag string around my cup handle, and stared at the distressed wooden tabletop. With any luck, only Jaycee had caught my little encounter with Riley.

A. J. lifted off the back of his chair and leaned onto his arms, forming a triangle with his coffee cup at the peak. "Maybe Rico Suave will let you have a turn on the stage after all."

He *had* seen.

The steam searing the inside of my cheeks rushed up my forehead while a streak of tea seeped down my chin. Arms flailing, I reached for the nearest napkin and the quickest way to extinguish my escalating level of embarrassment.

I should've expected Trevor would make that impossible.

In a comic-induced reflex, he swiped the napkin from the table before it ever cleared my fingertips. He tilted his chair onto its back two legs and dabbed the napkin over the dry corners of a simpering smirk. "What do you say, Em? Up for a little guitar showdown?"

I dragged my sleeve over my chin and thoroughly contemplated lunging across the table to dump the rest of my tea into his lap.

A. J. pried my whitened fingers off my mug handle, rested my hand in his palm, and met my gaze. "I bet this guy isn't half as good a player as Emma is."

"I think we're about to find out." Trevor dipped his head toward the stage in the corner.

The young shop owner jumped onto the platform. Dwindling conversations followed chair legs screeching across the floor. "All right, everybody, I think we might top last Friday's performance. You ready for another local artist to bring down the house? Give it up for Mr. Riley Preston."

The packed café lit up in sound. Claps and whistles from the crowd joined the noisy coffee grinders and steamers in a melody of applause.

Riley adjusted the microphone in the stand. "Thanks, guys. I don't usually perform in public arenas. So, if I run off the stage in a panic, don't worry. It was all planned." The crowd laughed on cue. Riley rubbed the overgrown stubble along his cheekbone. "No, seriously, I write my own music and don't often get the chance to share it. So, I hope you enjoy it."

His bronze hair, short around the sides with a longer, messy layer on top, glowed under the lights. In worn jeans, navy-blue flip-flops, and a tan, long-sleeved T-shirt, he could've been any other college student in the room. Yet, even though he'd just announced he rarely performed in public, it was clear he was made to be on stage.

His acoustic guitar's melancholy tenor set off a level of emotion in his song that reached places I hadn't realized ached until right then.

With his feet propped on the stool's bottom bar, he kept his eyes closed as he sang. "Where do you turn, where do you run, when the war for your heart's already won? When rules hedge you inside a colorless page, while notes and strings beg for an open stage?"

Emotion clung to his voice, his fingers to the strings. "How do you stay when everything feels wrong? How do you escape into this song where you belong?

"If this is a lie, then someone tell me why I can't stop wishing dreams won't fade with daylight."

The longer I watched and listened, the further the music transported me into a world of beauty completely outside the borders of the coffee shop's stone walls. Past the obvious fact that I didn't know anything about him. To a place of connection that warmed and terrified me at the same time.

I twisted my necklace over my chin, too captivated to look away from him. Minutes blended into the notes. Each song he played caused everything else to disappear until the hum of conversations gradually drew me back to my surroundings. People swayed while they talked, treating his set like background music. Didn't they sense the complexity in each chord?

Riley's fingers slowed over the strings. He lifted his head, eyes on me. "Over doesn't mean over when your heart's afraid. But how long can I chase this song, this song of a runaway?"

Several minutes passed before his focus drifted from me to his guitar, but not before I caught a note of sadness—one I wished I could've taken away.

Whoops and hollers rang from the back wall all the way to the stage as he gave a short bow with his final strum. Aside from the commotion of a group of girls prancing across the floor in their heels to reach him, the increasing buzz of conversations confiscated the momentary limelight Riley's music had held. Something inside me constricted.

"Now that we've all had our shot of caffeine for the night," Trevor said, "how about we take the long route home and hit up Portland first? See what street bands are out tonight?"

Becky wiggled the ends of her glasses behind her ears, sending the front bobbing up and down on her face in an enthusiastic, *Yes!*

Ashlea ran her hands over her bare arms. "I don't know. I wasn't planning on going out. I didn't bring a jacket."

"Don't worry, Ash. I've got some extra coats in the car." Trevor rocked onto the back two legs of his chair again and laced his fingers behind his head. "It'll be fun."

Jaycee tossed her crumpled-up napkin at his face. "Just because you're always up for an escapade, doesn't mean everyone else is."

The clamor of my friends' discussion grew faint in the shadow of the only thing drawing my attention. A tall brunette, who looked like she spent more time in a tanning booth than in classes, propped one stiletto heel on the stage next to Riley's knelt body. She twirled her Pantene-commercial-worthy hair around her finger, rhinestones on her nails catching the overhead light.

I polished off the last quarter of my tea to keep from gagging.

A. J. peered into my emptied mug. "Easy, girl. It's a cup of tea, not a shot glass."

Might've preferred the shot right about then.

I turned in time to see Miss Can I Be Any More Obvious sending two dramatized hair tosses over her shoulders while huffing toward the cluster of friends ready to help her blow off Riley's apparent disinterest. With her out of the way, the spotlight gleamed across the grains of the stage and spread onto Riley's back. I rose, not saying a word.

A. J. set his hand over mine. "What do you think, Emma? You game for a Portland run?"

"Um, probably not. I don't think I'm up for a night on the town." I slid my hand out from under his and grabbed my cup. "I'm going to go say hi to someone before we take off."

The intensity in Riley's music still had a hold over

me, drawing me across the room with a knot in my throat. The clan of offended sorority girls sat perched on their bar stools. With glares sharper than their four-inch heels, they laser beamed a message into my skin. *You're nowhere in his league.*

My gaze trailed down the length of my solid, navy-blue shirt, tripped over the holes in my jeans, and landed on my five-year-old Converse sneakers. They were probably right.

Wait, what did it matter? I just wanted to pay the guy a compliment. It wasn't like I was falling all over myself to get his autograph or something.

Squaring my shoulders, I smoothed out my shirt and shoved the knot in my chest back down.

Riley raised his head while fastening the brackets on his guitar case. His boyish grin stopped me a few feet away. "Did you enjoy your tea?"

"It was perfect." I swung my empty cup as corroborating evidence and braved another step closer. "Thanks again. You really didn't have to buy it for me."

"Let's just consider it a conversation starter."

His smile carried far more effect than any one person should be allowed to have. I stabilized my cup on the table beside me and tucked my hands in my back pockets—safe from drawing any more attention to my ridiculous nerves. "I'm Emma, by the way." The girl who was usually far more sensible and sophisticated than this.

He hung his head for a suspended moment. Standing

up with his guitar case in one hand, he extended the other. "Riley Preston."

Maybe he didn't notice the tremor in my handshake. Either that or he was as good an actor as he was a musician. Something gave me the impression it was the latter.

I scuffed my sneaker along the floor panel in a scramble to remember why I came over to begin with. "I wanted to let you know I think your music is really beautiful." *Beautiful?* "Um, sorry, beautiful sounds inadequate." *Along with every other word leaving my mouth.* "What I mean is, there are layers underneath it that I imagine few people understand."

He stilled.

What was I doing? If my sudden words-turned-leaky-faucet syndrome didn't make him question my competency, my presumption of understanding his music probably did. I snagged a napkin from the table, wishing I could hide behind it.

"I'm sorry. I don't mean to come off sounding like I know you or anything." *Way to make it worse, Em.* "It's just that the level of emotion I sensed in your music really gripped me. And I thought, as an artist, you might want to know you're connecting with people on a deeper level than entertainment. That's a special gift, and I wanted to tell you I hope you keep pursuing it."

By the time I'd finished sputtering, I'd folded all four corners of the napkin enough times to pass it off as an origami masterpiece. Nice. I crumbled it into a ball and shoved it in my pocket.

Riley rubbed the back of his neck.

"Em, you coming?" Jaycee called across the room.

"Guess we're leaving. I'll... um... see you around." *Or go crawl into a dark hole and pretend this never happened.*

No response.

*Now would be the time to move, not stand here like you're dying for him to say something—anything.*

The silence followed me in an awkward about-face and drove me into the near-jog I should've made to begin with.

A screech from behind brought me to a stop and drew me back around.

Mid-stride, Riley pushed the rogue chair he'd bumped into out of his path to catch up to me. "Emma, can I give you a ride home?"

I turned from Riley to Jaycee and back again. A rush of adrenaline slowly gave way to rehearsed practicality. I pointed over my shoulder. "I should probably go with my friends." Friends. The safe kind. The ones who didn't smell like Nautica and play ballads capable of undoing my heart.

Riley nodded. "Right. Yeah, sorry, of course."

Trailing another hesitation, he walked alongside me toward the exit, neither of us saying anything. I skidded in my tracks and almost stretched my arm in front of Riley the way Mom did when she hit the car brakes too hard. Trevor's ornery grin greeted us from the doorway, where he, A. J., and Jaycee were waiting. No telling what he was about to do.

"Hey, what's up, man? I'm Trevor Andrews."

*That's it?* I exhaled.

Riley cocked his head like he was trying to place Trevor's face. "Don't we have Marketing Research together? Mondays at nine, right?"

Of course they did. Trev was so going to enjoy this.

"Yeah, I think you're right." The red exit light zeroed in on the grin hiking up the corners of his mouth. "Great show tonight, bro. I think the crowd *really* got into it."

I almost elbowed him, but A. J. slid beside me. "A. J. Bowers." He gave a short chin flick toward Riley. "You're not half bad up there."

His complimenting skills must be limited to ladies only.

Riley balanced his guitar case on the floor and leaned on his hands. "Thanks. I think."

Jaycee rolled onto the balls of her feet. "We should probably get going. Ashlea and Becky are outside waiting for us."

A. J. held up my sweater for me to slip my arms through. "I'll get the car for you."

There went avoiding date territory.

Riley's shoulders drooped slightly as A. J. left, but then he clasped Trevor's hand again. "Guess I'll see you Monday. Good to meet you guys."

Another exhale seeped through my nose the second Riley passed the threshold.

Trevor bent over with amusement. "What's wrong, Em? You look a little... *riled* up."

"Don't even think about saying anything to him, Trev."

Flashes of white teeth beamed back at me. "Wouldn't dream of it."

My punch to his arm shoved him all the way through the door.

Jaycee handed me my purse. "Now aren't you glad I made you change before going out?"

Between the two of them, there was no point in trying to conceal my humiliation. Still, I waited for the heat to drain from my face before I ventured to the parking lot. I slipped into A. J.'s car and met a sideways smile from the driver's seat. Yet, rather than propelling me from one mortifying moment to the next, he turned on the car stereo instead of saying anything.

The soft music ransomed the tension trekking across my shoulder blades. With my elbow on the door panel, I watched the evergreens pass along the side of the road and pulled the pearl charm along the delicate silver chain around my neck.

"That's a pretty necklace."

"Hmm? Oh. My father gave it to me when I turned sixteen." I stared out the window again. "It's the last present he ever gave me."

"Which would explain why you seem to treasure it."

I dropped the charm, tucked my hands underneath my legs, and pressed my palms against the grooves in the leather seat.

A guitar solo on the radio waded into my lack of response.

A. J. looked from the windshield to me. "I'm sorry. Did I say something wrong?"

"No." Why couldn't I find my voice? "Well, I mean, it's just that tonight's the first time we met, but it's like you already know me."

He kept one hand on the wheel and rested his arm across the back of my seat. "I happen to know your best friend's fiancé. And you might find this hard to believe, but you're not exactly easy to overlook. You hardly let go of your necklace tonight. I figured it had to hold some pretty special meaning to you." He pulled up alongside the curb in front of my apartment, his expression genuine and disarming.

Maybe I shouldn't have forced him into a stereotype.

"For the record, A. J., I think you'll make a great trainer. You have the right eyes for it." Warm brown. Charming yet sincere. The kind that never held back but still made you feel known, rooted for.

The sound of his seat belt buckle clicking open caught the tail end of another laugh. "What do eyes have to do with it?"

"Everything."

He continued to gaze at me, unknowingly confirming what I saw in him.

"Well, I still think you could've won that showdown on stage." He cocked his chin. "For the record."

A breeze trickled through my half-open door and

carried my laugh on its way out. "You definitely overestimate my skills."

"Then maybe you should prove me wrong."

Maybe not. "Night, A. J." With my foot already on the curb, I waved behind me and smiled in spite of myself.

Okay, so Jaycee was right. He was a nice guy. Definitely on the charmer side, but sweet. He'd make a good friend.

As Jaycee and I filed into our bedroom, Riley's music kept flooding my mind, along with another wave of the feelings it had awakened. I stared vacantly at the wall above my dresser while unfastening my earrings. Were some emotions worth the danger of being swept away with them?

Jaycee tugged my sleeve. "Emma? Hello?"

"Sorry, did you say something?"

"I was asking what you were thinking about, but I think that look on your face already answered my question. I take it that was Mr. Mystery Eyes from the other day."

"Yeah, Riley Preston." What other mysteries did he hold?

She ran a brush through her hair. "You know, I thought A. J. would've been a good match for you, but I can see why you find Riley attractive."

I whirled around, hand in the air.

"Fascinating?" she said in exchange, but my hand-turned-stop-sign didn't budge. She set her brush down and motioned for me to insert my approved adjective.

"Intriguing." I yanked my pajama top over my head. The static electricity raising my hair made me look as ridiculous as I sounded.

Her earrings jingled, cackling at my response. "Right. Okay, clearly, I see why you find him *intriguing,* but I want you to be careful. You don't know anything about him."

"Jae, really? There's nothing to be careful about. He's the kind of guy who can have any girl he wants. Did you see the way those sorority chicks flocked to him?" He didn't rise to the attention like most guys would've, which made him even more intriguing, but still. "He won't remember my name tomorrow. And I doubt I'll run into him again anyway. I've only seen him on campus that one time."

Jaycee didn't answer my blabbering. She didn't need to. Even after she turned off her lamp, her intuition continued to glow in the light from her alarm clock.

I stared at the shadows sprawling over the ceiling. With any luck, the darkness would send me straight to sleep. Of course not. I let out a long sigh and rolled over to face Jaycee's bed.

"Fine, I think he's attractive. *Really* attractive. Which is exactly why you gotta help me not to get caught up putting his face onto some silly daydream of falling in love." I couldn't let myself go there. Especially with someone like Riley Preston, who could unhinge my resolve with a single glance. I hadn't dated the last two years for a reason.

"You got it. But," Jaycee warned, "don't go getting all defensive on me when I step in if I have to."

She knew me so well. "I promise."

My mind retreated to Nuts and Jolts the second I closed my eyes: Riley center stage and his music weaving a connection I doubted anyone else there understood—a connection I shouldn't have been thinking about. But with his voice singing me deeper into a dream, all I could do was lug my reversible comforter over my head and wait for the escape of daylight.

## 4

## COLLISION

MY CELL PHONE buzzed against my desk. With only one leg hoisted through my workout pants, I hopped across the room like the anchor in a potato sack race.

"May I speak with Emma Matthews?" a man asked.

I swatted the wreckage of hair away from my face. "Speaking."

"Jack Peters from Xander Technologies, returning your call about an internship opportunity."

It hadn't been filled?

"The position requires a minimum of twenty hours a week. There'll be some training, of course, but we're looking for someone who's self-motivated and hard working. This isn't a work-study job where you'll get to do your homework in between answering phone calls or—"

"I'll take it." I smacked the heel of my palm against my

forehead, then slumped against the chair. "I mean, unless you require an interview." *Great first impression.*

"No interview necessary. Your advisor sent over your transcripts. Your grades speak highly of your performance."

Thank goodness.

"Just to clarify, you do know this isn't a paid internship, correct?"

My elbows slipped off the chair back. Unpaid? Why hadn't Mr. Oakly told me some on the list weren't paid? I padded around for my desk and the footing I'd just lost. Deep breath. As long as it helped me keep my scholarship, everything would be fine.

"No problem. I'm grateful for the opportunity to gain on-the-job experience." There was a scripted response if I'd ever heard one.

"Well, then, you start Monday. My assistant will get you settled in."

Settled. The word made its way 'round and 'round my mind in search for a place to sink its roots. So what if it was a boring desk job? It was an internship. At a prestigious computer company, no less. Checklist, done. I should've been relieved, not... unsatisfied?

A sense of apprehension followed me down to the sports center for my step-aerobics class. Techno music blared from a small stereo in the corner of our sectioned-off portion of the gym. Bass vibrated inside my rib cage, but Riley's songs kept setting me off balance.

*"Where do you turn, where do you run, when the war for your heart's already won? When rules hedge you inside a colorless page, while the notes and strings beg for an open stage."*

I dropped off my step. *When the war for your heart's already won.* Something fanned inside me. A call without an answer. What would it be like to have my heart spoken for?

My classmate Megan tripped into me and roused me from my half-dazed stare. Her expression whiplashed right along with her shiny blond ponytail. "Jeez, Emma, try listening to the instructor. We're doing around-the-worlds, not stand-arounds."

"Sorry." Great. They guy had a hold on me even when he wasn't nearby. Definitely not good.

In the locker room, a wave of chlorine threatened to knock me over. I held my breath while flushing the perspiration from my face. With my hands braced on either side of the sink, I stared at my disheveled reflection and let the air ooze out of me. So much for wiping away my tension with my sweat.

Megan sauntered up to the sink on my left, undid her ponytail, and began twisting her hair into a loose side braid. "What's up with you today, Matthews? You're not lost in some Riley Preston daydream, are you?"

I lost my grip on the sink. "Excuse me?"

She erased the gleam from her brow with a stroke of mineral powder. "I saw you last Friday. At Nuts and Jolts.

I get the appeal, obviously, but don't get your hopes up. Riley Preston doesn't date."

"Excuse me?" Didn't I know any other phrase?

She turned in five different angles in front of the mirror, probably double-checking to make sure she hadn't lost her curves sometime during class.

"My roommate went to a football game with him once, and the guy didn't make a single move. Nada. And trust me, the girl's gorgeous. The entire football team would've trampled the bleachers to take the wide-open shot she gave Riley. But instead of taking it, he kept her at arms' length all night like some delicate piece of china he thought he'd break if he touched her."

"You say that like it's a bad thing."

She snapped her compact shut. A scrutinizing once-over equaled the sharp noise. "Maybe not for some of us."

What was that supposed to mean?

Megan flitted off, apparently not finding the conversation worth continuing.

"Me either," I said to no one.

My sneakers hit the back of my locker and fell onto the metal bottom with a *thud*. I shoved on my flip-flops, tied my jacket arms into a knot around my waist, and backed through the door leading to the atrium.

Dozens of "Books for Sale" flyers pinned haphazardly on a bulletin board flapped in the breeze and fanned an irritating reminder of the international business test I had tomorrow. The one I hadn't studied for yet. Perfect.

I started for the exit and the urgent need for caffeine reinforcements. Midway into a turn, my feet anchored me to the floor. A crowd of students zipped by me as if I weren't standing there, gripped by Riley's gaze.

In a pair of khaki carpenter shorts and a rust-colored T-shirt that matched the bricks behind him, Riley should've blended in with the crowd, not made me feel like he'd stopped inertia just to smile at me. He lifted off the wall and waved. "Emma."

He remembered my name.

Someone crashed into me from behind and jerked me out of place. "Watch it," a gel-haired kid in an SSA blazer yelled. A stack of papers spilled out of his hands and sprawled across the floor like a bucket of Pick-up Sticks.

"I'm so sorry." I caught one of the flying papers with my foot and bent to snag another one with my hand. Wow. In case bumping into someone hadn't drawn enough attention to the way I'd been staring at Riley like some roadie, now I was having a one-man twister game in the middle of the hall. Classy.

Riley knelt beside me and gathered the rest of the scattered papers. A glance my way sent the corner of his lips creeping up to the left. Why couldn't the floor have a trapdoor right here?

He tapped the pages into a neat stack and handed it to SSA Dude, who suddenly appeared to have learned some manners. "Thanks, man. I appreciate it."

Riley seemed oblivious to the effect he had on people.

He helped me up from the floor and eased me toward the wall—away from any more traffic collisions. "Thanks," he said. "I needed a little rush to get the day going."

"Wouldn't want to miss the chance to offer some more stellar conversation starters." *Stellar conversation starters?* An edgy laugh chased a surge of self-consciousness up my cheekbones. One day, I'd say something halfway normal around him.

Riley's grin pillaged my remaining reserve of dignity. The exit sign called louder this time, but he blocked my path before I could make a run for it. "How was aerobics?"

I twisted and untwisted the jacket sleeves hanging at my waist. "Oh, you know. Nothing like a few sets of pointed-toe leg lifts to really make things exciting."

"Who can argue with that?" He stuffed a small notepad into his side pocket. "Do you have any plans this afternoon that could possibly compete with that level of excitement?"

Plans? This afternoon? Was there any time or space outside of right now? "Um... actually, I was just thinking I should probably study for an international business test I have tomorrow morning."

"Ah, yes, that's definitely more exciting than leg lifts."

"A close second at best." Genuine laughter. Finally.

"If you have Professor Roberts, focus on the notes from his review session. You'll do great," he said without an ounce of question on the matter. Or in my abilities, period. The strange part was, I believed him.

"You're a business major?" I asked.

"Marketing."

Right. Same as Trevor. Hence the shared class. Speaking of which. "So, what are you doing here? I've never seen you in the sports center. Not that I've been on the lookout for you or anything. It's just that I would've remembered seeing you. You know, well, you sort of stand out. I mean…"

I dropped my jacket sleeves and waved at some random girl across the atrium. Seeming distracted had to be better than coming off like a nervous schoolgirl. Fat chance I'd pulled *that* one off. What was with this guy making me nervous? Just because I was attracted to him didn't mean I literally had to trip over myself when I was around him.

Riley tugged on his ear. "Actually, I was waiting for you."

My fingers slid down my ponytail, that single sentence down my body.

"I'm not sure I can compete with all the excitement you're trying to cram into one day," he teased, "but I wondered if you'd take a walk with me." His gaze strayed to the floor long enough for me to remember how to blink again.

A breeze from the exit doors urged me to escape now before I pulled another Nuts and Jolts mistake. Giving into his attractiveness once was bad enough. I didn't need to give him room to get any closer. Not if I wanted to keep my heart intact.

He looked up at me again, head and hand pointing toward his unanswered invitation.

"S… sure." Apparently, I didn't have any control over my eyes *or* my mouth.

"Great." A few paces ahead, he turned, arms splayed to his sides. "You coming?"

Sliding one foot forward, I inched toward Riley and the beginning of an afternoon that had serious potential to leave me undone.

## 5

## FORFEIT

RILEY HELD the door open to let four girls decked in soccer gear pass through in the opposite direction. They practically stampeded each other without garnering so much as a glance from him. Either he was blind, or he really didn't notice the way girls gawked over him.

He motioned toward Canyon Trail. "Ready?"

*Doubt it.*

Each time my flip-flops slapped my heels, I gave myself an internal head slap to knock my resolve back into place.

"I wanted to thank you," he said after a few minutes. "For the other night."

My memory catalogued through a rapid inventory. "For?"

"For what you said. I don't perform for audiences that often. I've sort of kept my music to myself lately." He stowed his hands in his pockets and lifted his shoulders.

"It's not that I've been afraid people won't like it. More that they won't understand it, you know? That they'd miss the meaning altogether and lump it in with any other source of entertainment."

An undercurrent of sadness pulled his head down.

"I really appreciate what you said to me that night. I know most people come out to enjoy a nice atmosphere and listen to good music. And don't get me wrong, I'm cool with that. I get it."

He dug his fingers through the top of his hair and faced the sky. "But as an artist, I always hope there might be something deeper. That people will connect like you did." He released a gruff exhale. "It's pretty rare anyone ever does."

His pause seemed to beg me to say something in return, but I didn't want him to stop talking. He opened up with the kind of transparency he would with his best friend rather than a random acquaintance. My nerves around him all of a sudden felt completely out of place.

Riley was a down-to-earth guy. The kind who helped uptight underclassmen pick up their papers from the floor, held doors open for girls without craving a response, and poured everything he had into his music simply because he was a true artist. Not some star with a celebrity complex, as A. J. had said. The kind of guy I could be friends with. Friendship didn't mean losing my heart, right?

He laughed, sounding almost self-conscious. "Sorry. I

don't normally talk about this with anyone. I didn't mean to unload on you like that."

"No, it's totally fine. I know what you're saying. I mean, not that I have any clue what it's like to have your kind of talent, but I understand the fear of being vulnerable with people, the reservations of opening myself up."

We stopped halfway across the footbridge leading to the other side of campus. Arched over the railing, I peered into the creek bed. "My dad used to tell me life's a lot like being an artist. It's not as much about mastering technique as it is risking the cost of opening your heart to the song you're meant to share."

Amazing how he'd made that so easy to believe. That I had a song, a purpose. I wanted to prove him right more than anything. I'd promised.

My internship at Xander stirred to mind, and an unexpected assurance rising in my spirit waged war with my doubts. I almost didn't recognize His voice. It had been so long since I'd given up on trusting God that it didn't make sense for Him to still be fighting for me.

I clutched the rail, caught in between remembering how much I missed the peace of a father's love and the pain of answerless hurts rebounding against it.

Riley eased alongside me.

I froze face forward, praying my mess of emotions would drain into the creek bed before he noticed.

He folded his arms over the rail next to mine. "Your dad sounds like a wise man."

My shoulders relaxed. I hardly knew Riley. Still, he

made it feel safe to be real. "He was. A natural dreamer too. You would've liked him. You share a similar passion. I can tell."

The creek's soft cadence drew the last of the tension from my muscles the way my dad's songs always had.

"You know, you're probably connecting with more people than you realize. There's something about music. Even if you're not aware of what you're missing, you walk away after hearing it, knowing—"

"You can't live without it."

"Exactly." I turned and met eyes locked on mine, as if he hadn't looked away the entire time I was talking. He held that same expression from the first day I saw him— torn between surprise and fear of finding something he'd lost.

"The way you understand things, it's… refreshing," he said.

His sincerity turned my throat dry. So much for relaxing. The bridge's hazy blue lights lit up an exit route. If only my feet moved as fast as I rambled.

On the other side of the bridge, we stopped along the edge of the empty sports field. Sunlight glistened across the freshly mowed lawn, trickled down my entire body, and washed away any trace of unease. "Wow, I guess I don't usually come to this part of campus when practices aren't going on. It's sort of serene, isn't it?"

I slid out of my flip-flops and sank my heels into the cool earth. "When I was a kid, I practically lived in my backyard. Spent hours chasing shapes in the clouds."

Blades of grass wove through my toes with each step toward the center of the field. It might not have been as unique as the creek bed, but the field and its bordering fir trees held their own tranquility.

"Do you mind if we sit for a while?" I spun around.

Riley was still on the sidewalk, staring with enough enamor to be admiring an intricate painting.

I peered behind me and back again. "What?"

Glimpses of a hidden expression followed him across the grass and stretched into a pause filling the time it took him to lift his head toward mine. "Sorry. The beauty of artistry still catches me by surprise sometimes."

*You and me both.* I sat down before my knees could buckle and tried to shift my focus to the beauty around us instead of on the artistry lying right beside me on the grass. Rays of sun sifted through the clouds. "I haven't done this in ages."

"What, no cloud chasing in between aerobics classes?"

"Ha. It might be a better workout. You know how many times I ran in and out of my house to get my dad?" A burst of sunlight warmed my face but didn't reach the ache inside that never really left. "The shapes were always gone by the time I rushed him out to show him. He said it was because the clouds had made that shape just for me." I knotted my fingers through the top of the grass. "Sad part is, I believed him."

"Some things are easier to see from the outside

looking in." Riley slipped his hand behind his head and studied me instead of the clouds.

My pulse chased after two dragonflies zipping past us. I balled the hem of my shorts in my fists. If I could harness my nervous energy to my hands, maybe I could short circuit the electricity surging through me.

Not even close.

"Do you ever wish you could go back to that time in life when everything was so much less complicated?" His arm brushed mine as he rolled onto his side. His torso cast a wide enough shadow to shield the sun's glare from my eyes, but I bolted face forward.

"It's ironic," he said. "As kids, we couldn't grow up fast enough. So sure some great *thing* was waiting for us." Another note of sadness—or regret, maybe.

Summoning any molecule of courage I had left, I turned toward him.

He twisted a small twig between his fingers and tossed it onto the field. "But somewhere along the way, we stopped chasing the future and started wishing we could postpone it."

I thought I was the only one who felt that way. He could've been reading straight from my journal. It didn't make sense. He was the last person I'd expect to understand. How could someone so talented be anxious about the future? He had a world of opportunity at his feet. He'd already discovered what made him somebody. Didn't he see how people were drawn to him? Even now, I couldn't turn away.

The cool, moist earth soaked into my skin through my T-shirt. I grabbed the backs of my legs, towed myself up, and settled my chin on top of my knees.

"Guess we always want what we can't have, wishing we were either in the past or future. It's kind of sad, actually. Sometimes I wonder if we realize what we're forfeiting by not living in the present."

Riley sat up, his attention never leaving me. "Maybe we've just been waiting to find the right reason to live in the present."

A damp breeze—and something far more penetrating —shivered down my arms.

"Getting cold?"

"A little," I admitted.

"We should probably get you back to the exciting world of international business anyway."

"Ugh, don't remind me." Why didn't I ignore the chill in the wind?

Riley leaped to his feet and reached to help me to mine. I clasped his hands, hopped up too quickly, and nearly toppled into him. The whiskers on his chin grazed my forehead as he placed a stabilizing hand to my waist. Warmth crawled up my back. For a second, I pulled even closer. His lips slid into a grin, and I had to grasp his shirt for balance.

"You all right?" he asked.

*Back up, Em. At least let go of his arms, for heaven's sake.* Arms. Maybe not as bulky as A. J.'s or Trevor's, but full of enough strength and tenderness to place his upper body into a whole other category. One I had to escape, and fast, before I looked as starstruck as Miss Too-Tanned-Brunette from Nuts and Jolts had. His smile wasn't exactly helping my sudden case of vertigo.

I tried out my feet and took a spacious step backward. "Yeah, sorry." Sliding my arms through my wrinkled jacket sleeves, I ambled over to my flip-flops and the chance to regain any measure of sensibility.

Some chance. Halfway along our stroll back, the desire to spend the rest of the day with him made each step harder to make.

*Stop swooning already.* Guarding my heart from him might not be the easiest goal I'd ever tackled, but I could handle being his friend. Like I'd told Austin, I wasn't the same naïve girl I used to be.

"Which apartment do you live in?" I asked.

"Actually, I live off campus, about fifteen minutes away off Holgate Boulevard. I do most of my classes online."

No wonder I'd never seen him before. I crisscrossed the sides of my jacket over my stomach. "Will you be playing at Nuts and Jolts again soon?"

"Nah, probably not."

I felt like a runaway train, each of his answers derailing my attempt to find potential ways to bump into him again. I stalled in front of my apartment building—the last stop before my impending collision into Patheticville. Then again, I was pretty sure I'd already crashed into that station back on the field. Doubted there was any recovering.

"Thanks, Emma," he said slowly.

"For what?"

He rubbed his jawbone. "For starters, for spending part of your afternoon with me. Hope it was more exciting than leg lifts."

I tucked my arms under one another and dished his crooked grin back at him. "I don't know. That's some pretty tough competition to beat."

He laughed. "Maybe you can give me a second chance. I ran into Trevor earlier today. He invited me to hang out with you guys tomorrow night."

*He did, did he?* "Tomorrow it is."

"Great. I'll see you then." Riley lingered a minute longer in a half-turn. Something unspoken seemed to pull him in two directions. Rather than say it, he started toward the sports center, where he'd left his car. "Oh, and Emma," he called up the walkway. "Don't worry about Professor Roberts's test. It'll be easier than you think."

Certainly easier than other challenges. I strolled to the door, lost in thought until I remembered. *Trevor.*

The front door welcomed me with scents of percolated coffee—a trademark of Jaycee's presence. Cozied up on the sage microfiber slipcover she'd bought for the abused couch the previous tenants had left behind, she rested her mug on a stack of library books. "Hey."

"Doing research?"

"What gave it away?" She glared at the looming pile beside her. "I'm drowning in theories on childhood development."

"You were made to be a teacher, Jae. Just think how your studies will impact all those kiddos you'll be teaching."

She sighed. "You're right. It'll be worth it."

I opened and closed every kitchen cabinet door in search of something to calm the dragonfly wings still fluttering inside my stomach. "So," I called into the living room, "you'll *never* guess who I ran into today."

"Are you serious? I'm gonna kill Trev. I told him to leave it alone."

I poked my head around the partition wall separating the kitchen and living room. "Don't worry about it." I twisted the drawstring at the bottom of my jacket. "It was kinda nice, actually."

She scooted back the books that were about to fall and stared at me. "Nice?"

"Well, other than the fact that he came to see me after aerobics, of all things. Nothing quite like the sweaty, hair-slicked-back, old-ratty-T-shirt-and-mesh-shorts look to really make a lasting impression."

Jaycee clasped her forehead. "Did he run away in horror?"

I nabbed the accent pillow from the chair closest to me and hurled it at her. "Funny."

"You're not supposed to be falling for him, remember?"

"I'm not." But after today...

"So, what does it matter what you looked like? Keep your head in the game, girl."

I slumped into the chair, my heart following. She was right. I was supposed to be focusing on keeping my scholarship, not traipsing around the campus with Riley Preston. That reminded me. "Hey, do you know a girl named Miriam? Short. Asian. Kind of shy."

"Miriam Chen? Yeah, she helps me tutor at Duniway Elementary."

"Tutor? Wait, isn't she a business major?"

"Yeah, but she volunteers with all kinds of things. She's a sweetheart. Soft spoken. Bright girl. Just a little unsure of herself. I think it might be because of money issues. Her parents are missionaries."

*Great. I'm up against Mother Teresa. Fabulous.*

Jaycee traded her pencil for her coffee mug. "Why? You know her?"

"Not exactly." I swiped a plum from the wire fruit bowl on the kitchen table and picked off the little produce sticker. "I think Mr. Oakly's pitting her against me for my scholarship."

A splash from Jaycee's mug ran down her hand. "What?"

"Don't say anything to her, okay? I've got it under control." I hoped. I tossed the plum between my hands over the silent warnings blaring from Jaycee's expression. Better to change the subject. "What fun exploit does Trevor have planned for us tomorrow?"

"I'm not sure. He said we're meeting up earlier than usual. Oh, and he said to wear comfy shoes."

No telling what that meant, but Trevor's suspense would have to wait. I exchanged my workout clothes for my black fleece pants, my light gray college hoodie, and a pair of plush striped socks that never matched anything. After grabbing a cup of chai, I hit my mattress and my schoolwork. Back to reality.

My international business textbook's binding dug into my thighs. I wedged a pillow underneath it, set my mug on top, and breathed in the invigorating aroma of Indian spices. What were the chances the steam could pass for some sort of head-clearing humidifier?

Evidently, none. The longer I stared at the page, the more my walk with Riley replayed over top of the words I was supposed to be reading. *"Maybe we've just been waiting to find the right reason to live in the present."* The right reason. He'd said it with such conviction, like he knew exactly what he wanted. Maybe even had found it. I'd spent so long chasing the future, I'd forgotten how to crave the present, forgotten the things I'd forfeited.

The passion Riley carried tore at the edges of a hole in my chest that I'd spent years numbing. I chucked my pillow on the floor and let the hardbound book burrow into my legs. If nothing else, pain would help me focus. Always had.

My cell phone screen lit up my hunter green sheets with an incoming call. "Mom, sorry I haven't called you back. It's been a bit of a hectic week... Mom? Is everything okay?"

Something pulsed through the phone line in the absence of Mom's response. Something far too familiar.

Fear.

## 6

## COMPETITION

GONE. What little money I had saved—gone. Just like that. The repercussions of Mom's call last night had kept my stomach in a vice grip all morning.

Glimpses of the late afternoon sunshine snuck through the venetian blinds and stretched across the living room carpet. I peeled my leg off the kitchen chair, shook out the pins and needles, and glared at the clock on my laptop.

How could I have been working this long and still not have had a solution? I pushed back from the table. With my scribbled notes in hand, I paced across the linoleum.

Okay, my living expenses ate up my loan refund. Work-study positions were already filled for the term, though it wouldn't hurt to check on a waiting list. Not having a car made an off-campus job more challenging, especially since I was already going to have to bum rides to my internship. And could I really fit in a part-time job on top of that without sacrificing my grades?

I smacked the paper to my forehead. *There's gotta be an answer. Think!*

Jaycee stopped short on her way from the kitchen to the bedroom. "You okay?"

*You mean aside from the bombshell Mom dropped on me last night? Super.* The tail end of my thought seeped out in a sigh. It wasn't Jaycee's fault the bank had drained our joint account to cover Mom's overdrawn balance.

I probably shouldn't mention the call. It would end up sparking another round of the same circular questions I'd been wrestling all day. What if this unpaid internship was a mistake? What if I couldn't afford to come back next term? What if Mom lost the house?

Downing the rest of my tea, I swallowed the gnawing frustration of not having any answers and let Mom's response repeat in my head like anti-virus software. *"Emma, honey, don't worry. It's going to be okay. I promise."*

The same reassurance I'd felt during my walk with Riley calmed my heart again. It'd be okay. Somehow.

"I'm fine, Jae. Everything's fine."

Hands on her hips, she lowered her chin. "Fine enough to come tonight? I can always get A. J. to keep Trev from coming up here to drag you out."

Trevor's mysterious Friday night outing. I'd almost forgotten. After the way Jae had lit into him for sending Riley to find me at aerobics, the last thing I wanted was to cause another issue. Better to go along tonight and channel Trev's carefree outlook so Jae wouldn't worry.

"Yep, it'll be fun." I headed down the hall before she could argue.

In the bathroom, I tucked my necklace under my long-sleeved turquoise tee, hidden along with my concerns about my finances. At least for now. Hopefully getting out would give me the recharge I needed to sort through this mess.

"You ready, Jae?" I called on my way past the bedroom.

"On your six." She locked up behind us, jogged down the stairs, and hopped off the last step.

I held the door open and tipped my head toward her bright pink New Balances. "Look at you, styling."

She shrugged. "Trev said to wear comfy shoes. That doesn't mean they can't be cute."

Ashlea and Becky climbed into A. J.'s Acura at the same time Jae and I reached the curb. A. J. revved his engine.

"You got nothin' on me, bro," Trevor shouted back.

I opened the door to his Outlander. "And so the competition begins."

From inside, Riley offered a hand to help me into the back seat—the seat he was going to be sharing. With me.

I shot Jaycee a *help me* plea, but what could she do? If Riley and I didn't ride with them, it meant riding in his car. Alone.

"How'd that test go?" he asked.

"She aced it," Jaycee said from up front.

I pulled my seat belt out. "You were right. It was as easy as you said it would be."

"Or you're as smart as you are modest."

It didn't make sense for his voice to sound that familiar. Or for his confidence to overflow until it became my own. Still, my shoulders sank a little deeper into the seat, and pressures from my scholarship ordeal deflated with an exhale.

"Trev, you gonna share whatever exciting adventure you have planned, or what?"

One hand on the wheel, Trevor withdrew a piece of paper from his coat pocket. "Wait for it..." Building suspense, he shook out the folded creases and flashed a bright orange flyer at us with dramatic flair.

"The Labyrinth Trail," I read.

Trevor dropped the flyer onto our seat. "You're going to love this place, Em. Forget studying for a change and remember how to be a kid with the rest of us."

Riley's knee bumped into mine. "Chase shapes in the clouds," he whispered from the side of his mouth.

With him there, maybe the clouds wouldn't be out of reach.

Parked on abandoned Highway 14, A. J. and Trevor scuffled over who beat whom. From this far off, the Coyote Wall resembled a columnar castle perched on the edge of a mountainside—captivating and intimidating all at once.

Becky scuttled up beside me and buttoned the last

two notches on her knit sweater. "You didn't bring a jacket? It's gonna get cold once the sun goes down, especially up top."

Before Riley could finish unzipping his coat, A. J. jogged to his trunk and back, then held a leather jacket in the air for me to slip on.

Swallowed whole, I curled my hands in the excess protruding past my fingertips.

"You're cute in my clothes." He slid a brown woolen beanie over his ears, his gaze never leaving mine, and eased his thumb across my now-warm cheek. "Come on, Rosy, Trevor's got a whole night planned for us."

"A night that's waiting for us to get a move on." Ashlea laced her hands around A. J.'s arm and tugged him forward.

Along the slender dirt trail, Riley kept his face forward and jaw flexed. "You, uh," he said without turning his head. "You and A. J. together?"

The front of my sneaker snagged an overgrown root. I caught my balance, resituated A. J.'s jacket, and considered hiding inside it. Or maybe chucking it back at A. J. "No, just friends. Acquaintances, really." *Same as us, right?* Two crows cawed on their way past us, like some kind of omen warning me to bury the question trekking up my throat. "Would it matter if we were?" *Way to go, Em.*

He edged close enough for the scent of his skin and cologne to devour the last of my levelheaded reflexes. His fingers grazed my neck as he folded down my collar. "You tell me."

That would require speaking. And breathing.

The uneven terrain had nothing on his smile.

Silly, nonsensical butterflies.

Jaycee jogged down the hill and looped her arm through mine. "C'mon, slowpokes, everyone's waiting on you." Ahead of Riley, she gave me an operation-rescue wink.

Why did she have to be so good at the job I assigned her?

Trevor corralled us in front of a dense forest of white oaks with spindly branches twisting toward the open sky. Something about the aged trees made it feel like we were about to infringe upon an enchanted forest.

"Okay, guys. There are several trails leading to the top of the cliff. Let's split up into three groups. Ashlea, you're with us." He rubbed his hands together. "Let's make this a little friendly competition."

Leave it to Trev to peer into a haven of ancient beauty and see an opportunity for an adrenaline rush.

"Does it always have to be a competition?"

"Emma..." He had a gift for drenching my name in the most mollifying tone possible.

"I know, I know. *It'll be fun,*" I said in my best Trevor-voice. Why did I bother asking?

Becky skipped forward. "I'll go with Riley."

Riley turned from me to her and back again right as A. J. dipped his shoulder into mine. "That leaves you and me, Emma."

Of course it did. Maybe a race was a good idea, even

if it meant partnering with A. J. I'd take any diversion right now. Especially one that gave me the chance to show up Trevor. "We'll see you fools in the dust."

The corner of Riley's mouth followed his arced brow. "Trash talker, huh?"

I laughed. "Fun facts you'd never guess about me."

"I'm learning something new every day."

A. J. toed the line next to him. "Ready to do this?"

Jaycee elbowed Trevor, and he flung his hands in the air to signal the start of the race.

I took two steps for every one of A. J.'s. "I'll try not to slow you down."

"You just concentrate on making sure we don't end up in circles."

"Too bad I don't have red lipstick to mark the rocks." I chuckled, doubting he'd follow my movie reference.

"At least it's safe to say we wouldn't have any creatures flipping around the arrows."

"You've seen *Labyrinth*?"

He peeked behind him. "You sound surprised."

"Um, to be honest, yeah. Not what I would've expected."

"Oh, c'mon. David Bowie, big hair, cheesy music… it's a classic."

He kept breaking every stereotype I tried to place on him.

Still laughing, we squeezed through the maze of narrow canyons and winding passageways and toppled out of the exit with the hope of being the first to arrive.

We wouldn't be that lucky.

Beside Jaycee, Trevor lounged on a large boulder with his ankles crossed and hands behind his head. All he was missing was an emery board to pass the time. He exaggerated a yawn. "Glad you guys could finally make it."

"Nice." I flicked a twig at him. "Seriously, Jae, at least try to tame his gloating."

Jaycee hooked an arm around his neck and pecked his cheek with a proud kiss. "Sorry, Em. When you're just that good, you're just that good."

I bent over my shoulder to gag.

"Wow. The view's amazing," Riley said from behind us.

Becky skipped over and linked arms with Ashlea, leaving Riley alone at the edge of the trail opening. Standing against the expansive backdrop with the wind rustling his hair, he looked like he could've been filming a music video.

My throat turned impossibly dry.

"Come check this out, Em." Jaycee waved me toward her and Trevor.

Riley wasn't exaggerating. The altitude swept us into a panoramic view of the Columbia River under a painted sky as vibrant as the wildflowers we'd passed on our way up.

I leaned into Trevor's bulky shoulder, stunned by how he managed to time our ascent to the top of the mountain with the sunset. "Not bad."

He rocked his backpack into my side. "The night's still young—"

A shrill gasp drew all of our attention toward Ashlea cradled in the crook of A. J.'s arm, her face a sheet of white against her fiery hair blowing in the wind.

"It's okay," A. J. said to the rest of us. "She tripped, that's all. Standing this close to the edge of a few-hundred-foot-drop can unnerve anyone."

The wooed look on Ashlea's face complemented the chivalry on A. J.'s. He continued to guard the edge of the cliff even after the dust settled. Trevor hugged Jaycee to his chest and wrapped the sides of his jacket around her arms. And Riley humored Becky with a game of hacky sack using a pinecone.

Standing amidst my friends, gratefulness swelled. They weren't like the guys I was used to. The ones who pretended to care to get what they really wanted. These three couldn't help but be genuine. Maybe some mamas still knew how to raise their boys right.

My walk with Riley around campus rushed to mind again. His transparency with me, how he related to the things I wrestled to put into words, the way he stirred feelings I hadn't experienced in other relationships. Could things really be different with the right guy?

Another gust of brisk air ripped across the cliff and poured down the inside of my jacket. I flipped up the collar, zipped it the rest of the way, and clung to the last glimpses of daylight bowing to an early autumn evening.

"Come on, guys, the fun's not over yet." Trevor

hopped in the air to draw attention to his backpack and whatever mystery it held inside. "I pulled a few strings and got permission to have a campfire here in the park. We can stay as late as we want. My buddy even set up a fire pit for us."

Riley caught the pinecone in one hand and snapped his head in Trevor's direction. "Wait a sec. You know someone who oversees this state park?"

"Trevor knows everybody," I said. "You learn not to be surprised when he has some kind of bizarre connection."

He tossed the pinecone and caught it again. "I'll have to remember that."

"Cody was really cool about it," Trevor said. "But you might not want to mention it to anyone else. I don't want to get him in trouble."

Jaycee and I exchanged a glance of reservation, but Trevor drooped his bulky arms across our shoulders and lugged us forward before we could protest.

Ahead, Becky stopped at the edge of the pit and covered her mouth. "Aw, Trevor, this was so sweet of your friend."

Cody had outlined a fire pit with four wooden benches. A pile of long, thin branches rested against the one closest to us. Trevor dug out a book of matches from his bag and set the pre-built fire ablaze. Blanketed in the seclusion of the mountain, it was hard not to mimic Becky's bubbling-over gushing.

We all huddled on the benches as a series of burning

ashes launched into the air and floated around us like fireflies. Jae and I eased forward until steam rose from the soles of our sneakers.

Under a moon outranking the fire's glow, the night could've been extracted from a score of childhood summers with Dad.

"There's something about campfires, isn't there?"

A. J. tossed a handful of pine needles into the pit. "You had campfires in California?"

"Why does everyone assume all of California feels exactly like Los Angeles? You'd be surprised how chilly it gets in San Francisco."

A. J. raised his hands. "Easy, cowgirl."

I smiled in spite of myself. "To be honest, most of my campfire memories are actually from Lake Tahoe. My family spent a couple of weeks at my uncle's lake house every fall and summer."

Riley sat back and considered me a moment. "That would explain your love of the outdoors."

His attentive observation magnified the heat sprawling over my face. I bit into my s'more and looked away.

A. J. passed the bag of marshmallows to Ashlea. "You should've brought your guitar, Em." He flicked a glance at Riley's surprised expression. "She didn't tell you she plays?"

Riley looked at me, and a chunk of my s'more stopped dead in my throat.

7

FALLING

"Aw, man, I should've thought of that." Trevor stretched a gooey string of melted marshmallow from his mouth. "You and Riley could've had your showdown right here."

Jaycee poked Trevor with her stick.

"Ow, what'd I say?"

Please tell me they weren't actually having this conversation. I unzipped A. J.'s jacket, tugged the collar away from my throat, and braced myself for Riley's deluge of questions about why I hadn't mentioned my guitar playing to him.

None came.

He set his stick across his lap, his focus rivaling the intensity of the fire. "What inspires your music?"

No one had ever asked me that before. He scooted forward on the bench. An honest desire to connect with another musician's heart poured through his eyes and overrode all the questions he was more than entitled to ask.

Except I wasn't a musician. Not like him. Yet the way he looked at me, I almost believed it didn't matter.

"My dad," I answered. "I've played off and on since I was eleven. He gave me lessons growing up, but, um, I wasn't exactly the best student. He never gave up on me though. Even when I did." I stared into the fire and into memories charred with loss. "I picked it up again a few years ago. Playing…"

"Makes you feel close to him," Riley said.

I managed to nod. Was there anything he didn't understand?

The grooves on the bench pressed into my palms, the pain of missing Dad piercing deeper.

Riley's gaze met mine with clear perception and then darted around the group. "Hey, Becky, why don't you do that impression of Dean Scott you were showing me on the trail?"

Everyone followed Riley's intended distraction.

"Thank you," I mouthed across the circle to him.

He dipped his chin, and my heart slipped a little farther through my walls.

Ashlea peered into the sky. "Check out the stars, guys."

Out this far away from any light pollution, the sky's clarity made the stars feel close enough to touch—just like at my uncle's lake house. "Whenever I see the sky like this, it reminds me of the *bigness* of it all. That I'm just a small piece of the puzzle, you know?"

While everyone surveyed the heavens, Riley kept his eyes on me, as if what he saw across the fire captured him more than a breathtaking sky ever could. What was he thinking about?

Trevor's cell lit up with a text message. He thumbed a reply and hopped off the bench. "Time to roll, guys."

We started our descent following the edge of the mountain. I had to hand it to Trev. He knew how to pick out adventures. I looked over my shoulder at Riley. "When was the last time you spent a Friday night scaling old volcano rock?"

"Have to say, this might be a first. Emma, look ou—"

The rock under my foot rolled off the edge, taking me with it. The trail disappeared above me. I clawed at the mountainside. Dust filled my nose, my mouth. Jagged rock fragments poured into my socks and swallowed my ankles deeper into the mountain the harder I strained to keep from sliding any farther.

I couldn't regain my balance.

Couldn't breathe.

No air.

No sound.

And for a second, I thought I heard Dad's voice.

Riley caught my arm and anchored me in place. Adrenaline and paralysis ripped through my muscles. My pulse hammered against my eardrums and alternated with my friends' shouting until every noise dissolved but the sound of Riley's assurance.

"Emma, look at me. I've got you. Give me your other hand." His grasp tightened around my wrist. Strength and masculinity teemed in the raised muscles on his forearms as he towed me up to the top of the cliff in a single motion.

Clouds of dirt stirred under our feet. He held on to me, hands pressed tight around my back. I kept my cheek on his chest and his coat balled in my fingers. "Thank you."

His heart raced beneath my ear, his breath and whiskers over my hair. I raised my head but froze when his lips hovered above mine. Neither of us moved.

"Em!" Jaycee flew toward us.

Face creasing, Riley let me go like I was the breakable piece of china Megan had talked about in the locker room.

Jaycee clobbered me in a hug. "Girl, you almost gave me a heart attack."

"I'm good. Promise." Mostly. I waved her off. "We should keep moving."

A. J. bounded forward. "Maybe I should carry her."

"Don't even think about it." I backed up. "The last thing we need is both of us tumbling over the side."

"She's right." Ashlea clasped his hand. "It's dangerous. We should walk side by side, watch each other's back."

A. J. resisted her tug. "You sure you don't need—?"

"She's good. She's got Riley. Now, c'mon." Ashlea nudged him forward before he could protest again.

We all eased the rest of the way down. Though Riley didn't say anything about what had happened a moment ago, he stayed by my side with his pinky grazing mine, ready to move at the slightest indication I needed him.

I stood my ground until we reached the car. But once inside Trev's Outlander, the woodsy smell of smoke left on our clothes clouded my senses. Being with him tonight awakened a desire to know him more—his music, his passions, even the thoughts that held his eyes captive.

The dark sky streamed above the tree line outside my window. I wound my necklace around my finger, my promise to Dad twisting in my heart. Did that promise have room for more than a career?

Riley's coat crinkled against the car's leather interior. I turned and followed the moonlight draped across the back seat onto his body. So much for breathing. The same electricity from earlier kept us both in place.

Jaycee's door opened, and I almost hit my head on the ceiling. Nice. How was I supposed to be friends with someone I couldn't even handle sharing the same seat with?

Ashlea met A. J. as he circled around his front bumper behind us. "Thanks for the ride."

"My pleasure. I'll never pass up the chance to beat Trev in a race."

Trevor hopped over the curb. "Keep talking smack,

and we're gonna end up on the courts tonight." He hooked Jaycee in his arms and reclined against the car door. "Hey, Em, come train with A. J. and me in the gym for a few weeks, and you might just fit into that jacket."

*The jacket.* I shucked my arms out of the lined sleeves and returned it to A. J., being sure to give Trevor a good whack in the face with it in the process.

"I'd let you hang onto it," A. J. said. "But I don't know. I kinda like being able to take care of you in the moment." His dimples sank so deeply in his cheeks they probably touched each other on the inside.

My heels dropped off the curb. I gave serious consideration to slinking down the storm drain beside me, but I caught Riley's shirtsleeve instead and made a beeline for his silver Civic parked a few spaces down from the other vehicles.

"I had a good time tonight," Riley said. "Trust me. Most people on campus come up with far less creative ways to have fun. You've got some good friends."

"The best." Even with Trev's and A. J.'s antics, I couldn't deny that truth.

We ran out of walkway sooner than I wanted. Beside his car, I twined my arms behind my back and one leg over the other. I was even more tongue-tied, but I had to ask. "What were you thinking about?" I blurted out. "At the fire, I mean." There went all subtlety.

A passing car's bass filled the now-awkward silence.

Riley stared at the ground. "I was thinking that you are a very unique girl, Emma Matthews." He looked up slowly. "You don't even realize how you view the world, do you? Like an artist. You should trust that more. It's inspiring."

Me? He was joking, right? "You're the artist." The one whose music awakened things in me I'd suppressed after losing Dad. Creativity, dreams, desire. Things I was starting to crave again. I twisted my necklace. "Maybe…"

Two pixie-like girls purposefully swayed their hips as they sauntered by Riley. Not that he noticed. He closed the distance between us, eyes locked on mine. "Maybe what?"

*Breathe.* "Maybe you could play… for me… sometime?"

He dropped his gaze to the asphalt.

My pulse throbbed in his pause. What was I doing? Stupid. I never should have—

"I'd like that," he finally said.

This close, the smoky campfire scent clinging to him absorbed every other thought.

The corner of his mouth slanted. "On one condition."

## 8

## LIABILITY

MY BREATH CAUGHT the same way it had the first day I saw him. Except this time, his eyes didn't let me go. I leaned against the hood of the car to steady my balance. "What condition?"

With his head lowered again, he scuffed his shoe against the sidewalk divider. The streetlight's glare fell over the curve of a grin. "I'll share my music if you promise to let me hear some of yours."

My hand slid off the hood. He couldn't be serious.

The door hinge creaked in place of the response locked up somewhere inside my rib cage. He stepped into the driver's side and smiled over the top of the car. "Night, Emma."

I couldn't manage a response. I simply stood on the curb like a statue glowing in the fading trail of his tail-lights. Play? In front of him? No way. What was I thinking asking him that?

Stars strained to bleed through the charcoal-gray clouds. At some point along the ride home, the sky had lost its clarity, and I'd obviously lost my common sense.

I trudged toward the stoop without looking past the square inch beyond my footsteps. Someone appeared from the shadows. I jumped two feet back, gasped.

"Whoa, it's okay, Em. It's just me," A. J. said. "Didn't mean to scare you."

"Oh, sorry." I continued up the sidewalk. "I thought everyone already went home."

"Yeah." He rubbed the backs of his fingers over his five o'clock shadow. "I started to head to my place but wanted to make sure you were all right first, after the fall and everything. Tonight, you seemed... I don't know, off."

Off. Yeah, that's exactly what I was. Between the pressure from Mr. Oakly, Mom's financial issues, and memories of Dad resurfacing, what else would I expect?

"Thanks for checking, but I'm fine. Really."

He dipped his chin. "I didn't know unsteady fit into the *fine* category."

Unsteady? I squared my feet. "I think I can handle standing on level ground."

He edged closer, backing me into the door until my shoulders pressed against the cool glass. "Sure about that?"

The buzz of the streetlight answered for me. I lifted my palm to his chest. The second the corner of his lips flirted with satisfaction, I dropped my hand to my side. He tucked a finger under my chin.

"A. J.," I warned.

He paused, brow crinkling, then winked. "See you around, Rosy."

The air in my lungs oozed out as he swaggered down the sidewalk to his car. Okay, maybe his advances were more than testosterone wars after all. Which meant I needed to set him straight—and fast. The same way I needed to set myself straight about Riley.

I banged my fist to my forehead. Ugh, what was wrong with me? I dug my cell from my pocket and called Austin.

"There's this little thing called sleep, Em. Ever heard of it? It's what normal people do at this time of night."

"I wouldn't exactly classify you as normal. And don't act like you don't have a venti Starbucks cup sitting next to you right now."

"Guilty," he said after an exaggerated gulp. "To what do I owe the pleasure of this late-night call?"

Despite his teasing, I grappled for an honest answer. "I was thinking about Dad tonight. Remember those crazy teepee fires he made at Uncle Rick's?"

"Yeah. But, I don't know, I think his real talent was keeping Mom from making him put them out. Gotta give the man some bonus points for those saves."

I laughed. "Poor Mom. She didn't stand a chance against his charm."

"Guess that's what happens when you're in love," Austin said with an audible shrug.

His comment sank into my chest to the place where hope always wavered.

I picked at a scratch in the metal door handle. "Do you think it's pointless to search for that kind of love?"

"So, *that's* what this call is about. Giving up already? I thought you banned fairy tales for good."

"I have, but… Stop avoiding my question."

"Look who's talking."

"Hey, I have enough stress in my life without worrying about chasing after love," he said. "Besides, if I ever need a little drama, I have a kid sister I can call."

"Hilarious." The joke that never got old. He and Trev could have their own stand-up act. "Are you ever serious?"

"Occasionally."

He was lucky I loved his laugh.

"For real, Em. I don't think you have to worry about searching for love. When you're ready, it'll find you."

"But does it really matter? Mom and Dad were lucky enough to find each other, and now he's gone." What was the point in putting faith in something that could be stripped away from you?

My last word hung in Austin's pause.

"Some risks are worth taking," he finally said with the same resoluteness Dad had always held.

I wished I could believe them both the way I used to,

but too much had happened since then. Still, it helped to hear my brother's voice.

"Love you, Aust."

"Love you too. Now you better get to sleep before Jaycee starts thinking I'm a bad influence on you."

"Yeah, I think it's a tad late for that one."

His caffeine-amped snicker ended our call. I pocketed my phone and looked back at the empty spot where Riley's car had been. Austin was right about one thing. I had clearly lost my battle for sanity.

I let my forehead drop against the door and prayed all my impulsive feelings would funnel down the walkway into the gutter where they belonged. Ready or not, the only risk worth taking was waiting for me to face it head-on tomorrow.

## 9

## UNCOMPLICATED

WITH LAST NIGHT shoved inside a back drawer of my mind, day one of my internship at Xander Technologies took the forefront.

I rolled my chair up to my desk and resituated the stapler and tape dispenser. A quick shake of my mouse roused the computer monitor back to life. After signing in, I looked around and exhaled. *This* was sensible. No charming guys or romantic notions complicating matters. Just black and white, measurable work.

The clock on my PC announced the end of my lunch break. I aligned my training manual beside a yellow legal pad, then swapped the two, set a pencil on top of the binder, and drummed my fingers over my laminate desk.

The ceiling vent blew ice-cold air tainted with a burnt coffee stench onto my shoulders and hovered inside my tiny cubicle. Why hadn't I thought to bring a sweater? And what was the deal with this annoying restlessness? I'd already soared through the morning training. I should have eased right in with everyone else by now. This was what I'd prepared for, what I was good at. Why did I feel out of step?

Jack Peters's secretary, Renee, peeked over the partition wall. Curved wrinkles rippled around the corners of a motherly smile. "Relax. You're doing great, honey. No need to be uptight."

I slumped my shoulders a little. "Better?"

She let out a raspy laugh. "It's a start."

"Sorry. I want to make a good impression, I guess."

"You already are, deary." She rolled in a chair beside me. "Now, where'd we leave off?"

I thumbed through the binder to the flagged page headed "Financial Reporting and Control" and felt the blood drain from my face. "Um, Renee, I've only had one class on interpreting financial reports."

She retrieved a giant stack of papers from the overhead shelf and plopped them next to my adding machine. "That's what practice is for." She lifted up the red-hued reading glasses chained around her neck. "These are all past statements that've already been reviewed. Jack wants you to study the first half along with the notes he included. Then you'll provide your own analysis on the second half."

My own analysis? Either the cubicle just shrank a size, or the air cut off. Maybe I didn't need that sweater after all.

Renee lowered her glasses to her floral-patterned

blouse. Even though I'd just met her, she held a sort of mother-hen look toward me. "Trust your training, honey. If you walk away with anything, remember that."

A man craned his neck around the cubicle opening, something apparently catching his eye. He backed up and stepped inside. Skinny tie, Italian-looking suit, sleek hair, not a whisker in sight. Seemed kind of young to be the boss, but everything in his demeanor screamed confidence, including the unabashed stare fixed on me.

"Renee told me she was impressed with you. Seems she left out a few details."

What was that supposed to mean?

Renee coughed as she swiveled her chair toward the desk.

"Jack Peters." He extended a hand. "Sorry for the late intro. I was tied up in meetings this morning. Renee tells me you're picking things up faster than she anticipated."

I straightened the stack of reports. "I think she might be a tad on the gracious side."

"I doubt that. You don't earn your kind of grades by relying on grace." He stretched an arm over the partition. His oversized silver watch rapped against the molding. "The same principles apply here. Push hard, find ways to make the boss look good, ace your performance reviews, and reap the benefits."

At least someone understood how things worked. "Uncomplicated," I said. "That's the way I like it."

He slanted a brow. "My kinda girl."

Renee swung around and bumped Jack's knee with the binder on her lap. "We should get back to training."

He wiped off his pant leg. "I'll take it from here, Renee. Thank you."

She didn't move at first. When he cocked his head, she skirted past him, mumbling something undecipherable.

Jack took her spot in the chair beside me and ran a hand down his silky tie. "Okay, show me what you got."

"I'm sorry?"

Flaunting a devilish grin, he motioned to the stack of reports without ungluing his gaze from mine. "Profit Loss statements."

Right. What happened to that air conditioning? "Do you mind if I get a drink of water before we get started?"

"Be my guest." He swept his arm toward the hall. "Actually, why don't you grab that and meet me in my office instead. It's less distracting in there." He stood in the opening, so I had to squeeze by him. "Sometimes you need a little privacy if you want to make any real progress."

The floor of clustered cubicles sandwiched beside each other suddenly felt like an open courtyard compared to the *privacy* of an office's closed walls. At least they were see-through.

I hunched over the water fountain and tapped my fingers against the chrome base. What was with the whole *Suits* routine? Did he think this was some USA drama series where he'd pick up the naive girl hoping for kickbacks?

Or was I over-reading his signals? It wouldn't be the first time. Surely, he was a professional. Either way, he'd find out I could hold my own. I pushed off the fountain.

A guy, who looked young enough to have been interning from high school, rolled a cart out of a cluttered room. "If we add any more junk in there, it's going to turn into Hogwarts' Room of Requirement." Snickering, he swept his Bieber hair from his face.

I peered through the window on the door. Dozens of monitors, towers, and keyboards filled the room like some kind of forgotten computer graveyard. "They're not usable anymore?"

"Usable? Yeah, I guess. If you don't care about things like HD graphics. But who wants to wait on slower frame rates when you can get the latest Intel Core chip?"

How old was this kid, and what language was he speaking? I waved it off, pretending to have a clue what he was talking about. "Yeah, totally." I peeked inside the room again. "Seems like a waste though."

"Welcome to the nonstop evolution of technology." With a quick shrug, Shaggy-Haired Boy steered his cart toward the elevator.

The company wouldn't toss all that hardware because it was a little out of date, would it? Then again, that was the way most things worked. Always those who got discarded, value discounted. I swallowed. I couldn't afford to be one of them.

Inhaling, I straightened. This internship was the goal I'd trained for. Maybe even the one I was meant to have.

My forehead landed on the doorframe a second later. So, why did that goal still feel as meaningless as this overlooked room of abandoned computers?

The air conditioning kicked on again and ignited a reminder of Riley's comment. *"You don't even realize how you view the world, do you? Like an artist. You should trust that more."* I wanted to. There was just one problem. I didn't know what to trust anymore.

## 10

## RUNAWAY

IN OUR APARTMENT, I dropped Jaycee's keys in front of her on the table and trekked to the kitchen. "Thanks for letting me borrow your car."

She swallowed a bite of a ham, egg, and cheese sandwich. "How'd it go?"

Aside from an awkward one-on-one session with a boss who kept his eyes on me longer than on the computer? At least he'd kept his hands off. Well, other than that one brush against my knee. I was probably blowing it out of proportion. The last thing I needed was for my boss to think I was some inexperienced schoolgirl, trigger-happy on making accusations.

I tugged two cabinet doors open. "The way it's supposed to." Work's work. You train, you produce, you earn respect. Just as I'd been expecting.

The near-empty fridge glared at me. I flipped around,

tossed my head back against the freezer door, and stared at the flat white ceiling.

Cereal would suffice. Uncomplicated cereal.

I plopped onto the chair across from Jaycee, swiped a banana from the fruit bowl, and ripped it open a corner at a time.

I was fine with my plan. Fine with aiming for a lucrative job. So what if the internship lacked potential for fulfillment? That was a luxury anyway. As long as it provided security and helped me take care of Mom and myself, that was what mattered. It's what I was on target for.

Until I met Riley.

I slapped the empty banana peel on the place mat. Why did he have to unbury things better left alone?

Jaycee's stare joined the light boring into me from the ceiling fixture.

I dropped my spoon into my bowl. Milk splashed across the Formica tabletop. "What?"

She lowered a piece of her sandwich onto her napkin. "I warned you not to get all defensive when I was probing."

"Jae, you haven't even said anything. You're just..." I waved between us. "Staring."

"I was reading your thoughts." She swirled her cup of coffee, releasing hints of caramel and intuition into the air. "It's easy to interpret people's thoughts when they don't think anybody's paying attention."

"Oh, really?" I slumped back in my chair, grinning. "And what do my thoughts tell you?"

She pinched off another piece of bagel and rolled it into a tiny ball. "That you're already in too deep."

"Is that something only mind readers understand?" I shrugged off her psychoanalysis and resumed my cereal eating, but my intentional slurping couldn't drown out her silent response.

My spoon clinked against the Corelle bowl again. "Fine, hit me with it."

"You asked me to help you not to rush with Riley, remember?"

That was what she was worried about? "Jae, relax. There's nothing to rush into. Riley and I are just friends." I shoveled in another bite of my now-mushy Cheerios, which was almost as hard to swallow as my comment.

She pinned her arms over her V-neck sweater. "Just friends, huh? I don't see you brooding over me."

"I'm not brooding." Okay, maybe a little.

Jaycee caught my gaze and held on. "It's obvious you guys have a connection. I just want you to be careful. There's been some talk."

I circled my spoon in the air when she stalled. "About?"

She scooted her chair closer to the table and shifted her hands to her neck, to her lap, and finally onto the place mat. If she got any antsier, she'd knock over her coffee cup. "About Riley having a bit of a past."

My arched shoulders leveled out with an exhale. "I'm pretty sure we all have one of those. Kinda goes with the whole life-cycle thing."

"You know what I mean." She twisted her necklace into a spiral. "I heard he lived in Nashville for a while. That he got into some trouble that almost got him arrested."

Arrested? I dragged my spoon around the bottom of the bowl and tried to imagine Riley in trouble with the law. Maybe he did have a little darkness in his past. It might explain some of his melancholy music. But that could also be what added depth to his artistry. What made him real, authentic. Part of what set him apart from any guy I knew.

She let go, and her necklace uncoiled. "Maybe you should ask him—"

"And maybe you should leave it alone." My chair screeched with a resounding exclamation point as I pushed away from the table. I snatched a handful of napkins from the center and dabbed them over the spilled milk and the words I wanted to take back.

"Sorry. I didn't mean to snap. I just have a lot on my mind." I pushed my hair out of my face, off my neck. "I'm gonna go check my mail." I could use some air. Or at least a distraction.

This time of day, the campus center turned into a revolving chain of frenzied students rushing between their classes. I scurried through the maze, squeezing through one free space to the next until I saw Miriam a few feet away.

With a backpack twice her size hunching her forward, she glanced up from her loafers and looked right at me. My heel caught a snag in the floor and launched me straight into A. J.'s uncanny timing.

"Better slow down, there, killer," he said, clearly enjoying the opportune collision.

Miriam continued advancing. I grabbed A. J.'s forearms. "Quick. Hide me." My back hit the wall behind us. A. J. hovered above me with his palms flexed against the bricks on either side of my shoulders. I peered under his sleeve and caught Miriam's gaze again. But instead of coming over, she lowered her head again and kept walking past us.

A. J. leaned in. The bangs peeking out from under his turned-around basketball cap touched my forehead. "Who are we hiding from?" he whispered.

Someone I couldn't afford to get close to. Which reminded me… I ducked under his arm before he got the wrong impression. "Don't ask."

"O-kay." The dragged-out word joined the noisy squeak his basketball shoes made over the tiles.

"Headed to the gym?" Like I had to ask.

"I'm supposed to meet Trevor at one. Thought I better come a little early to warm up. You know how competitive he is."

That I did. We walked side by side toward the endless

rows of student mailboxes mounted on the wall in the atrium.

"You should come play a couple of games with us." He flipped his Trailblazers ball cap off and tucked it onto my head. "You can be on my team."

In the two-inch heels I borrowed from Jaycee against my better judgment? Yeah, maybe not. "I'm not exactly dressed for basketball."

His gaze flashed up and down me like a strobe light. I snatched off his hat and shoved it over his face. He slipped the cap backward onto his head again while a mischievous grin regained its regular hold on his lips. I maneuvered around him, but he hopped in front of me. "Oh, c'mon, Em. Or are you worried you can't hang on the basketball court?"

My hands gravitated to my hips before he finished. "I nail my layups every time, thank you very much. But I wouldn't want to rob Trevor of his enjoyment in beating you all by himself."

"Ohh…" A. J. flung his hand over his chest to cover the blow my little faith in his basketball skills had landed to his pride. "So, that's how it is? I'm hurt, Emma, really."

My eyes rolled with the same dramatization as the ones pouting at me. I unlocked my mailbox and withdrew a cluster of envelopes.

"Fine," he said, "we'll ball another time. Come grab a quick bite with me instead. I'm going to need some energy if I'm going to prove you wrong about Trevor winning."

The need to set him straight about us resurfaced. "Um, that's probably not such a good idea. Listen, about last night after the campfire... I appreciate you staying to check on me. You're sweet. But I hope—"

"Easy, girl. A guy can only take so many blows in one day."

His smile eased the sting, but I hated seeing the strain it took to keep the playfulness in his voice.

I really did want to be his friend. I twisted the stack of envelopes. "Maybe we could..."

Riley strolled toward us, stealing my words, my thoughts.

"Could what?" A. J. angled in front of me until he blinked into focus.

I rubbed my arm. My coarse wool sweater burrowed into me right along with his perplexed expression.

Riley stopped beside us. The creases over A. J.'s forehead shifted again, pulling taut with the muscles in his neck. How could a bustling hallway have turned this quiet? I backed against the mailboxes. I should've run—away from hurting A. J. and away from falling for Riley. It wasn't fair to any of us.

Riley budged his stare from A. J. to me. "What are you guys up to?"

"Trevor and A. J. are gonna ball at one," I said quickly.

A. J. squeezed the bill of his hat, biceps twitching. "Wanna join the competition?"

In Jaycee's high heel boots, I shouldn't have felt this small standing between them.

Riley smiled curtly but didn't rise to A. J.'s insinuation. "Actually, I'm heading back to my apartment to work on some music. I swung by campus to see if Emma wanted to help me."

The envelopes in my hand hit the tiles and fanned across the floor. I scrambled to gather them into a stack and whirled up from the ground in time to see A. J.'s expression transition into a wall of indifference.

"You two have fun this afternoon." He darted a chin flick at Riley, backed up, then strutted to the exit.

Something prodded me to go after him, but Riley touched my arm, his unanswered request still hanging between us. "What do you say?"

Help him with his music? I returned the crumpled envelopes to my mail slat. "I think you're overestimating my skill level. You've never even heard me play. I might ruin it."

"Doubt that." He lowered his head in front of mine. "Trust me. Music's a part of you. I can see it."

He made it so easy to believe. Too easy. I should listen to Jae and stay away from him if I wanted to guard my heart.

Grasping for any shred of resolve, I clasped my elbows across my chest. "I thought you weren't crazy about playing in front of people."

He scrunched his lips to one side. "Let's just say, sometimes it's nice to change up your audience."

His smile undid my arms. They drifted to my sides and left my heart exposed once again.

He held out his hand. "C'mon." Without expounding, he led me toward the exit. With my hand in his, no explanation mattered anyway. You can only run for so long before you run out of excuses.

## 11

## DEFENSELESS

A FIVE-MINUTE DRIVE shouldn't have left my muscles tighter than an hour-long aerobics class. Then again, the gym didn't smell like Riley's shower-damp hair.

As soon as the tires skimmed the curb in front of a short row of brick apartments, I pried my fingers from my innocent seat belt and jetted into Oregon's misty fresh air.

*Breathe.*

At the door, Riley turned the key halfway in the deadbolt. "Brace yourself."

As if it would've mattered. Hints of the shower he must've taken before coming to get me billowed from inside, right before an adorable chocolate Lab pounced on me with the full force of the day's pent-up energy.

"Emma, meet Jake." He squatted down and rubbed the dog behind both ears. "He gets a little excited when we have visitors."

Jake lapped his slippery tongue against the backs of my fingers. "I can see that."

"He'll calm down in a minute." Riley motioned toward a sliding glass door along the opposite side of the living room. "Would you mind letting him outside?" He tossed his keys onto a narrow table in the entryway. "I'll grab us some waters."

Jake sprinted between both doors two times before I made it across a bare-walled room that would've put Jaycee in home-makeover heaven. But there was something to say for practicality over style. Something I could relate to.

I tugged on the door handle. Snout first, Jake pushed the sliding door open wide enough to squirm through and darted outside.

"I'm surprised you're allowed to have a pet in an apartment."

"I lucked out getting a landlord who's a dog lover. Double bonus getting an apartment with a fenced-in backyard." Riley peered around the edge of the hollow doorframe separating the kitchen and living room. "I'm gonna cut up a lime for my water. You want some?"

"Um, sure." Fresh limes? I thought a single guy's kitchen was supposed to look like the rest of the bachelor pad: sparse. Though, Riley's pad didn't exactly fit into the normal category. Instead of where someone would've typically placed a TV, he had an upright piano. Right beside it, a laminate bookcase with a bowed middle shelf leaned to one side. Obligation beside passion. Responsibility beside dreams. A perfect depiction of the same inner conflict I knew too well.

I traced my fingers over the black and white keys. "I didn't know you played the piano." Was there anything he didn't do?

"I took lessons as a kid."

"Me too, but I quit before I really got the hang of it." One of many regrets added to a list of more than I cared to count.

I glanced at the half-emptied coffee mug sitting on the piano top next to handwritten sheet music and two chewed-up pencils. "When did you start writing your own music?"

"Sometime between the first day I snuck my dad's guitar into my room and the day I'd saved up enough to buy my own."

"Wait. Your dad's a musician too?" Something else we had in common.

"He tried to be. He dragged my mom, my two little sisters, and me to Nashville when I was fifteen, hunting down the dream of getting signed." The cutting board vibrated against the kitchen counter as he sliced. "Don't get me wrong. I'm all about chasing dreams, but sometimes you gotta learn when to let it go."

If he only knew.

"Not that he wasn't talented. He was. Determined too. But he couldn't accept he didn't have what record labels were looking for. And his family took the brunt of it." The edge in his voice could've replaced the knife. "I used to think the pain of rejection was worse than the pain of regret. I'm not so sure anymore."

The room fell silent.

"I'm sorry." I didn't have to know the details of what he went through to recognize the ache in his words.

"Don't be." His voice grew somber. "If nothing else, he's kept me from making the same mistakes as him."

My forehead pinched. "Are you saying you think pursuing your music is a mistake?" He couldn't honestly believe that. "You and your dad are two different people. Just because it didn't work out for him, doesn't mean—"

"I'm his son, Emma. I have the same genes." A resigned exhale swept in from the kitchen. "And he's never let me forget it."

The implication speared into my chest to the chasm separating loss and love. I spotted his guitar stand beside a faded faux leather recliner, and my heart broke a little more. How could anyone think Riley's music didn't measure up? That *he* didn't measure up? Especially his father.

I jumped at the sound of the blade colliding with the cutting board again.

"I quit playing when I was sixteen and didn't pick up a guitar again until after I came here and tried to remember what it was like to play without anyone to approve or disapprove. No ulterior motive, just the free feeling of music, you know? It's been..." He let out another slow breath. "Well, let's just say it's been more than a little challenging. I'd almost given up on falling in love with it again. Until recently," he added so softly I almost didn't hear him.

I lifted a picture frame from the piano top—his two sisters, I assumed. "I can't imagine how hard it must've been to live under your dad's disappointment, but please don't let his experience discourage you." His path would lead to a different outcome than his father's had. I was sure of it. "Believe me. I know how much it costs to hope, but have you ever thought about just going for it?"

"Once," he said slowly. "A long time ago." A sad laugh echoed off the kitchen walls and into the living room. "Your arms get weary when you keep them stretched toward something that'll always be out of reach."

I hugged my own weary arms to my sides.

"At this point, it's time to sober up. I'll graduate in the spring and get a normal job like everyone else."

Like me? Something flared inside me. "You're just going to settle? You can't. You're too talented. You can't give up and do something you're not even passionate about. Think what a loss it'd be for everyone you could touch with your music."

Even if he'd never been able to please his dad, had his perception of himself become so skewed that he couldn't see how amazing he was? I set the picture down, turned, and almost ran right into him. The intensity in his eyes cranked my heart higher up my throat.

He handed me my water without releasing my gaze. "You're flattering, but I don't have what it takes to get a record deal. Even if I did, I can't go down that road."

"That's your dad talking." The words flew out before I could stop them. I clamped a hand over my mouth. "I'm sorry. It's just that you have a real gift. I felt it as soon as I heard you play. I don't have a single doubt in my mind that a record label would jump at the opportunity to sign you. But I shouldn't have said—"

"No, it's fine." His eyes smoldered above his royal blue pullover. "It just catches me off guard sometimes. The way you can read me so easily. It's like every shield I normally have up is defenseless against you."

Though he didn't move an inch, his expression did. The level of emotion he held sent my own feelings spiraling. Swallowing hard, I fled to the corduroy couch and to the hope of finding my voice again.

The cushion dipped beside me a second later. "Are you okay?"

With his hand nearly grazing mine? Not even remotely, but this wasn't about me.

I set my cup down, rubbed my moist palms over my jeans, and faced him before I lost my ability to talk completely. "Listen, I promise I'm not trying to overstep my bounds. And I won't pretend to understand the scars your dad left on you. But I do know how it feels to wake up every day to doubts. I think, sometimes, believing in someone else is easier than believing in yourself."

I set a hand on his knee. "I know you don't see it—I knew when I heard you play at Nuts and Jolts that you didn't see it—but you're an incredible artist. You were made for this. I hope one day you'll be able to see all you have to offer."

Something unspoken burned in the way his focus drifted to my mouth. I withdrew my hand, the affectionate touch all of a sudden registering. He scooted back and downed his entire glass of water. The empty cup's *clink* against the coffee table jutted into the groan I was mortified for releasing out loud.

Thankfully, Riley didn't seem to notice. He ran his hands along the cushion's grooves as though debating something. A minute later, he led me up from the couch. Over by the recliner, he cleared off a pile of papers from the ottoman, motioned for me to take a seat, and retrieved his guitar from its stand.

From what he'd told me about his dad, no wonder he wanted to avoid the spotlight. "It's okay. You don't have to play for me."

"It's different with you." He sat on the chair arm and brought his guitar to his lap. "I don't feel like I'm performing. I feel like I'm living."

Without reservation, his fingertips kissed the strings, and it took everything in me not to wish I could trade places with them.

"Can we stay right here," he sang, "in this sweet refrain, where memories last and tears don't stain?

"Can we stay right here, in this timeless space, where hope is a song and love is a place?"

Each chord deepened a connection to him that I still didn't understand. When his eyes found mine again, it didn't matter. Nothing did. The emotion fueling his voice wrapped itself around me, and I knew right then. This was home, where I belonged. No matter how hard I tried to heed Jaycee's warning, I'd already lost. Whatever Riley's past held didn't frighten me. The grasp I was losing on my heart did.

"How do you hold on to somewhere you don't belong?" he sang. "How do you stay away from a dream that calls your name? Can we stay right here, for just a little longer?"

I inched toward him until a sharp noise at the sliding door nearly knocked me off the ottoman. We both looked toward Jake clawing at the glass. I'd never been more grateful to see a dog before. Another verse, and I surely would've made a fool of myself.

"Sorry about that," Riley said on his way to the door. "Jake's usually my only audience."

"Ah. So, *that's* what you meant about needing a change of audience." My tension eased as I wiped the dog hair from the seat of my pants. "He must be a good sounding board, 'cause seriously, Riley, that song was amazing. You definitely don't need any help from me."

With a soft smile on his lips, he rubbed his neck. "Except you've already helped write it."

What did that mean?

Jake barreled inside and saved me from asking. My unfamiliar scent must have been some sort of magnet. He bolted across the room on a mission to sniff me inch by inch. I could've kissed him for interrupting, wet nose or not.

"Get over here, Jake." In trained obedience, the dog flanked Riley's side while panting with the energy of a puppy. "Don't worry. He'll get used to you. You'll just have to come around more often."

And withstand *that* smile? Apparently, my guitar skills weren't the only thing he overestimated. I fled to my abandoned glass of water on the coffee table and dabbed the cool condensation from the cup onto my neck. Still burning, I yanked my sweater sleeves up my forearms.

Riley materialized next to me and stretched his guitar in my direction. "Your turn."

I choked on my water halfway through a swallow. As if I could possibly follow his flawless perfor-mance. "Sorry. Hard pass."

"You've got a little bit of a stubborn streak, don't you?"

More like self-preservation.

I scoured the room for a form of distraction—*any* form. Seeing the pile of ruffled papers on the floor, I dropped to the carpet beside them. "Are all of these songs you've written?"

"Yes. Or at least have started writing. I can work on one for hours and get stuck banging my head against this invisible roadblock. Know what I mean? I've learned it's better to lay it down for a while and pick it up later when my head's clear."

Already beside me, Riley collected a handful of pages of unfinished sheet music. "My songs usually come out of something I'm going through. Sometimes the music flows the easiest when the emotions are close to home. And other times, I can't break through it. I don't know if that makes any sense."

More than it should have. I traipsed back over to the couch, like it would do a lick of good to try to distance myself from how close I felt to him.

With his eyes never leaving mine, he strode across the room. My pulse followed each step bringing him closer. He settled beside me on the couch but didn't say anything. He didn't have to. The electric current channeling through the seat cushions between us said enough. Heat crawled up my back again and rendered my own defenses useless.

I unclasped my death grip on the cushion, but the inward battle hung on. Reason clashed with hope. Yearnings slayed logic. I couldn't do this. I had to get out of there.

"I should get back to campus," I blurted out while leaping off the couch like some crazed trapeze artist.

"Are you sure?"

I nodded. "Positive." Thirty more seconds sitting there, desire would've won the war over caution, and I'd be kicking myself for making a move I'd regret later.

He followed me to the entryway. "You know, you still haven't told me what you're passionate about?" Riley fished his keys out of the bowl on the table—the one I was now latching onto for sheer stability.

"I'm sorry, what?" I managed.

"Earlier, you said you think we should invest our lives doing something we were made to do."

"I was talking about you." I scooted the throw rug back and forth with the tip of my boot, afraid he'd see straight into the emptiness where vision was supposed to be. "Creating music isn't something you do, Riley. It's who you are. You can't afford to settle—most of us can."

"How can you say that?" He set a tender hand over my forearm.

The confinement I'd felt in my cubicle closed in on me again. Did he really want to see inside those gray walls?

"I'm not like you, okay? Growing up, when all the other kids were daydreaming about being doctors, firefighters, and veterinarians, I was the one shrinking down in my chair, praying the teacher didn't call on me." I traced the edge of the bowl and dodged his eyes. "Jae's always telling me I don't have to have everything figured out right now, but it's more than that."

His hand slid down to mine. "What is it then?"

The vulnerability I'd feared risking swept between us —too late to hide, too real to ignore.

"We all had a hard time dealing with my dad's death. Except Mom almost didn't recover. Emotionally. Financially. It shattered her entire world. Austin and I practically had to force-feed her for a while. We spent months afterward trying to break her addiction to anti-depressants. The helplessness we felt…"

I clutched my arms against the memories pressing in. "But I guess you find out how strong you can be when you have no other choice."

Jake came up beside me like he understood. I rubbed his head. "The day I had to drag her out of Walgreens after threatening the pharmacist was the day I vowed I wouldn't end up like her. No more waiting around for a career I was *made* for. As long as I could find a way to build a more stable life for us, then that's all that mattered."

I straightened but sighed a second later. "Which is why I should be happy with my internship. It's exactly what I've been pushing for. A lead to a promising job. Opportunity for advancement, financial security. But…"

Riley moved closer. "But?"

Some parts were harder to admit than others. I curled the edges of my sleeves under my fingers. "I've been so set on avoiding Mom's footsteps that I've buried Dad's in the process. He taught me to believe I could do something meaningful with my life. That I could make an impact, you know?"

Jake pushed my hand over his wet snout back onto his head. "But the truth is, I'm scared. Scared he's right, and I'm totally blowing it. And even more afraid he's wrong. That this is all there is." I faced Riley, too exposed to put up a front. "He promised me my life had a song worth sharing. But what if it's not enough?"

"That's not possible." He leaned forward, voice urgent. "Don't you see it?" His eyes held the same belief that had died in my heart the same night Dad did.

"See what?" I whispered.

He glanced at his cell, then back at me. "Showing you requires taking a little field trip."

A field trip? Where'd that come from?

Riley grabbed my hand. "Trust me."

Tell that to my heart.

## 12

## EXPRESSION

My BROWS ARCHED toward the green exit sign for downtown Portland passing above us. "You're taking me to work? Because that's definitely not gonna help your cause."

Riley merged into the left lane. "We have enough work in our lives. Sometimes we need a little adventure instead."

"An adventure. Thanks, Gandalf, but I'm all set."

A grin slid across his face and settled over his whole demeanor. "Breaking your borders is good for you."

I hunkered in my seat. "Not so sure about that."

"Look where it led Bilbo."

"To a fire-breathing dragon? Again, not helping your cause."

Riley pressed his tongue to his cheek to keep from laughing. "Courage, Em. It led him to find courage." He hooked a right onto Southwest Broadway.

He was taking me to the Cultural District? Made sense. The latest creative trends and the artistic roots of old-time architecture turned the streets into a group mural anyone could contribute to no matter what color or form their imagination used. It was a world where dreams were real. Riley's world. Maybe he'd let me borrow his paintbrush. Just for the day.

At least five free parking spaces came and went, but Riley kept driving. Past the stately brick buildings and quaint corner pubs. Past the abstract sculptures and tree-lined sidewalks. Shadows from skyscrapers stretched behind us in a goodbye wave. *Where's he taking me?*

At a stoplight, exhaust from the city bus in front of us leaked through the vents until the light finally turned green, and a left-hand turn led us onto a dead-end street.

The tires rumbled over the clunky gravel and came to a stop. I stared out the window. "An abandoned building. You shouldn't have."

He opened my door and extended a hand. "Trust me," he said again.

Jaycee's warning about his past cropped up but vanished the second I gripped his hand. It was hard to remain sensible with someone who sabotaged every shred of willpower I had.

I followed him to an opening in the wall that must've lost a fight to a sledgehammer. "Guess it wouldn't be *Nightmare On Elm Street*-ish enough if we used a door?"

He pointed to the crumbled concrete at the base of

the opening. "Apparently, cinder block was easier to break than padlocks."

"Why is that not comforting?"

A cop car rocketed past the side street, siren blaring. I retracted my hold from the wall. It probably wasn't such a good idea to leave any trace of fingerprints.

Riley's hand found the small of my back. "Relax, I won't let anything happen to you. Promise."

His assurance buried one fear behind another. Trusting him wasn't the problem. Trusting myself was. I doubted I could hide the way he made me feel when in the safety of his arms.

Two crows launched off the ground the minute we stepped inside the open-ceilinged building. "Watch your step." He pointed to breaks in the pavement where overgrown weeds had uprooted the foundation, and to piles of cinder blocks that had fallen from the tops of the walls.

Aside from two city benches that someone must've transported inside, the place could've been an old fortress, plundered and left in ruins.

He fanned his arm in a semicircle. "What do you see?"

"Cement walls."

He led me into the center and spun me around by the shoulders. "Look deeper."

I shielded the sun's glare from my face. "Colorful graffiti?"

"Don't get hung up on preconceived ideas. You have

an artist's heart, remember?" He tapped his chest. "What do you see from here?"

Inhaling, I focused on the details around us—intricate details of walls turned into murals. Some sketches were rushed and ragged. Some painstakingly beautiful. Others unfinished.

Visions of people escaping their circumstances to come here to paint blurred into the scene in front of us.

"An outlet," I answered. "Art. Creativity."

"Exactly." Riley beamed. "Most people see an abandoned, useless corner of the city. Same way they see the kids in this neighborhood. Even the way some of them see themselves. But here, something changes."

He approached the wall and traced his hand over the designs. "Here, they find their own voices and tell their stories without holding back."

He circled the perimeter. "I come sometimes to jam with the kids. Their expression is always unfiltered. No refined renditions or picture-perfect molds. Just straight from inside." He raised his head toward the open-ended sky. "They remind me to live without borders. Kind of like being with you."

Me? And all my prescribed plans? I surveyed the freestyle artwork and almost snorted. "I think you got the wrong girl."

"Or finally found the right one," he said softly.

I turned. Right in front of me, his eyes cradled me in an embrace sweeter than any touch.

"You don't recognize your gifts, do you? The way you

see potential in me and aren't afraid to call it out." He cocked his head. "With some force, I might add."

He nodded to the clouds. "You take time to see the world through a lens most people rarely do. Like these kids, you have a story to tell. Just have to find your own expression. You can do anything, Emma."

Except breathe from the way he looked at me. Similar to how he'd taken in the art, he studied me as if he felt what was inside rather than only seeing it. Like he believed in me and saw past my walls.

They'd been there so long—erected to safeguard my heart and keep the pain of loss out while holding the fear of disappointment inside. Suffocating me from both sides. If I lowered them, I might fall apart with the piles of cinder rubble. I couldn't risk that.

Riley touched my hand with such tenderness, I had to grip his sleeve to keep from melting through the cracks in the pavement. There wasn't a single foundation he couldn't break.

His lyrics replayed inside my heart again. *"How do you hold on to somewhere you don't belong? How do you stay away from a dream that calls your name? Can we stay right here, for just a little longer?"*

Somewhere you don't belong. That's where I'd been living. In school. At work. I wanted to believe there was something more. Something—or someone—calling my name.

The same whisper from the other day on the sports field sang in the wind. I closed my eyes, swallowed.

Riley's hand constricted around mine but then let go and brushed through the knee-high weeds as he turned away. "This place has been sort of a refuge for me. I've written a lot of songs here."

With his back still turned, he raised his shoulders. "I thought it might bring you inspiration too. Help you see your dad was right. You're already making an impact. You just have to see it for yourself."

His sincerity caused something in me to wince with longing.

"Thanks for sharing this with me. You're right. Maybe a little adventure is a good thing."

"I'm sorry, what was that?" His grin toppled his whole head sideways. "Was that just Emma Matthews conceding?"

I glared at him with all the pessimism I could fabricate. Pitiful. "Okay, Mr. Smarty Pants, I concede."

He raised his fists in the air. "Sweet victory."

"You know gloating doesn't become you, right?"

"Really? That's funny because sore losing is adorable on you." He laughed when I shoved him backward. "Yep, definitely adorable."

"Hope you're happy now."

"Almost." He headed for the trash can. "Adventure's not over yet."

"Um, sorry, but I draw the line at garbage diving."

He slipped his arm underneath the bag lining and withdrew two spray paint cans from the bottom of the receptacle. "Things aren't always what they seem."

"Secret stash, eh? Who are you? Music Composer by day, Count Vandalizer by night?"

He made a superhero pose and laughed. "I wish I was cool enough to have dual identities."

Arms crossed, I tapped my foot. "You really need to step up your game."

He returned my feisty grin and handed me a spray can. "You first."

"You can't be serious."

"Sure I can." He sprayed a three-dimensional box on the wall. "Think of this box as your life. You can turn it into whatever you want."

He *was* serious. *Turn it into whatever I want. Like it's that easy.* I shook the aerosol can as I walked up and down the wall. "I can't believe I'm committing vandalism."

"Technically, you're stalling."

"I'm thinking."

He stopped me. "Don't think. Feel."

*Feel.* I breathed in, out, shook the can once more, and sprayed a daisy rising from the box with its face lifted to the sun. Free, flourishing—everything I wanted to be.

Riley's gaze swept between the picture and me. He shook his can, added a lid flipped open along the back edge of the box, and sprayed the word *Unveiled* underneath it. "My favorite art piece so far."

I cracked a smile. "It's terrible."

He tilted his head and stroked his chin. "I might not plan on a career in painting if I were you." He shielded his face when I raised my can in a threat to spray him down. "But sometimes it's good to color outside the lines."

"Mm-hmm. At least I did it."

"Yes, you did."

Despite his teasing, I yielded to a genuine smile. "Thanks for this. For inspiring me."

"It's only fair I get to return the favor." He edged closer. The same intensity from earlier flowed in every movement, pouring over me until the ground felt like mud instead of cement. His fingertips found mine. "We all have a song to share, Emma. Sometimes we just need someone to help us remember how to hear the music."

His words squeezed across my chest with the terrifying tenor of something I'd lost.

Hope—a song I wasn't sure would continue to play outside these walls.

## 13

# WALLS

Days later, A. J. and I cruised up in front of Xander Technologies in his Acura. He eased his sunglasses down his nose and peered at the mirror-glassed building. "Fancy, schmancy."

"What would Corporate America be without a few flashy skyscrapers, right?" I unbuckled my seat belt, thankful for the last-minute ride and even more grateful A. J. hadn't let any awkwardness between us hamper our friendship.

He stared at me and tapped the steering wheel. "You like this internship?"

I gathered my purse and briefcase from the floorboard and smoothed out my skirt and blazer. "It's great." If I said it enough times, maybe I'd believe it.

"Wow, good thing you're not a theater major."

I shoved him and that goofy grin of his toward his door. "Fine, it's a job, okay?" It wasn't that I didn't like it.

But after spray-painting with Riley, the unrest that'd been gnawing at me dug even deeper.

Reflections of men and women hustling around the corner traveled along the mirrored siding. I didn't want to end up as just another suit.

"You don't strike me as a girl who settles."

I whipped a glance at him. "I'm not." My focus slowly returned to the busy street corner. "Maybe I'm waiting for the right possibility to come along."

"I'm counting on that."

He got another whipped-around stare, but no words came out this time.

The side of his mouth hitched up his cheek. "Relax, Rosy, I know what you meant." He jutted his chin toward the blinking crosswalk sign and a horde of incoming commuters crossing the street. "It's five to nine. Time to get a move on. Word of advice though?" He tipped his head. "Try working on those acting skills before you use them on anyone else today."

"I'll see what I can do." I resituated my purse strap on my shoulder. "Thanks for driving me. Sorry it was last-minute notice. You should tell your best friend to man up and take care of Jae's car inspection before it's past due next time."

"Now, why would I do that when his slipup gives me the chance to rescue a pretty lady?" he said in a western accent right before kissing the back of my hand. "You know I like taking care of you."

"Uh-huh. You sure *you're* not a theater major?" I

opened my door. "You might want to roll your windows up on the way home. I think you lost your cowboy hat on the drive in."

He chewed on the side of his sunglasses like it was a piece of straw. "The hat isn't what makes a cowboy, honey."

"You don't even have to try, do you? That stuff just flows right off your tongue."

"Raw talent."

I bent over the open window. "You're special, A. J. Bowers. Anyone ever tell you that?"

He slid his glasses on and set one wrist on the wheel. "All the time."

"Yeah, I don't think it means what you think it means."

Laughing, he stretched across the passenger seat. "Later, Corporate."

I waved behind me and fanned into the revolving door.

"Hiya, Miss Emma," the janitor said as he rolled his mop and bucket across the entryway.

"Morning, John."

He motioned to the windowed walls. "It's gonna be a beautiful one today."

Hoped so.

The familiar office-coffee smell trickled into the elevator each time the chime let another wave of people off. On my floor, a stretch of cubicles stared at me from the other side of the open doors. I sighed. Being a theater major might not be so bad.

A steady hum of clinking keyboards led me down the hall in a processional of routine. I passed workstation after workstation with mounted name tags. Credit Analyst. Budget Manager. Accounts Receivable Specialist. Titles. Jobs I could do. Things I was good at.

On the outside, it made sense for me to belong here. There'd even been moments when I'd dared to wonder if God might've actually opened the door for me to get this internship during a time when all other options seemed closed. But after being with Riley, the murals he'd shown me spurred a hunger for something more.

My fingertips drifted down the partition's thatched lining. These walls weren't so different from the concrete ones bordering that downtown corner—a gray canvas, urging me to find courage to add color to it. I'd hidden that palette of creativity so long ago, the paints had dried out. They'd hardened and cracked. Like I had.

I wasn't fully mended. I wasn't fully sure what broken colors could create. I only knew I couldn't settle for a whitewashed backdrop anymore. For my dad, for me, I needed to find where I was meant to be.

I booted up my computer and toyed with my necklace, wishing more than ever he was still here to tell me what to do.

Renee whizzed by with a cardboard coffee carrier in her hand. She backtracked, hoisted a cup out of the tray, and set it on top of my wall. "Chai," she said with a wink.

I popped up from my chair. "Free drinks?"

"More like combat reinforcements, dear."

Steam poured into my face when I lifted the lid. "For?"

Renee hiked up a foreboding brow. "Mr. Johnston's coming to the office today."

A woman in a pair of high heels she had no business trying to balance in bumped Renee's arm as she rounded the corner with her nose in a stack of papers. The tray of coffee cups teetered, but I grabbed the opposite end before it could topple over.

In a matter of seconds, the dormant floor turned into a maze of scurrying employees. Was a visit from the company's president that big of a deal? One of Jack's tips on success rushed to mind with the obvious answer. *Make your boss look good.* That would explain the palpable stress level buzzing throughout the floor.

Renee's purse strap slid down her arm. "You have those capital planning reports ready? Jack will want them first thing."

"Right here."

Hands full, she gestured for me to put them under her chin.

"I'll set them on your desk."

"Thanks, sweetie. It's gonna be a long one today."

A long and muscle-tightening one if everyone kept up this anxiety level. It was a shame we couldn't all have the janitor's perspective.

After I dropped off the reports, my trek back to my

desk passed by the computer graveyard. I peered into the darkened room and dipped inside. Though dusty and cluttered, at least it was peaceful. I maneuvered through piles of printers, cords, and PCs, and sat on a tiny cleared-off section of a desk.

*"What do you see?"* As with that rundown building, it was easy to see what everyone else saw. Waste. A lost cause. But if I closed my eyes, an entirely different scene came to life. Rows of desks. Computers set up with after-school learning programs. Kids engaging in another outlet.

The overhead light blinked on. "There you are," Renee said. "You hiding? It won't be that bad, sweetie. I promise."

"Not hiding. Just thinking."

She considered me a moment. "Thinking," she repeated. "In the dark. In a junk room. You sure you don't need something stronger than that tea of yours?"

Probably, but I couldn't stifle the energy rising in my chest.

I lifted up a keyboard and blew off the dust. "What if it's not all junk? What if we could use it for a good cause? Invest in the community and maybe even get some grant money." Ideas swirled. Mr. Oakly wanted to see some ingenuity. This could be it. This could be the reason I'd been sensing a reassurance that things would work out. That maybe this really was the place for me.

Renee lowered her glasses on their chain. "Emma,

our job is to provide companies with profitability and capital planning tools, strategy management—"

"But why not use our resources to make a difference instead of only money?"

She glanced behind her and shut the door until only a sliver of the hallway peeked in. "I'm not saying it's a bad idea, but Mr. Johnston doesn't like new ideas unless they're his."

Really? "Well, Jack's sort of one of his yuppies, isn't he? Maybe he'd help me."

"I'm sure he would." She crossed the room and set a hand on my arm. "Look, honey, I like you. You got spark to ya. It's somethin' special. But this isn't the place for dreams."

"Don't you ever want to do more?"

"More than what? Work? This is reality, Emma. The sooner you stop hoping for more, the better. Take it from me. You'll only end up getting hurt going down that road."

Maybe so, but it couldn't hurt more than staying trapped inside colorless walls.

She pinched her bottom lip and drummed her fingers over her arm. "I can't change your mind about this, can I? Just make sure it doesn't interfere with your regular work." She weaved through the clutter. "And don't say I didn't warn you."

Jack nudged the door open and poked his head halfway inside. "Found a secret hideout?"

Renee cleared her throat, and Jack's face fell. He adjusted his tie knot. "Renee." He gave her an acknowledging nod, to which her lips quirked in reply. His gaze slanted past her to its original fixation. "Hiding from me?"

"Actually, I was hoping to run into you."

His smug smile beamed under the overhead lights. Renee launched a warning brow my way. Smug or not, he might be the key to helping me nail my performance review.

"I have an idea I wanted to run by you. A project, actually. But I think I'm gonna need your help with it."

He eased a little closer. "I like it already."

The elevator dinged from down the hall. Jack shook his watch forward on his wrist. "I'll be tied up in meetings most of the morning, but I'll tell you what. Meet me in my office at noon, and you can tell me all about it over lunch. I know the perfect café on 12th Avenue." He swept the door open, apparently not needing to wait for a reply.

Figured.

A secluded lunch? Fine. But there was someone else I needed to share the idea with first. I scrolled for Riley's number and typed a quick text. *I think I might've found my own paintbrush. Fill you in later tonight. See ya soon.*

With my hand on the light switch, I glanced around the room once more. If discarded computers had a chance at making a difference, then maybe there was hope for me too.

## 14

## UNTAMABLE

THE WEEK FOLLOWING my lunch meeting with Jack pitted a lurking apprehension against my excitement for the after-school project.

It was hard to tell if he was really on board or only interested in an ulterior motive. Especially after he'd invited me to his place for lunch instead of going to the café. Though, he hadn't rescinded his offer to help when I declined.

I polished off the last of my tea and swallowed my concern. Nothing I could do about it anyway. I'd probably lose my internship if I said anything to anyone. And the bottom line was, I couldn't get around needing his help. We'd be presenting the proposal in a few weeks. I could stick it out until then.

Jaycee padded down the hall with her hair swept up in a towel. Hints of her papaya shampoo blended into the hazelnut-scented steam rising from the coffeemaker.

Her forehead scrunched into the towel when I handed her a mug. "*You* made coffee?" She lifted it to her nose for inspection.

I fanned a dish towel at her. "Oh, stop. I can brew a pot of coffee, for Pete's sake."

She took a cautious sip and held it a second before daring to swallow. "And added the right amount of creamer. Okay, what have you done with my best friend?"

"Very funny." I rinsed out my mug and set it in the drain rack. "I got an early start to the day. Thought I'd be a nice roomie for a change." I slid onto the kitchen chair beside her, sobering. "Jae, I'm sorry for snapping at you the other day. You were only doing what I asked you to do."

"Which you're completely ignoring, by the way."

I curled the sides of the place mat into the center and let them unfurl. "I know. I was scared Riley would be like every other guy, but he's turned into a good friend."

She tucked one leg under the other. "A friend you find *intriguing*?"

She was never going to let me live that down. I flicked a crumb at her. "Yes. But it's more than that. He inspires me. Challenges me to dream instead of settling for status quo. He makes me feel... real, I guess." Trying to put it into words sounded painfully insufficient. All I knew was that for the first time in forever, I'd found passion for life again.

Jaycee lowered her mug. "Em, I shouldn't have

listened to what those people were saying about his past. He's good for you. When you're with him, you're... I don't know... who you're supposed to be. Like, you're alive. Feisty," she clarified, brow darting my way. "But alive."

She consumed a giant swig of coffee. "And yeah, I get he's a good friend, but it's obviously more. So, stop fighting it already and tell the boy how you feel."

My heel slipped off the chair. "And risk ruining our friendship? No way. He's too important to me. I can't mess this up."

Jaycee tilted her head. "Did you ever stop to think he might be thinking the same exact thing?"

But what if he wasn't?

She hunched over the table. "What are you afraid of?"

I towed my legs into the chair again and laced my arms around them. "Everything. I'm afraid of the way he makes me feel when I'm with him, and even more afraid of how I feel when we're apart."

Jaycee chuckled. "I think that's called love."

A knock on the door rippled across the entryway.

I grabbed Jaycee's mug, guzzled the rest of her coffee, and zoomed up from the table. My chair wobbled in place with as much grace as the way I glided across the linoleum.

Steeling myself before I opened the door, I flashed Jae a silent plea to forget everything we'd just talked about. The risk was too high.

"'Sup, Preston," she said without an upward glance from the coffeemaker when Riley stepped inside.

He laughed. "Nice impersonation of Trevor."

"It's a talent."

Leaning against the table, I balanced on one foot at a time while sliding my boots over my fuzzy socks.

Riley picked up a sweater draped over one of the kitchen chairs and held it out for me. "I have to warn you, it's a little chilly out."

He gathered my hair in his hands and lifted it from under the sweater. His fingers grazed my neck. Tender and warm, the sensation launched a fleet of wings flapping in my stomach with enough power to airlift me outside. I clasped the top of the chair.

A sideways grin snuck around the rim of Jaycee's newly filled mug. If she hadn't missed my response, chances were Riley hadn't either.

I stumbled toward the door, desperate to escape the borders of the conversation we'd just had. As soon as my boots touched the stoop, a burst of fresh air came to my rescue. Leaves floated to the sidewalk from tree branches swaying in the breeze like paintbrushes sprinkling colors over a white page. Pure, heavenly distraction.

"Autumn's incredible, isn't it?" Amazing how the distinct smell of fallen leaves could trigger old memories with such vividness, I would have sworn I was eight years old again.

"Every October, Mom took Austin and me on these

scavenger hunts to find the brightest leaves to take home. You'd have thought we were searching those sidewalks for some hidden treasure."

Riley pressed his arm against mine. "It's the little things."

I pushed him into the street. "You're patronizing me, aren't you?"

"No, no, I promise." He laughed softly. "I think it's cute, actually."

"Mm-hmm." Regardless of how it sounded, autumn always reminded me of what I didn't want to lose. "Don't you miss it?"

"Miss what?"

"Childhood. Spinning in the rain until we fell to the ground." I twirled in a circle, head lifted, arms in the air. "Being satisfied with a tree to climb and a swing set to fly on. Fears of the future never outranking the belief in happy endings. That's why I'm so excited about this after-school program idea. What if it's the key to a kid believing he'll get his own happy ending, you know?"

Like Dad taught me to believe for myself?

The thought rattled against walls in my spirit. I'd finally found the dreams he'd wanted for me, hadn't I?

Confirmation swelled.

At the curb in front of the car, I turned back around from the empty space where Riley should have been. He stood a few feet behind me with his hands in his pockets, watching my every move.

"Was I rambling? I'm sorry. Sometimes my thoughts

run over before I have time to stop them." My hand soared to my mouth. "I'm doing it again."

Riley started toward me—slowly, resolutely. Sunlight caught an expression I couldn't interpret, and my pulse spiked all over again. I shouldn't have drunk that coffee.

With any luck, the wind blowing my hair in every direction would hide my blazing cheeks. Two leaves scampered past my feet, one chasing the other. I almost ran after them.

Right in front of me now, Riley secured a strand of untamable hair behind my ear. "I warned you it was chilly out." The world came to a standstill at his touch. "I'm not sure which fascinates me more. The way you manage to keep so much depth tucked away in this little body of yours, or the fact that you don't even realize how special you are."

Special? My heart raced. His words crashed into past words from guys who'd already found out he was wrong. Insecurities crept in with memories of the looks on their faces after I'd turned them down. Or worse, after I hadn't. It wouldn't take long for Riley's face to mirror the same disappointment once he realized I was just another girl.

His forehead pinched. He lowered his hand from my hair and stalled in a half turn toward his car. "Can I take you somewhere today?"

*Say no.* "Jaycee's sister and nephew are stopping by later. I don't want to miss them."

"We won't be long." With earnest eyes conquering my

resolve, he retrieved a coat from his car and held it up for me. "I promise to get you home before it gets too cold."

As if being cold around him would be a problem. Ever.

He tossed me a water bottle from the back seat. "Don't worry, 'I'm a tea kind of girl.' I'll bring chai next time."

I pressed the cool bottle to my face. "You remember that?"

"Are you kidding? With those red cheeks after you said it, how could I forget?"

He started the car, and I almost crawled out of it. "Hey, cut me some slack. I was a little starstruck." *Might as well be honest.*

"Over another student?"

"A student who's insanely talented." And devastatingly gorgeous. I twisted my seat belt into a spiral. "And you don't know the power your smile has." Why, oh, why didn't I know when to stop talking?

"I'll try to work on that." He scrunched his lips together, but it only made it worse. "You don't exactly make it easy."

That made two of us. I looked out the window, away from the grin that left me in a puddle on the floorboard.

After twenty minutes of driving, the tires crunched over an accumulation of pinecones along the side of the road. Nothing but miles of woods stretched up and down either side of us. I slid Riley a questioning stare. "Where are we going?"

He unbuckled his seat belt and dangled his keys around his finger. "You'll see."

Tight-lipped, I clambered out of the car. But once we hit the trail, all frustration with his deliberate evasiveness evaporated with the last trace of nerves left from my conversation with Jaycee. Nothing existed except here and now—nature's serenade, a backyard-pile-of-leaves fragrance, and scenery that could've been taken straight from a poem.

"It's gorgeous."

"It gets better." He pointed ahead of us. "We're almost there. Just past that bend."

"I thought we were just taking a walk in the..." A circular field bordered with sparkling boulders and bright green ferns stole my voice.

Riley stepped beside me. "What do you think?"

"You didn't tell me we were hiking into the middle of a Bob Ross painting."

His face lit up with the thrill of showing me his own hidden treasure. "The way you were talking about your love of fall this morning, I knew you'd like it here."

A glimpse of the skyline showered through the opening in the treetops. He stood in the middle, the sole performer on a handcrafted stage as unique as he was.

How much longer could I pretend I wasn't falling for him?

Riley shielded his eyes from the sun and peered to

the edge of the grassy field, where a rise of unease kept me locked in place. His face fell. "What's wrong?"

"This is obviously a special place for you. I'm not sure I belong."

"Emma." His mouth quirked. "I invited you, remember?"

"I know, but…"

He picked up a leaf from the ground and twirled it in his fingers on his way toward me. He lifted my hand and set it inside it. "I want to share this with you. All of it. Help you see what I see."

His fingers lingered against mine. Forcing in a breath, I dropped my gaze to the treasure in my hand. A medley of burnt oranges, auburn reds, and golden yellows blended into childhood memories. After all these years, it still astounded me how a single leaf could embody the splendor of an entire forest.

Instead of absorbing the vibrant fall colors, Riley kept his eyes on me.

The leaf's momentary diversion vanished without any chance to reclaim it. I pulled my hair to the side and shifted the coat he'd lent me. "What?"

He squeezed the back of his neck. "You're not making this very easy for me."

"Not making what easy?"

He rolled a branch on the ground under his shoe. "Holding back hope," he said quietly.

Hope for what? I couldn't ask. Not with the vulnerability written on his face—the same vulnerability conquering my heart.

Desperate for a diversion, I fled to the boulders and studied the moss's bristly texture. "How'd you find this place?"

He headed toward me. "By accident, actually. I was stuck on a song and needed to take a step back from things. So, I grabbed Jake, and we kept driving until I saw that trailhead. Jake must've caught the scent of a squirrel or something. You should've seen the number of scratches I had from plowing through all the underbrush to catch up to him."

He ran a finger down his forearm, where he probably had some scars under his long sleeves. "But it was worth it. One step in here, and I knew I'd found something special."

Every inch of him teemed with emotion as he looked right at me. "It's funny. You always find the most extraordinary things when you're not searching for them. But once you've found them, it's hard to let them go." He lowered his head. "Even when you know you should."

He had no idea. I searched for my voice, which I'd lost somewhere in the collapsing space separating his body from mine.

I shuffled backward. "Who else have you brought here?"

I gnawed my lip, not sure I wanted to know the answer or why I asked it to begin with. The way girls ogled him in public, he could have his pick from a list lined down the street.

He toyed with the hem of his pullover. "Only you, Emma."

The wind rippled over the leaves, his words over my heart.

"Oh, I assumed…"

"What? That I didn't mean it when I said you're special?"

The entire forest paused, awaiting my response. I snapped a branch off a fern, stroked its feathery leaves, and prayed for even an ounce of serenity to return.

Riley drew me around by my hand. "You've been hurt before. I can see it."

"That's what happens when you give your heart away."

A mixture of compassion and sorrow creased his face.

I wanted to hide and prevent him from looking at me the way others had. But I couldn't run from him any more than I could from my past. "It's my own fault. In high school, I let myself get caught up in the ideal of love. Turns out it was only a competition. Guys competing for the sexiest trophy girlfriend. Girls willing to give anything for affection. Even their self-worth."

I chucked the branch into the forest and cringed at the way I'd played the game of seduction. Maybe I'd played a part all my life. One role after the other, trying to find approval. Trying to be who others wanted. "It's kind of sad, but the longer you give in to the label people place on you, the easier it is to believe. No wonder they expected—"

Riley's hand fell from mine. "Expected what?"

"The only thing they saw when they looked at me." And I'd been stupid enough to give in to their empty back seat promises. I offered them everything, believing I'd found what my parents had.

"I thought college might be different. Hoped I'd find what my dad taught me to dream for, but the first half of freshman year was a complete disaster." I braided the fringes on the end of my belt and dodged Riley's gaze.

"If I wasn't already letting Dad down enough by having zero idea what career to choose, then I had to go and top it off with falling for a charming upperclassman who ended up being ten times the jerk my high school boyfriends were. The worst part is, I knew better."

A deep inhale raised my shoulders. "But I got my head on straight by midterm. All that practice being strong for Mom kicked in. I poured myself into my studies, got on the dean's list, and stopped tripping over relationship roadblocks. Simple as that. You can't get hurt if you can't feel, right?"

Riley's jaw twitched. "It's not your fault. Passion blinds people. I should know." He looked at the sky, pinched the bridge of his nose, and exhaled slowly. "Your dad wouldn't be disappointed in you for wanting to find a guy with enough control to treat you right. You deserve that."

The vast blue of the sky filled his eyes when they met mine again. "Don't give up on that dream, Em. One day, you'll find it."

The gravity that came over him cut through my feigned confidence and nearly pulled me to the ground with a realization I couldn't keep ignoring. Despite everything I'd just said about guarding my heart, I stood there, holding it in my hands in front of the guy I'd already given it to.

Jaycee's words echoed between each pulse. *Tell. Him. How. You. Feel.* My mouth turned to cotton. "Being with you..." *Breathe.* "Riley, you help me to have faith to dream again. To believe the risk is worth taking."

His gaze jerked away from mine. "You give me more credit than I deserve."

"And you don't give yourself enough."

He turned toward the fir trees and shook his head. "What if I'm not the guy you think I am?"

"Is this about your past? Because whatever happened doesn't matter. You're..." Every word I'd said to Jaycee pounded in my chest. Words that would expose how much I'd fallen for him. Needed him.

I plucked off another fern branch and tied it in a knot as tight as my insides felt. "You're different from other guys."

An edgy huff clipped off my response. "You're wrong." He turned again, and the pain in his eyes bored straight into his voice. "You don't know what I'm capable of."

My heart wept over the lines of turmoil etched across his face. I moved toward him, but he held his hand up to stop me.

He raked his fingers through his hair and released a long breath. "I never resented my dad more than the year he dragged us to Nashville. While he was out trying to convince agents he had enough talent for a record deal, my mom had to work two jobs to make ends meet. That left me to keep an eye out for Melody and Jasmine."

He kicked a loose rock into the woods. "We rented an apartment in the only part of the city we could afford. Our landlord was a total skeezeball, but Dad insisted we stay on his good side, not do anything to get us kicked out. It was hard enough restraining myself when I saw the creep hit on my mom. But when I caught him with Melody, I lost it." He balled his hands into fists at his sides.

"All those years of pent-up anger toward my dad—all the emotion I'd stifled for him—took over. I heard the guy's rib break with the first punch, but I couldn't stop. Nothing mattered. Not the amount of blood. The broken bones. I didn't stop swinging until some neighbors wrestled me off him."

Seeing the guilt Riley still carried from a mistake he'd made all those years ago thrust blows of their own into my chest.

I crossed the boundary line he'd erected earlier and rested a palm on his unshaven cheek. "You were protecting your sister. She was just a little girl."

"That doesn't justify losing control. You didn't see what I did to him. Who I became. I could've killed him."

"But you didn't."

He looked away and knotted his fingers in the back of his hair.

I angled my face under his. "You're wrong. About what you said earlier. I know exactly what you're capable of. Fighting for those you love and believe in. Putting them above yourself. Living with transparency, passion—"

"That's the problem." He laughed sadly. "At least my dad had one thing right. I should keep my passion buried. I've seen what it does to people. Myself included." His strong, confident features languished behind the image of a boy who lacked his father's acceptance. "I try, Em. Try to be who I'm supposed to be. But sometimes…"

"Being passionate isn't a flaw. It doesn't discount your value. It adds to it." Couldn't he see that?

Glassy eyes found mine. "You don't know how much I wish that were true."

"It is." My hand drifted to his shirt. "I'm not saying what you did to that guy was right. I'm saying grace is as much a part of life as passion is."

Part of me winced from the pain believing that had caused me in the past. It was one thing to believe Riley needed to forgive himself for making a mistake out of love. Believing it wasn't a mistake to trust that God's grace and love were sufficient in my life was another thing entirely.

Sunlight fanned through the treetops. Warmth spread through me, and somehow I knew. I'd already started to believe it again.

Riley's chest rose and fell underneath my palm. Each breath deepened the way he looked at me until a damp draft blew across the field. He tucked one side of the Columbia coat he'd lent me inside the other.

Was this how Mom felt when she first fell for Dad? Caring about him more than she understood? Willing to risk everything she was afraid of to be close to him?

I set my fingers over his, drew his palm toward my lips, his body closer to mine, and leaned in. My heart, my mouth—nothing withheld. His forehead furrowed at my touch. He shrank back and inhaled, taking my heart with him and leaving a cold realization in its place.

He didn't want to kiss me.

He traced his fingers over a frayed tear along the front of the coat he'd given me, his expression equally as torn.

"I'm sorry, Riley." *Please tell me I haven't ruined our friendship* and *his coat.*

"It's always been there," he said, voice painfully soft. "Some tears are harder to hide than others." He dropped his hand from the coat. "Don't ever settle for anything less than your dad's dreams for you."

He backed up, paced toward the trailhead, and stopped. He turned and met my gaze then, but something had changed in his eyes. "I promised I'd get you home before it got too cold."

His words chilled far more than the dropping temperatures. Had I imagined the way he looked at me? Misinterpreted? I squeezed the sides of his coat tighter across my torso like a tourniquet to keep the truth I feared from reaching inside.

He didn't want me.

## 15

## PRESERVATION

PARKED in front of my apartment, the car's overworked engine echoed the churning in my stomach.

Riley met me around the bumper, and the walkway to the front door seemed to stretch even farther than the silent drive home had. What was I supposed to say to the guy who pulled away when I almost kissed him?

Head down, he stalled on the stoop. "Emma, I—"

The door blew open behind us. A red-eyed, sniffling version of Jaycee's four-year-old nephew bounded from inside. Jaycee and her sister scurried after him, Trevor right behind.

"Enough with the whining, kiddo." Sabrina stopped beside us with a once-neat bun half-unwound down the back of her neck. She massaged her temples. "Sorry. We're overdue on nap time."

I squatted to Marc's level and brandished the best

private eye look I had. "Hmm. Freckled cheeks. Chocolate mustache. Looks sorta like the Marc Toberty I know." I leaned in and took a whiff. "Smells like him, too, but I think we might have an imposter here."

Marc dragged his runny nose over his sleeve. "Miss Emma, it's me."

Arms folded, I tapped my foot. "I don't know."

"It's me! See?" Hands in the air, he twirled in a circle, and I had to bite my lip to keep from giving in to his cuteness.

"Well, there's really only one way to be sure."

He must've known what was coming. With a running start, he tore down the sidewalk, giggles erupting. I scooped him up and tickled him under his flailing arms. The raspberry I landed on his chubby neck almost out rang his high-pitched squeals.

"Now, there's the Marc I know." I tapped his chin. "See, aren't giggles way more fun than tears?"

Cheeks reddened, he caught his breath and nodded.

I winked at Sabrina. "All better now."

"You're a gem." She squinted at my face. "Ooh, sorry about the chocolate. Luckily, it didn't get on your clothes." She waved on her way to the driver's side of her Volkswagen while Jaycee helped Marc into his car seat.

Riley drew close and wiped the fingerprint-sized chocolate residue from my cheek. "You have a way of touching a boy's heart, Emma."

Trevor's line of sight ping-ponged between us. A

minute later, he patted Riley on the arm. "You staying for dinner? Em can make you her specialty. Frozen-meal-in-a-bag."

"Hey, don't knock my frozen meals. They're a classic."

Riley rubbed a knuckle over his jawline. "Tempting, but I should get going. There's a song I need to work on tonight."

Trevor clasped his hand. "Next time, bro." He intercepted Jaycee on her way to the porch and steered her into the apartment, leaving Riley and me outside. Alone.

Riley's attention fell on my coat. *His* coat. I started to shuck it off, but he stopped me with his hand over mine. "Keep it."

Why did he have to make my heart beat like that?

He stowed his hands in his pockets and dragged his shoe up and down the front of the stoop. "Emma, what you said today... being with you... I... I had a nice time."

Nice but not enough. Was he trying not to hurt my feelings? I swallowed the sting. "What are friends for, right?"

He looked backhanded. His shoulders followed his crestfallen stare at the ground. "Right. I should get going then."

I managed to nod. Words wouldn't come out even if I tried.

His taillights bled into the distance, and for the second time that night, my heart stopped.

In the stairwell, I took off Riley's coat—his scent, the

warmth he provided, the feeling of his arms—and folded it into a tight, compact square. I shut the door and leaned into it, my grasp on the knob the only thing keeping me standing.

"Everything all right?"

My lids blasted open to the sound of Jaycee's voice coming from the couch.

Trevor took one look at me and broke into a karaoke version of Taylor Swift's "Love Story" in perfect falsetto.

"Really, Trev? How old are you?"

"Twenty-two," he said right before busting out another of Taylor's singles.

"How do you even know the words to that song?"

He tossed his arm around Jaycee. "Have you ever taken a road trip with my fiancée?"

She swatted him in the chest. "Hey, if I gotta listen to Dave Matthews Band, you can listen to Taylor Swift."

He scooted forward, hands out. "See, Em? Love's a give and take."

"Wow, we are so not having this conversation right now." I tugged off my boots. They could be useful weapons, even if they were flats. "Riley and I are just friends." He'd made that clear enough.

Trevor exaggerated a head roll. "Right. I always come home from hanging out with a *friend* all flustered and having difficulty breathing."

The leather boot crinkled in my hands. "You're seriously trying to get yourself smacked, aren't you?"

Jaycee set her coffee mug on the end table. "All right, babe, give her a break."

"Oh, c'mon. You know my badgering is out of love. I'll stop. I swear. At least for now," he amended with another obnoxious grin. "Honestly though, sometimes you can really be blind. I know you have to figure it out for yourself and all, but we'll be on the sidelines if you need us to kick you into reality."

"Thanks, Trev. I can always count on you for a good kick in the rear." But the only reality check I needed was the reminder that I shouldn't let my heart escape any further than I'd already let it roam. Hadn't I learned anything?

Evidence of Jaycee's trip to the grocery store greeted me from the kitchen counter. Four bottles of flavored liqueur bookended the coffeepot. I opened the freezer and caught a domino ripple of boxes spewing out. Classic. I punched in the minutes on the microwave.

With my frozen dinner tray in hand, I ducked past the living room, hoping to bypass Trevor this time.

"Oh, Em, wait." Jaycee sprang up from the couch with a business card in one hand, a book in the other. "Miriam gave this to me a week ago. It's contact info for an internship possibility. One she didn't get, I guess. Since you already have one, I stuck it in my book to give to you later but ended up totally forgetting about it. I'm so sorry."

I turned the card over and read a scribbled note above two underlines: *Paid internship. Guaranteed job lead.*

"Do you know why she didn't get it?"

Jaycee shrugged. "Something about needing a recommendation. She was bummed but said she thought it'd be a good fit for you if you wanted it."

She was willing to help *me*? Her competition?

"Thanks." I tucked the card in my back pocket and lugged the ironing board out of the hallway closet. Shame followed me down the hall to my bedroom and joined the shriek of the ironing board as it expanded into an upright position.

Swallowing my frustration with generous bites of mashed potatoes, I cleared the entire tray in the amount of time it took for the iron to reach the appropriate temperature. I pressed Riley's leaf between two sheets of wax paper for preservation the way Austin and I used to do as kids.

With a tiny piece of the forest in my hand, everything about being in the clearing with Riley rushed in and grounded me in my desk chair before I could stop it. The way he'd looked at me. Like no matter what I told him, he'd do anything to make me feel safe, valued.

Then when he'd opened up to me, emotion had plagued his eyes like he was terrified of what I'd think of him. He was probably looking for a friend in return. Someone to believe in him, someone he could trust.

I buried my face in my hands. *He needs a friend, Em. Not someone who misreads his kindness as an invitation to kiss him, for crying out loud.*

My arms dropped onto my desktop. Lamplight flickered over the picture in the corner of Dad and me. I nestled the frame in my lap. His embrace had always left me with the assurance of what to do next—an assurance I'd been seeking ever since I'd lost him.

I hadn't forgotten my promise to make him proud. Nor had my feelings for Riley replaced the importance of that promise, but being with him made the hole inside me feel smaller, less jagged. Like it was safe to dream again. Maybe I'd gotten it all wrong.

"*Prove your merit.*" It always came down to that, didn't it? I set the frame in front of the leaf. In the war between dreams and responsibilities, some treasures were meant to stay hidden.

I rolled onto my bed and turned the business card Miriam had given me around in my hands. Had I chosen the right internship? The weight of that question crushed me into the mattress, the answer coiling with the springs. It didn't matter. Same as today, I couldn't rewind time. I'd made my choice. I shoved the card in a book, lugged my economics text from the floor, and draped it over my face. Maybe this was one time osmosis would actually work.

The bedroom door opened and closed, followed by the sound of Jaycee's mattress squeaking. I knew what was coming.

"There's nothing to say," I mumbled from underneath my blockade. "You were wrong. Riley doesn't feel the same way."

"How do you know?"

"Something about him bucking away from a kiss he didn't want gave me a clue."

Saying it out loud made it ten times worse. What a fool I must've looked like.

"Are you sure he knew that's what you wanted? Maybe you guys should talk about it."

The edges of my book sawed into my palms. "I'm pretty sure I did enough talking today." I'd let my heart ooze out like a complete imbecile. "Look, it doesn't matter. Riley wants friendship, and that's what I'm going to give him. Romantic feelings only get in the way."

"Yeah, I don't think you can just turn those off."

I had no choice. "He's been a good friend to me. He deserves that much in return."

"Friends fall in love, you know."

"This isn't a fairy tale, Jae."

"No, you're right. This is your life. The one you're gonna let slip by."

My book torpedoed onto the floor and landed with a *thud*. "What do you want me to do?"

"Stop letting fear hold you back." She strode to the door and stopped with her hand on the light switch. "That dream of *ever after* you're too stubborn to admit you want? It's not just for heroines in fairy tales. You know who it's for? Those who believe in themselves enough to accept love when they find it."

*Wrong again. I can't accept something that's not being offered.*

The streetlight outside our window cast a glow over

the laminated leaf peeking from behind the picture frame. Two pieces of my heart. One I'd spent years running to. The other, years running from. Two races I'd never win. When was it time to give up? I curled in bed, tucked my pillow under my arms, and waited for sleep to overshadow an answer I didn't want to face.

## 16

## ON LOAN

DAYS of intense work were starting to take their toll. I plodded up the stairs and into my apartment. Dusk's shadows crept through the windows and yawned across the living room carpet.

"Another late day?" Jaycee asked from the kitchen.

I jostled my bulging book bag. "Gotta get this research done."

"I could've sent Trev to pick you up." She planted a hand on his shoulder.

"Jack offered." I snagged an apple from the fruit bowl. "He's been staying late, too, helping me with this grant proposal. We're so close to having it ready." So, no need to mention his latest advance. We were both tired, stressed. If I could push through a little longer, it'd all be worth it. I couldn't afford to lose everything now.

A yellow sticky note pinned on the bulletin board

above the phone waved underneath the vent. *Mr. Oakly called for an update.*

"No calls from Riley?"

Jaycee shook her head. Trevor crept up behind me and stole my apple in one of his famous basketball moves. He crunched into it, splattering me with juicy overspray.

I wiped my face with my sleeve. "Thanks."

"My pleasure." He dipped his head toward the board. "You and Riley avoiding each other or something?"

"No." Maybe. He probably thought it'd be better that way. Less chance of hurting my feelings. And it was certainly easier to handle being only his friend from a distance. But not seeing him for days caused something inside me to ache like a bruise. An acute longing throbbed around a dull pain as soon as someone put pressure on it.

Jaycee ladled a heap full of soup into Trevor's bowl on the table. "Want some minestrone? There's enough for one more helping."

"No, thanks. I think I'm gonna go for a walk." With any luck, the night air would clear my head. I kept my bag on my shoulder and grabbed my guitar case on my way out the door.

Cicadas zipped around me along the trail leading to my favorite alcove between the roots of a hemlock tree. I settled in and listened to the creek's soft current. If only the rest of life could've felt this serene.

An exhale pressed the bark's grooves deeper into my

back and doubts about the after-school program deeper into my thoughts.

I cradled my guitar in my lap, but the strings felt brittle, the wood heavy. I set it aside. Clutching my legs instead, I closed my eyes and listened to the memory of Dad's music harmonize with the crickets.

A coarse, wet tongue slurped up the side of my face. I opened my eyes to Jake's snout wiggling its way to my ear. "Hey, boy." I laughed and pulled him down by the collar.

A short distance away, Riley took in the scene with pensive eyes.

He made it impossible to view his unexpected visit as an intrusion. Same way he made it impossible to deny how I really felt about him.

I lifted a hand instead of speaking, lest those very feelings came spewing out.

He moseyed up, looking uncertain. "I'm sorry I haven't called," he started. "I—"

"Don't need to make excuses." I didn't want to bring up what had happened. I wanted things to go back to the way they were. I needed him in my life, as a friend if nothing more.

Head down, I twisted a thread on the bottom of my jeans and jumped on the chance to divert topics. "Seriously, don't worry about it. You've probably been as busy as I have. This project is a killer—on my mind and my back."

I motioned him forward and heaved my bag into his

arms. It almost fumbled to the ground with a weight he obviously wasn't expecting.

"See? I won't have to go to the gym for a week."

"No kidding. What's in this thing?"

"Library books, case studies, notes, reports for work, my economics text." I rubbed the crook of my neck.

His forehead crinkled. "Sounds like a lot to carry on your shoulders."

"Tell me about it."

Riley nodded to the guitar propped against the tree trunk. "May I?" He set some things down and plucked a series of chords as stirring as any of Dad's music. "That's a good guitar you've got there."

"I think it might have something to do with the player."

Casting a frown of doubt my way, he traded the guitar for a cardboard cup he'd put down a minute ago and handed it to me. "Maybe this'll help ease the tension."

He squatted and rubbed Jake behind the ears while the dog licked the sweat from his temple. "We stopped at Paradox after our run. I was actually on my way to your apartment. Trevor told me you've been coming home around eight each night. I thought you might need a pick-me-up."

An alluring scent of cinnamon and cloves danced from the cup of chai. My lashes fluttered.

He chuckled. "I take it I was right."

"Mm. You have no idea." A timely yawn added its

corroborating evidence. "I didn't realize how much would need to go into this project. I'm exhausted. More like flat-out drained, if I'm being honest."

The skin around his eyes wrinkled as he stood. "Maybe you should take a step back from things. Not drive yourself so hard."

"I thought you were the one who wanted me to break through borders." I nudged my backpack. "I don't have any spray paint cans in here, but I know where we can find a secret stash if you need a reminder."

Riley didn't return my laugh. "I never meant to push you." His jaw flexed. "See, this is why—"

"You didn't push. You inspired. But coloring outside the lines can take hard work. Especially with a performance review riding on the outcome." I sighed and stroked the guitar strings beside me. "Truth is, I'm scared it won't be enough."

"You're already enough, Emma." Light from the lamppost amplified the full spectrum of blues in his eyes. But rather than hold my gaze, he looked off to the tree line and dug his fingers through the back of his hair the way he did when he was torn over something.

*Please don't let it be us.*

After a painfully long minute, he looped Jake's leash around his wrist. "I know it's getting late, but would you be up for coming to my place for a little while? I have something I think might help."

I breathed a prayer of relief for not driving him away.

"As long as it doesn't include any more adventures," I teased.

A hint of the smile I loved flickered at me under the light. "No fire-breathing dragons this time. Promise."

"That's comforting." Except he didn't know the fire he stoked without even trying.

"I won't keep you long." His earnest expression ravaged any chance of deflecting my attraction to him. Why did I even try?

I laced my arms over my ribs and repeated the same thing he'd said to me the night of the campfire. "On one condition."

He gave me a Sherlock Holmes stare. "Which is?"

"That you play a song for me." It came out more as a plea than a condition. There went downplaying how much I missed his music.

He mimicked my stance and pretended to deliberate. "Deal." He helped me to my feet. "But only if you play one for me. You got out of it last time, you know."

I braced the tree until my Jell-O legs solidified again. Not that walking right beside him or seeing how perfect my guitar looked in his hand was helping matters.

My nerves followed me like a shadow to his car. But once we reached his apartment, the angst finally eased. Even if it didn't make sense, I felt at home there.

Riley tossed his keys on the table in the entryway. Jake bounded for the dog bed in the corner of the living room and collapsed in a tight ball. Evidently, I wasn't the only exhausted one.

I dropped onto the couch and considered curling up in the same exact position while Riley headed to his bedroom. On his knees, he looked like he was digging through some kind of chest from the glimpse I caught through the doorway. He sat back on his heels, dusted something off, and joined me on the couch a minute later. Smiling warmly, he set a small, hand-carved wooden box in my lap.

"What's this?"

"Open it."

A soft cadence of high-pitched notes swirled around me in an unexpected song.

"When I first left for school," he said, "Jasmine insisted I take her music box with me. Said it was a reminder for me not to lose my song while I was away." He smiled again. "She'll be thrilled to know it helped someone besides me. I want you to have it."

Above the music player, the word *Dream* was stenciled onto the back of the lid in what must've been his youngest sister's handwriting. My throat tightened. "I can't take this, Riley. She gave it to you."

He set his hands over mine and moved the box back to my lap. "Consider it on loan then. Sometimes we need to borrow each other's songs until we learn to hear our own."

Tears filled in for words. I nestled close to him without thinking. He bristled at first but then settled his cheek over my head. His stubble brushed against my hair as his fingertips caressed my arm. Slowly, softly, he began the same song he had the first time he brought me here.

"Can we stay right here, in this sweet refrain, where memories last and tears don't stain?"

Even without his guitar, the tender melody drew me deeper. I held on to him, on to this moment, not caring about boundaries or promises. Not tonight. Tonight, my heart was on loan.

My fingers tightened around his shirt when the song ended. I wasn't ready to let go. But if there was anybody I could play for, anyone I could offer everything to, it'd be Riley. I lifted off him slightly. "Guess it's my turn." The words sounded slurred.

He pulled me close and brushed my hair back. "You're exhausted, Em. Just rest." He continued to hum softly. And as the minutes drifted, so did the remainder of my pretenses.

I nuzzled my head beneath his chin again, breathed in the scent of his skin, and dreamed we could stay right there—where everything made sense, and it felt safe to trust that God would work everything out.

"Do you think there are things worth hoping for?" I whispered.

Riley stopped humming. His fingers stilled over my arm. A minute later, his body relaxed again. "Sometimes," he whispered back, "hope is all we have."

Like dreams. When they're all you have, it's hard to let them go. I curled closer, sleep nearing. At least for tonight, I'd hold on to this one dream a little longer.

## 17

## CRUMBLED

ALL WEEK, I'd relived the feeling of falling asleep in Riley's arms. Any time my muscles ached from sitting in hard library chairs, I retreated to that night on Riley's couch and to the reminder that some things were worth hoping for. Just as some things were worth working for, even if it meant spending every spare minute double-checking my research on this grant project.

"You know, I hear you have higher odds of retention when you read while you're awake."

A sideways view of A. J. blinked into focus. I peeled my face away from the open book on the library desk and rubbed out a crease embedded in my forehead.

A. J. raised the front cover. "Webster's New World Grant Writing Handbook." He let it fall to the desk. "That'd put me to sleep too. You been here all night?"

All night? Faint traces of daylight traipsed across the

row of bookshelves two down from us. *No, no, no. It cannot be morning already.* "What time is it?"

He lounged an arm over the shelf above the individual-size desk. "Quarter to eight."

"What?" I rocketed up from the wooden chair, my body screaming with stiffness. The hardbound book teetered off the desk onto the floor and sent an echo across the quiet library. "I have to be at work in an hour."

"Need a ride?"

"Riley's taking me today."

He raised the back of his hat, scratched his head, and tugged it down. "Of course he is. And where is *lover boy*?"

"He's probably at my apartment, wondering where the heck I am." I checked my cell phone. Two missed calls. Great. I yanked my tangled book bag strap off the chair.

"Relax, Speed Racer, you have time."

"Not today. I have to give a presentation first thing. I need to get in early." *Stupid backpack.* I left the zipper half open, whipped the bag over my shoulder, and wrenched my hair out from underneath it.

A. J. picked up the book from the carpet and tapped it against his leg. "So, this is why I haven't seen you much lately? Burying yourself in research for a presentation. There's more to life than an internship, you know?"

I knew what he meant, but he didn't understand. "Everything's riding on this. I have a real shot at making a difference. I can't blow it."

He raised a brow. "I think you might be missing the big picture, Em. You don't have to try so hard."

My conversation with Mr. Oakly at the beginning of the term flooded to mind with reminders of how every other scholarship recipient exemplified the prestige I was lacking. Riley's voice rose in my heart to counter the thought. Weary of the tug-of-war, I pushed the chair out of my path. I couldn't handle the fight today. Too much was on the line. "Look, you don't get it, okay?"

A pang of hurt touched his eyes, and the tension straining my muscles tightened even more. "A. J., I... I'm sorry. It's just... I'm tired, in a hurry."

"In a hurry to make a difference. You're right. I don't get it." He turned but stopped. "It's one thing to invest in a good cause. It's another thing to lose yourself in the process." Without looking back, he strode away.

My fist banged into the top of the chair with regret for snapping like that, but I didn't have time to follow him.

Back at my apartment, I hustled up the stairs, taking two at a time. Thankfully, I'd thought to wash my hair and iron my suit last night.

Riley rose from the couch with a to-go cup in his hand the second the door opened.

"Sorry," I said before he could voice his worry. "My phone was on vibrate. If A. J. hadn't woken me, I'd still be asleep." I dropped my bag by the table and rotated my neck from side to side.

Riley's line of sight sailed over the rumpled outfit I

still had on from yesterday. Anxious eyes constricted above his tight jaw.

No telling what I must've looked like. "Give me five minutes to clean up. It was a late night."

He squeezed the cup. "Ow." Steaming tea dripped down his hand.

I grabbed a napkin from the table.

"I got it." He blew past me into the kitchen. His shoulder clipped mine with the same brusque clip in his tone.

Now I knew how A. J. must've felt.

I got dressed in a whirlwind. Teeth brushed, hair swept up in a clip, I sank into Riley's passenger seat. I flipped open the mirror on the visor and studied my reflection from all angles to check for any more creases left from my choice of pillow.

"Something wrong?" Riley asked from the driver's seat.

"Just making sure I don't have any marks left from last night. I'd rather not have any reason to be embarrassed today."

Riley shifted into the wrong gear. The sudden burst of acceleration jerked my head into the headrest. Good thing I wasn't putting on mascara. He wrenched the gearshift into third, the engine squawking.

I angled toward him. "Is everything all right?"

"Fine." He turned the radio on.

Apparently, "fine" meant no talking. I slumped in the seat. Could this day be over already?

Twenty minutes later, his Civic idled in front of Xander's towering building.

My nerves vibrated with the tired engine's rumble. I swallowed. *Man up, Em.* If I could handle being only friends with Riley, then surely I could handle delivering a proposal to a few bigwigs. I released my seat belt. "You'll be back at two, right?"

Riley nodded without turning in my direction.

"You sure you're okay? You've hardly said two words the whole ride."

A labored inhale rose in his chest. "Sorry. A little distracted, that's all."

"I know the feeling. What if I blank in the middle of my presentation?"

He finally faced me then. A look of turmoil gradually gave way to an assuring smile. "You've been prepping for weeks. The proposal is top-notch. The board would be crazy to decline." He lifted my briefcase from the floor and rested the strap on my shoulder. "You've got this, Emma."

With borrowed confidence maybe. I breathed in. No, he was right. As scary as it had been to trust again, I'd sensed God's hand was on this from the first time I'd walked past that room of forgotten computers. I had to believe it would work out.

"Thanks. I'll see you this afternoon?"

Though something torn still tugged at his eyes, he set his hand over mine. "Ready to celebrate."

I exhaled. With Riley cheering me on, I could face

anything. "Thanks." Another deep breath led me out of the car and into the building. "I've got this," I whispered.

The janitor peeked up from his bucket as I crossed the foyer.

"Hi, John." I waved, but he kept pushing his mop without saying hello. Weird.

In the elevator, Alicia from accounting hovered along the opposite side from me. Had I forgotten to put something on in my rush to get ready? I did a quick once-over in the mirrored walls. Everything looked to be in place. I nonchalantly whiffed my clothes. Since when was Downey fabric softener offensive? The doors opened. "Have a nice…"

Alicia maneuvered around me and trekked to her office.

"…day," I finished anyway.

Okay, I was definitely missing something here. A strange current of energy pulsed across the floor as if someone had rubbed a giant balloon over the felt cubicles.

On my way to my desk, Renee caught my arm and steered me in the opposite direction. "Why don't you make a Starbucks run?"

"Renee, what's going on? I feel like I'm in one of those awkward dreams when you walk into the school cafeteria and realize you forgot to get dressed."

And then I heard it. Yelling from Jack's office. Behind the glass walls, Mr. Johnston shook a folder in the air, ranting.

Renee raised her shoulders. "I tried to warn you, sweetie."

Warn me? He couldn't have been upset about my project idea. I hadn't even presented it yet. I started down the hall.

Renee followed. "Emma, wait."

Another holler from inside the closed office almost knocked me backward. I wasn't supposed to be nervous pitching to this guy? Right. Maybe I needed that Starbucks run after all. Tea! Shoot, I'd left the tea Riley brought me in his car. This morning couldn't get any better, could it?

I fought to tune out Mr. Johnston's muffled ranting from down the hall while I laid out copies of my proposal on the boardroom tabletop. Renee led five gray-haired gentlemen to their seats around the oval table. Jack followed a minute later. He slipped on his suit jacket, looking like he'd slept about as well as I had.

"Everything all right?" I whispered from the corner of my mouth.

"Stock's down," he whispered back. "That always sets him off."

Perfect.

"Should we postpone?"

Mr. Johnston barreled into the room past Renee.

Jack turned. "Too late now." He downed an entire bottle of water and resurrected his usual cocky stature before facing the group. "Gentlemen, thank you for allowing us to add a quick presentation to the beginning of your meeting. Before you dive into your regular reports, our newest intern and I have an exciting business venture to propose." He fanned a hand toward me. "Emma."

I cued the PowerPoint to the opening slide and tried to feed off Jack's self-confidence.

"An after-school program?" Mr. Johnston scoffed before I got a word in. "Is this a joke?"

Blank stares from around the table pummeled into me. I wiped my clammy hands on my skirt and forced down a dry swallow. "No, sir. I'm proposing a business plan to invest some of our resources into a secondary market. We have an entire inventory of unused computer equipment we could refurbish into a new venue of operations."

Mr. Johnston shooed Renee away from his water glass. "Jack, tell me you haven't pandered to this idea. You're supposed to be making me money, not proffering it out to the poor."

Jack lifted off the edge of a side table and cleared his throat. "There are tax benefits. And an investment in the community could add a philanthropic brand to the company's reputation. It might even help our stock."

"The community?" Mr. Johnston flexed out his collar. "I'm running a business, not running for public office, for God's sake."

He motioned for Renee to hand out the performance reports, clearly putting an end to our presentation before it even began. "You want to know the reason

Xander is ranked in the top six companies in Oregon? Because we know what our clients want, and we're good at delivering the goods."

He rose from the table and strode straight into Jack's face. "I'm supposed to be providing the board with budget forecasts and profitability measurements," he said in a hushed reprimand. "Not some socio-economic nonsense." He flicked the paper in his hand. "The board doesn't have time for this. And neither do I."

"It was just a proposal," Jack said calmly.

At least one of them was calm. Mr. Johnston stared him down. "Can the proposal, Jack, or can your job."

The single glare he pinned on me carved right through my gut. No words necessary. Straightening his tie, he paced back to his seat.

The slide advancer slipped out of my hand to the floor. I gripped the table. "It was my idea," I said faintly.

Renee nudged me toward the door. "Let it go, Emma."

"I can't let Jack take the rap for me." Regaining feeling to my limbs, I unwound my arm from hers and braved facing Mr. Johnston. "Jack was doing me a favor. Please don't take your disappointment out on him."

The same scathing glare from a moment ago coursed over my profile with the stark assessment of one of his profitability tools.

I addressed the entire table. "I'm terribly sorry for wasting your time." With as dignified a smile as I could forge, I took my leave. Tears brimmed the second I crossed the threshold.

Renee stroked my back. "Emma, honey—"

My hand raised before my voice. "Please don't." I couldn't bear to hear another *"I tried to warn you"* comment. Thoughts of letting Dad down compressed until I felt as small and useless as the pulled-out staples collected on the carpet at my feet.

A murmur of conversations ignited across the cubicles.

Jack swept through the door. "Back to work, everyone."

Conversations fell behind sounds of wheels rolling over chair mats and fingernails drumming over keyboards. The anthem of routine resumed.

All except for my breathing.

I fled to the bathroom and dabbed cool water over my face, but the sting of disillusionment kept burning. How could this be happening? The excitement I'd felt, the affirmation I'd sensed… This was supposed to be it. The reason I was here. I was so sure of it.

I gripped the sink's porcelain edge. "I don't understand."

The squeak of creaky hinges followed a rap on the door. "Find another hiding spot?"

I jumped back from the sink. "Jack, this is the ladies' room."

He glanced at the emptied stalls. "I doubt anyone's leaving their desks anytime soon. Little privacy's a good thing, remember?"

Did that include crawling into a cave somewhere in a remote mountainside?

He crossed the tiles. "Listen, I can take an early lunch break. Why don't you let me take you home?"

My arms drifted to my sides. Home? Don't tell me I'd lost my internship over this. How would I explain it to Mr. Oakly? To Mom? My stomach twisted and wrenched me forward. "So, that's it? I don't get a second chance?"

"It's business, Emma. That's the way it goes."

How could I forget? Reprimand for relying on grace drilled into me. My palms found the cool sink again.

He set his hand over mine. "Don't take it personally. It was a good try."

"Is that a nice name for failure?"

"At least he didn't fire you."

Thankfully. Though, if I bombed my performance review, it really didn't matter.

"C'mon." He nodded behind him. "Let's get out of here. You can start fresh tomorrow."

There was only one person I wanted to be with right now, and it certainly wasn't Jack Peters. "Thanks, but I have a ride." I drew my cell from my pocket.

He gestured for me to make the call.

If Riley kept the radio turned up anywhere near how loud he had it on the drive in, he probably wouldn't hear the ring, but I had to try. *Please pick up.* "Riley Preston, leave a message."

I faced the wall and lowered my voice. "Hey, it's me.

Turns out I need a ride home sooner than two. If you haven't made it to campus yet, would you mind turning around to come get me? Mr. Johnston shot down the proposal." My voice caught. I pushed End before the quiver in my lip gave me away.

Jack's hands touched the tops of my shoulders from behind. I eased out from under them.

"Give your ride a few minutes. Then I say we go. Trust me. You're not going to want to wait around here."

Valid point.

People dropped to their chairs or dipped into side rooms when the bathroom door opened. Like it wasn't obvious they'd been listening. Good thing none of us were theater majors.

At my desk, I stuffed my notes inside my briefcase's front pouch and wished I could bury myself inside it too.

The image of A. J.'s hurt expression from this morning seared into the canyon left in my gut from Mr. Johnston's glare. I had to get out of there. I checked my cell. No missed calls. A tap on my cubicle stopped me in the middle of a text to let Riley know not to worry about coming back.

"Ready?" Jack asked.

"Yeah." I'd finish the text in the car.

A series of whispers traveled down the string of cubicles beside us like some kindergarten game of telephone.

A burst of natural light shined from the windows in the front of the building. I hadn't even felt the elevator leave the third floor.

In the parking lot, Jack toyed with his keys. "Are you as tight as I am?"

I looked up from the pavement. "Excuse me?"

"Your muscles. They aren't tight after all that work and stress over this proposal?"

I shook my head. The condition of my muscles was none of his business.

"Man, you're steel, aren't you? Ballsy too. All for the off chance the boss might actually go for it. That drive will take you places."

The off chance? My feet stopped. "You knew he was going to react like that?"

He turned, hands splayed. "I knew it'd be a gamble."

How could there be no air outside either?

He scratched his cheek with his key. "Why are you looking at me like that?"

My nails dug into my palms. "I've spent weeks working on this. I fell asleep at the library. Lost time with my friends. And now you're telling me you knew this whole time it'd be a waste? You let me do all this for nothing?"

"Not for nothing. If he'd bought into it, we both could've scored some serious points. That's the risk you take." He edged closer and traversed the side of his finger down my cheekbone. "Plus, we got to spend time together, didn't we?"

*You've got to be kidding me.* I backed up.

Jack looked around the lot. "Listen, we're both drained. Why don't you come over to my place for a while? Unwind." He slinked up beside me and squeezed my shoulders. "Let me work out that tension."

I pulled away, but he caught the side of my skirt. The fabric cinched at my waist as he whipped me around.

With one hand on my hip, the other slithered down my back until calloused fingertips pressed into the top of my leg. "I've been patient enough with your girl-next-door act, Emma. After all that work I put in to helping you, you owe me."

Owe him? "I'm sorry if you got the wrong impression, but we're not—"

He yanked me closer. My arms locked to keep the space from collapsing between us, but the buttons on his shirt bored into my palms the harder I braced them. I turned away from his breath scorching the skin on my neck. "Let go of me."

He transferred his grip from my waist to my chin and jerked it toward his. "See, this is your problem. You think you're something special. Out to change the world. Acting like you're too good for me. Why don't you drop the good girl routine and live a little already?"

Fists clenched, I slammed my heel into his foot and broke free from his grasp.

The venom in his four-letter response fueled my pace to a sprint.

"Where you gonna go?" he yelled with smug satisfaction.

I paused mid-stride, stumbling less over the rise of pavement and more over the truth in his words. Not only didn't I have another ride, I didn't have another internship. Somewhere in the shadows, a garbage can lid clanked onto its metal shell. The sound rattled across the street and straight up my spine.

Jack closed in again and backed me against a wall. "You need me. Admit it."

"Let me go."

A cup crashed to the ground and splattered tea onto the wall. Someone ripped Jack off me and pounded him against the bricks, arm against his throat. "She said, let go."

Riley'd come back for me. Relief collided with the panic still surging inside me.

"Who are you, her bodyguard?" Jack seethed.

The tendons in Riley's neck twitched. "I'm the guy who's going to shatter your trachea if you think of touching her again."

Jack tried to break free, but Riley caught his chin with his elbow. Jack's face turned a shade darker than his red tie. "Push me again, and you'll regret it."

"I doubt that."

I grabbed Riley's taut shoulder. "He's not worth it."

His chest continued to heave as if he hadn't heard me.

"Riley?" I set a hand over his trembling one.

His eyes strayed to mine. He looked at Jack, then back at me, and slowly slackened his hold.

Jack pushed him away the second he had room and reached for his neck through raspy breaths.

Riley guarded me with his body when Jack lifted off the wall. "Keep walking."

Jack wrenched his disheveled suit jacket into place and raked his fingers through his hair. Once he'd regained his composure, he squared his shoulders as if his arrogance made him untouchable. The longer he glared at me, the more his sharp glower crawled into a dark smirk. "You're done, Emma. Your internship. Any chance for a position in this company." He opened his hand like a puff of smoke. "Gone."

He scoffed at Riley's tight jaw. "You can thank your hoodlum boyfriend for that." He spit on the ground and wiped his chin. "She's all yours. Good luck getting her to put out."

Riley lunged at his words, but I caught his hand to keep him close until Jack disappeared around the corner.

An edgy breeze cut through the parking lot. Neither of us moved. Riley's chest rose and fell three times before he seemed to trust his voice again. "Are you okay?"

"Yes." The word sounded as hollow as I felt. "No." Nothing was okay.

Riley brought me to him without my needing to say more. There in his arms, I crumbled under the weight of a day I wanted to erase. The hurt on A. J.'s face, the whispered murmurs in the office, Mr. Johnston's deep-cutting stares, Jack's slimy hands. It all drained onto the front of Riley's coat with tears of regret.

He held me tighter. No words. Just protection. Safety.

In the warmth of his embrace, it was easy to believe the world wasn't as cold as it really was.

Time stilled until he lifted me into his car. He left the radio on during the ride home, probably for distraction. The level of adrenaline still steaming off him could've fueled the engine.

With my legs swept up in the seat, I cradled my knees and chewed my pinky. Scenery passed outside the window, but nothing came into focus. Questions ran together without beginning or end. I'd thought I'd finally found it—the plan God had for my life. It was supposed to work out. The project, the review—all of it. Why would He open my heart to something He knew was going to fail? Had I misinterpreted completely? Gotten it all wrong?

My hand drifted to the door panel, my eyes to the gray sky. Part of me wanted to ask Him why He'd give us dreams He'd never fulfil, but I knew better than anyone that not all questions had an answer.

Riley parked in front of my apartment building but didn't cut the engine. Each time the blades smeared the beginning of raindrops across the windshield, I wished a little more for a way to wipe away the cost of hope.

"I'm sorry." Riley stared at his hands in his lap, his voice sullen.

*He* was sorry? "For what? Protecting me?"

He gripped the wheel and looked up at the hood. "I shouldn't have—"

"You have nothing to be sorry for. If you hadn't come

back…" I shut my eyes against the possibilities of what could've happened.

My door opened a minute later. Riley led me out of the car and up to my apartment. The entire walkway passed without a sound, without a look.

I didn't know what to say. I dawdled in front of my door, hating how off things had felt between us today.

His jaw contracted and released half a dozen times under the stairwell light. The war of holding back what he wanted to say reached his eyes when he looked up at me. "Em, I—"

"Stay?" Vulnerability bled through my request, but I didn't care. Not tonight. I wasn't ready to be alone.

Riley's forehead creased. The minute he reached for his hair, I reached for the doorknob.

"Forget it. It's fine. Really." I dug for my keys and any ounce of stability. "I should get to sleep anyway. I'm gonna have a lot of work to do tomorrow and—"

"Emma." He edged toward me when I turned but stopped himself mid-step. A slow exhale lowered his chin to his chest. "I have to go." Though his hands had stopped shaking, his voice still quavered.

He started for the stairs, hesitated once more, then turned back and strode straight to me. A breath stood between us. He brought a hand to my cheek. Tender, earnest. Whatever battle he was still fighting beat through his pulse against my skin.

I didn't move, didn't breathe. I knew if I did, I'd make the same mistake I'd made in the woods.

His chest continued to expand and fall until he finally let go and stepped back. "I'm sorry," he whispered again.

I wanted to tell him it was okay. That everything would be okay—with us, with my internship. Trouble was, after today, I no longer believed it.

## 18

## SECOND CHANCE

FOUR DAYS LATER, Monday's catastrophe still burned in my lungs. My New Balances pounded the treadmill. Barely able to breathe, I forced my feet to either side of the moving runway, guzzled half my water down, and doused my face with the rest.

What was I thinking? I had one task—earn a stellar performance review. Not tout grand proposals about making a difference, like some wet-behind-the-ears idealist. And certainly not lay my dreams on the board table for corporate suits like Jack Peters to trample over. I should've kept my head down and got the job done. That was it.

My heart thudded against my sweat-soaked T-shirt. I bashed my fist into the rails—once with full force, a second time, lifeless. I'd messed up. Again.

I snagged my book bag from the wall, lumbered through the exit doors, and crashed smack into a walking Nike commercial, complete with white Jordans, a charcoal hoodie, and a basketball stowed under his arm.

"Whoa, Steamroller." A. J.'s grin was as lopsided as ever, even after the library incident. "You know, you're starting to make a habit of running into me."

The wind clung to my damp shirt and stung my eyes. I pushed past him before he could see.

"Hey, hey, hey." He drew me back around and lifted my chin. "What's wrong?"

I batted away all signs of emotion. "I'm sorry, A. J. For a lot of things, but I can't talk right now." If I did, I'd break. I had to keep moving.

*"You're done, Emma."*

The constant replay of Jack's words raged with the wind. I tried to outrun it. But whether inside on a treadmill or outside on the gravel, no amount of running could reverse time.

At the library, a gust from behind took another stab at me. I wrenched open the Book Return kiosk and whirled my bag around my arm. The books jammed the harder I pushed until I finally tore the pack off my shoulder and left it hanging there in the wind. A frustrated shriek shattered the composure I'd feigned all week. I slid down the kiosk's metal side onto the cold concrete.

A gut-level sense of self-disappointment almost curled me into a ball. I had to fix this.

With a deep breath, I pulled myself together and

dialed Mr. Oakly's number. He'd probably heard by now anyway. Bet Jack had a real blast giving him a blow-by-blow.

One unanswered ring stretched into another. My watch caught the lamplight. Seven o'clock. Of course he wasn't still in his office.

A high-pitched beep blared through the phone line. "Mr. Oakly, it's Emma Matthews. I'm calling about what happened at Xander. I made a mistake. It won't happen again. Trust me." A dry swallow scraped down my throat. "I have six weeks left to find another internship. I'll make this right. I promise."

I ended the call and tapped the phone against my leg. Six weeks. I could do this. I *had* to do this. Elbows on my knees, I dialed a second number. *Pick up. Please pick up.*

"Riley Preston, leave a message."

Another beep. Another pause waiting for me to fill in the silence. But after four days of leaving messages, no words came. On top of everything, I couldn't bear it if I'd lost him too.

An ominous backdrop of ash-colored clouds chased the last of the day's light away. I braced myself for another storm. Yet instead of rain, resolve kicked in. The clouds kept passing. The stars peeked through. And this time, a whisper in the wind renewed my strength to stand.

Trevor's bravado sailed around the corner of my apartment building right as I did. "About time you got here."

I glanced from him to the rest of the gang congregated on the sidewalk. "For?"

He spread his arms to his sides. "A night out with your friends. You know, that thing we do every Friday."

Except it wasn't every other Friday.

A. J. extended a hand. "A little fun with friends goes a long way." Though a hint of his earlier concern shadowed his tone, he didn't recant his smile.

I looked around my semi-circle of friends again. Honestly, it was too late to make internship calls tonight anyway. I'd work on it first thing Monday. If there were any left.

A. J. pulled me into a side hug the instant I nodded.

"Sweet." Trevor rubbed his hands together. "Since we have an even number, we should play some racquetball. Bowers, you're always up for a little competition, right?"

Testosterone-driven digs slung between them, the quest to win already surging.

Maybe sweating out my tension was worth another shot. "I'm in."

"Jae?" Trevor's look of expectancy met a devilish grin.

"You know me." She perched a hand on her hip. "I never miss the chance to show you up."

"Oh!" A. J. covered his mouth with one hand while giving Jaycee props with the other. "You just got slammed, bro."

Trevor closed in on her with a swaggering stride. "All right, lil' lady. Bring it on."

After Ashlea and Becky elected to watch a movie

instead, the remaining four of us traipsed down to the sports center.

"A. J., I'm sorry for the way I acted in the library. You were right. I got too caught up in everything."

He grabbed two racquets from the utility closet. "Already forgiven." He handed me one and winked. "Now, you ready to take these two down, or what?"

I poked my fingertips through the racquet strings. "I don't wanna trip you up."

Trevor approached us on cue. "You better let me pair up with her. I'm used to it." We exchanged a tight-lipped glance.

Thirty minutes of sneaker-squeaking fun ended with my scoring backhand. Trevor gave me a jumping double high five. "That's what I'm talking about, girl." He got up in A. J.'s face, arms in the air. "You just got slammed, bro."

A. J. darted a finger between the pair of us. "Wait a sec, here. You two totally played me, didn't you?"

I spun my racquet like a cowgirl with a pistol.

"Hustlers. Wow." A. J. turned to Jaycee. "How do you put up with these two?"

She looped her arms around our necks. "Bribery."

Standing there with my best friends reminded me of what Riley had said that day on the sports field. "*Maybe we've just been waiting to find the right reason to live in the present.*" The right reason still felt out of reach, but part of the answer had to include friendship—the kind filled with ordinary moments that mattered the most.

A. J. draped his arm across my shoulders as the four

of us started for the campus café. "You owe me a rematch, Miss Playah. But this time, on the basketball court. You're going down, girl."

"'Sup, Preston?" Trevor said.

My head snapped up in time to see Trevor give Riley one of those guy half-hug-handshakes. "Didn't expect to see you tonight."

That made two of us.

"Yeah, I ended up needing a break from the song I was working on." He scuffed his chin with the back of his hand. "What are you guys up to?"

"Not much." Trevor flexed his arms like he was posing for GQ magazine. "Just smoking Bowers and Jaycee in a little racquetball."

A. J. huffed. "More like hustling." He squeezed me closer. "Better watch out for this one. She's dangerous."

Riley zeroed in on A. J.'s arm still draped over mine.

Trevor nodded down the street. "We're headed to Paradox. Come hang out for a while."

Riley looked away from A. J. and me. "I should probably get back."

"It's Friday. Forget work." Trevor clapped Riley on the back, prodded him forward, and offered his notorious phrase. "C'mon. It'll be fun."

Though we only lagged a few paces behind them, whatever Riley and I'd left unsaid Monday kept a wall between us thicker than Paradox's double paned glass doors.

My unvoiced questions crashed into the horde of

people piled in the café. Huddled around tables and corners, students traded an evening away from their studies for a tonic of oversized coffee mugs and parchment-wrapped cookies.

We were no exception. A compelling tag team of chocolate and caffeine could undermine any source of stress. Usually. It might've worked on me if my line of sight hadn't intersected Riley's across the table. It looked like it pained him to be there.

Why wouldn't he tell me what was wrong, or what I could do to change it? I latched on to his gaze, silently pleading until a coffee grinder agitated in the background and broke the connection.

Riley rose to his feet so abruptly, I checked to make sure someone hadn't pulled the fire alarm.

Everyone stared.

Trevor stretched over the table. "You cool, bro?"

"Yeah. Yeah, fine." Riley grabbed his coat off his chair. "I'm gonna call it a night. You guys stay. Have fun." His eyes flickered to me for the slightest moment before he hustled to the side exit.

A gust of wind blew in through the door on the tails of his cool departure.

Already rising, I didn't bother waiting for my voice to catch up to my body. "I'll be right back," I called behind me.

Wind seeped into my skin with a chill that'd been building over days of not seeing him. I jogged through the obstacle course of tables and chairs. "Riley, wait."

He stood on the outskirts of the patio without turning around. "You should go back inside."

I stopped behind the unseen barrier still hovering between us. "Why?"

"Because I'm not as strong as you think I am, and you're making this harder than it already is. I shouldn't have come."

"Making what harder?" I turned him toward me. "What are you talking about?"

He stared at the pavement. "I want you to be happy, Em. Always have."

"And you think not talking to me is helping?"

"If it keeps me from interfering with you and A. J., then yes." His shoulders fell. "He's good for you, Emma. You should be with the right guy, and—"

"A. J. and me?" Where was this coming from? "You're not making any sense."

"Monday, you came home in the same clothes after..." He dug his hand in his hair.

"After what?"

"You said A. J. woke you up."

"So you thought, what? That I spent the night with him?" Did he really think I'd fall asleep in his arms one night and then run into A. J.'s a week later? My insides turned into a wrestling mat, relief in one corner, hurt in the other. The night's abrasive air joined the fight with a jab to my eyes.

"I didn't mean... It's just..."

"I fell asleep in the library, Riley. A. J. happened to

find me in the morning. That's all." I shoved my hands in my pockets, the hurt impossible to bury with them. He probably thought I'd egged Jack on too.

"Is this about the way I fell apart outside Xander? I never said anything about Jack because I was scared I'd lose my internship, but I should've seen that coming. I should've handled it better." Not have had a meltdown and shown how vulnerable I was. No wonder he thought I'd go crawling to anybody who opened their arms to me.

His hand, momentarily outstretched, recoiled like a reflex he'd trained himself to master. "Don't you dare apologize for that, Emma. He assaulted you." Knuckles whitening, Riley backed away and lifted his head to the sky.

The brokenness in his voice clamped around my heart. Fighting with Jack must've sent him right back to when he'd fought his landlord in Nashville. I can't believe I put him in the same situation he'd spent years trying to run from.

"I'm sorry. For everything." He turned, his voice a whisper. "I don't want to keep hurting you." He withdrew something from his pocket and turned it over in his hand. "The after-school program idea wasn't a mistake. I know that's what you're thinking."

The shadow of his movement flickered across the sidewalk as he neared. "Just because the rest of us blow it doesn't mean you should doubt what you have to offer."

He placed a folded piece of paper in my palm and curled his fingers over mine.

"What's this?"

"A second chance." The warmth from his hand spread to the look in his eyes. "If it's not too late."

Too late for what?

My cell phone rang into the stillness. I peeked at the number. Austin could wait.

Riley motioned to the phone. "It's fine. Take it."

I swiped the screen. "Hey."

"Em, have you talked to Mom today?" Austin asked.

"No. Why? Is everything okay?"

The pause from Austin's side of the line pushed me backward.

"Mom got next semester's bills in the mail today."

I padded for the nearest patio chair and dropped into it. Riley sat across from me. "What's wrong?" he mouthed.

"You know how Mom gets when she starts looking at bills and her bank account," Austin said. "She's talking about looking for another job."

"Another job? She's already working two. What's she trying to do, add so much stress she needs anti-depressants again?"

"I know. I'm trying to talk sense into her. We both have scholarships. I don't know why she's freaking out."

My pulse pounded.

"What?" Austin asked. "You still have your scholarship, right?"

"Yes." I hoped. Had I lost my only chance of keeping it?

"I thought you found an internship."

I cradled my legs in my chair with me. "I did, but… I lost it." I lowered my voice in the receiver. "Mr. Oakly gave me until the end of the semester to submit my review. I'm gonna fix this. Don't worry." My words turned into white puffs in the dark air and disappeared with my confidence.

Riley's face tightened. He wrenched backward.

"Listen, we'll figure this out together," Austin said. "If it comes to it, I have some money saved."

My feet dropped off the chair. "Absolutely not. You're not giving me the money you need for your last semester. Forget it. It's not going to happen."

I unfolded the paper Riley had given me. *Clear Channel. Paid internship opening for business and finance majors. Possible transition to full-time position. Contact: Mrs. Joan Weberly.* A second chance. I looked up at Riley. "Everything's going to be fine, Aust."

"You haven't gotten any less stubborn this semester, huh?" Austin reined in a laugh. "Okay, fine. Just don't forget you're not in this alone."

Riley pushed off his chair and strode for the sidewalk.

"Riley, wait," I called away from the phone. "Austin, let me call you later. I have to go." I caught up to Riley and grabbed his hand.

He pulled it back. "Please don't tell me everything's

fine. You wouldn't be in this position if it weren't for me. And now your mom—"

"Losing my internship isn't your fault."

He stood against the wind, a wall of doubt against my words.

"Jack Peters is a suit on a power trip. Don't let him make you second guess who you are." I stepped closer, wanting him to see what I saw in him.

He swallowed. Without apprehension this time, he lifted his hand to my ear, stretched his fingers into my hair, and studied me as if I weren't real.

Self-consciousness trickled over me. "What?"

"You really believe what you told me that day in the woods, don't you? About grace?"

Everything about my circumstances screamed the opposite. But somehow my dad's steadfast faith prodded me to place my hope in what I couldn't see.

"I have to believe it." I wouldn't make it through all this otherwise.

A pang of doubt clipped into my side. Fighting it back, I wrapped my arms around Riley's waist and rested my cheek on his chest. His cotton shirt felt like home. In his arms, everything else faded behind the only thing in my life I was sure about. I loved him.

He straightened sooner than I wanted him to. The same torn look from earlier ran into a sad smile when he let go. "Good night, Emma." He hovered a moment longer, then drifted out from under the lamplight.

Alone, the weight of the day closed in again. I curled

back into the chair and looked at the paper Riley had given me. I didn't know if I had what the company was looking for. But when sounds of the life I wasn't ready to part with rang from inside the café, I knew I had to try.

I stretched my shirt cuffs over my hands. In that cold wicker chair on the lamp-lit patio, I held on to the afterglow of being in Riley's arms and prayed there was enough grace left to keep me from losing everything.

## 19

## PARALYZED

BOLSTERED hope filled the next five days. Having an interview lined up with Clear Channel might've had something to do with it. Hanging out with Riley nonstop hadn't hurt either.

We'd spent every afternoon together, listening to music and enjoying Oregon's beauty. Despite an inward battle he strained to hide, he made each moment feel like a gift to savor—moments of friendship I should've been content with.

Like this one.

He sat less than four feet away from me on the sports field with his guitar resting in his lap, the strap unfastened, a small memo pad and pen in the grass inches from his knees. Captivating and inspiring as usual.

"So, when do I get to hear the song you've been working on all semester?"

His fingers froze to the strings. "I haven't finished the lyrics yet."

"Your songs don't need lyrics." I reclined across the blanket, propped up on my elbows as his attentive audience. "I'm sure it's amazing already."

Riley twisted the tuning keys and ran his sleeve across his forehead. Was he blushing?

"I'm not making you nervous, am I?"

He tossed his head back with a groan. "You have no idea."

But as his fingers mastered a melody more beautiful than the tree-lined backdrop behind him, I couldn't imagine a hint of nerves interfering with his talent.

Three girls passing on the sidewalk stopped to watch from a distance. I could practically hear their collective sigh from here. All giggly and doe-eyed, they probably thought Riley was playing a love song to his girlfriend. I might've been tempted to wish the same if wishing didn't cost so much.

"That was gorgeous." I traced the stitching along the blanket. "What's it about?"

"Thought my songs didn't need any words." His grin tipped with the guitar.

Darn smile. "So, you're gonna make me guess?" I sat up and crossed my arms. "It sounded like it could've been a love song."

He fastened and unfastened the guitar strap while avoiding my stare. "All music has a thread of love woven into it."

"Wow. Okay, Mr. Elusive, now you definitely have to tell me the lyrics."

He scratched his neck behind his ear. "Not today."

"Oh, *that's* fair." I hurled a guitar pick at him. "Those girls over there seem to agree with me. So, I guess consensus rules."

"What?" He turned and squinted. "There's no way they heard the music from that far away."

"Doesn't matter. Girls have a built-in love radar. I guarantee they're standing over there, dreaming about diamonds right now."

Riley set the guitar on the blanket. "C'mon, diamonds? They're probably just chatting about classes. I doubt they're dreaming up love stories on their way to Calculus."

"I'm telling you. It's a girl thing. After all those Disney fairy tales we grew up with, we can have our eyes open or closed and still be dreaming."

"Oh, really? So, you could be daydreaming right now."

I threw him a replica of his usual impish grin. "You'll never know."

"Now who's not being fair?" He tossed the guitar pick back at me.

I laughed with him, loving the sound. "Honestly, dreams are overrated. Diamonds too. When my dad proposed, he gave my mom a sapphire. Said it matched her eyes, and the ring was a reminder of the gift God had given him. He always told me I'd find that same gift one day." I lifted the pearl on my necklace and twisted it around. "I know. A sapphire engagement ring is a little… unique."

Riley shook his head but didn't lower his gaze from mine. "Actually, it doesn't surprise me. There's very little about you, Emma Matthews, that isn't unique."

The pearl dropped back to my shirt. It killed me when he said things like that. With such sincerity, such conviction, I could melt into every word and believe them.

Megan's comment from that day in the locker room rushed in again. *"Riley Preston doesn't date."* Would he ever? Could I be enough to change his mind? Enough to love?

I swirled my fingers through the grass folding over the edge of the blanket.

He tilted his head toward mine. "What are you thinking about?"

"Nothing." I plucked a blade of grass and drew figure eights over my palm with the tip. "Do you think love is one of those things worth hoping for?"

I couldn't bring myself to look up. Especially when he didn't answer right away.

"Do you?" he said slowly.

Deep inhale. I couldn't lie, not to him. "To be honest, sometimes I wish I didn't. It'd be easier that way. Less painful. But I guess your heart doesn't always cooperate."

His brow crumpled the way it had numerous times

today, as if he was caught between two opposing emotions. "Your dad wanted you to hope for love because he had faith you'd find it. And so should you."

I almost reached for him, but he broke eye contact and swallowed. He slid a notebook out from under the guitar and toyed with the spiral binding. "We should keep practicing for your interview at Clear Channel. We're running out of time."

Time. My dreaded enemy. I fell backward onto the blanket under the shadow of an approaching storm. "I'd rather listen to you play."

"That's not gonna help you nail these questions."

It might. His music had a way of soothing the restlessness in my heart like nothing else. If I could hold on to it during the interview, I might be able to squelch my nerves. As much as I loved music and art, applying for a position with a top entertainment company was more than a little daunting. No telling who my competition would be.

"How'd you find this lead, anyway?"

Riley stretched and rubbed out his hair. "I sort of pretended to be you."

"You what?"

"I sat through one of those job assessment sessions that Career Development offers. And at the end, I answered all the questions the way I thought you would. This Clear Channel position was one of the top fits." His cheeks turned a guilty shade of pink. "Then I might've scoured all the bulletin boards on campus and confiscated the ads for this interview."

I laughed. "Seriously? No you didn't… Did you?"

"Hey, I was doing everyone else a favor. Spared them the letdown of going up against the unstoppable Emma Matthews."

"Ha. Nice try. More like sparing me from more competition than I can handle."

He shot me a look of reprimand. "More like trying to teach you to believe in yourself. C'mon. A little more rehearsing, and you got this."

I flicked the blade of grass in the air and eyed the dark clouds rolling in. With any luck, the rain would cut our practice short. I pulled myself up by my shins and faced him, hands in my lap, spine straight.

"Ahem." He mirrored my posture. "Miss Matthews, why are you interested in this position?"

My lips scrunched to the side before I could stop them. "Because I got fired from my last internship, and I'm desperate."

Riley's forehead pinched again. He didn't still blame himself for that, did he?

"Kidding." Sort of. I sat tall and composed and cleared my throat. "This internship would be an opportunity for me to add hands-on experience to what I'm learning in the classroom. Clear Channel has an excellent reputation in the entertainment industry, and I can't think of a company I'd rather work for."

He fought to keep a straight face. "You're very wise for your age."

I chucked a pinecone at him, but he dodged it without missing a beat.

"And Miss Matthews, what are your greatest strengths?"

I covered my face with my hands. "Ugh. I hate this question."

"This is an easy one, Em."

Maybe for him.

Thunder echoed in the distance, but Riley didn't relent. He peeled my fingers away from my eyes. "You're compassionate, intuitive, driven. You view the world with creativity and innovation. See possibilities where other people see doubt. You have..." He waved his hand to prompt me.

"The heart of an artist," I recited.

He laughed. "Now there's conviction if I've ever heard any." His focus strayed to his guitar, his fingers tracing the strings. "One day you'll believe it."

"I do." *When I'm around you.*

He held his guitar out. "Show me."

The trees stilled. No air. The guitar almost slid out of my clammy hands when I took it.

Riley stretched into the same position I'd been in earlier, sassy expression and all. "I'm not making you nervous, am I?"

Nervous? With that sultry grin? How about incapacitated? I hugged the guitar close to my body as a safe barrier. If I could get my fingers to ignore the disjointed drumming in my heart, I might make it through it. I closed my eyes. *Breathe.*

With a storm nearing, we probably should've packed up and left. But once a few bars into one of Dad's favorite songs, all the memories of hearing him play it while growing up anchored me right there in an embrace I could almost feel.

A breeze danced over me as I strummed the last chord. I left my hands on the strings a minute longer, not ready to let Dad go.

"My dad wrote that for me. He played it for as long as I can remember. Even without any lyrics, it's something you feel, you know?" I pitched a brow at him. "Kind of like *your* songs."

"Emma…" He swallowed. "You're amazing. You have no idea how talented you are."

"It's just a childhood song."

An ache overtook his expression. He brushed back my hair and glided his thumb over my temple. "What would change in your life if you could see what I see?"

My pulse jackhammered. I scooted back—away from every desire propelling me into his arms, away from facing his rejection if I tried.

"You're the real artist. Speaking of which." I fished in my pocket for the paper I'd brought. "I did some research and put together a list of A&R reps." I pointed to the address column. "Here's where you mail in your demos. Record labels are gonna love you."

Riley stared at the page. "You didn't have to do this."

"I believe in you. Of course I did. And when you're on stages across the country, I can say I knew you before you were famous."

He didn't return my chuckle. Didn't look up. "I can't."

The first raindrop dotted our blanket. I rested a hand over his arm. "You're not your dad, Riley. You have what it takes to make it. One day you'll believe it." I held out his guitar as he'd done a few minutes ago for me.

He took it slowly but set it on the ground instead. The passion pouring through his eyes unwound every remaining thread around my heart. I couldn't hide how I really felt when he looked at me that way. The tree line blurred in the background, urging me to run before I gave in.

He lifted a hand to my cheek. My body trembled under his fingers as he raised my chin toward his. Fear of how much I wanted to show him collided with the fear of losing him. But this close, my love for him won. I covered his hand with mine.

The space between us disintegrated until his lips were only an uneven breath away. I met his eyes, plead-ing. An exhale broke past the last barrier and melded into a kiss softer than I'd ever experienced.

His thumb brushed the corner of my lips. "Emma."

Instinct kicked in. My fingers knotted in his hair. I drew

him closer and drank in every heightened sensation—the rapid flutter in his pulse, the gentleness of his hand on my cheek, the strength in his hold around my back. His arms carried me in an undertow of desire I wasn't strong enough to withstand. Grasping his collar, I pressed in with all the feelings I'd spent months fighting. Held nothing from him.

He groaned, lifted back. My hand slid down to his chest. His heart drummed under my palm as he rested his forehead to mine. One beat. Another.

I gripped his shirt, not ready to let go. All this time—all this waiting—had he really felt the same as me? Did he—?

"I'm sorry," he whispered.

My heart stilled. "What?" The broken word barely rose above a clap of thunder nearing closer.

"I'm sorry. I—"

"I'm not." The urgency still coursing through me pulsed with everything I'd wanted to say that day in the clearing—how I saw him, cared about him. "You're one of my best friends, Riley. I haven't wanted to do anything to jeopardize that, but I can't keep pretending it isn't more." I reached for his hand. "Your music, the way you feel life... It's what's inspired me. What opened my eyes to that grant idea and gave me faith to hope for love again. The kind I was scared I'd never find."

His brow furrowed. "Em..."

"I love you." The truth fanned such freedom, I could barely keep from kissing him again. "I've been falling for you since our first day back on campus, and I've been giving you my heart every day since. I—"

"Don't." He let me go.

"Don't what?" I strove to keep my voice intact, but the clouds moving in absorbed the sunlight and my momentary confidence.

Riley's shoulders caved. "Don't give your heart to me."

A knot swelled in my throat. He didn't want my heart? "What just happened a minute ago? That kiss. I thought..."

Still without looking at me, he clenched his coat cuffs. "I'm sorry. That was out of line. I shouldn't have let it go that far. Shouldn't have let you think..." A gruff exhale craned his neck to the sky.

Let me think what? That he might've loved me back? I couldn't bear to hear him say it. My heart flinched, then retreated to the place it never should have left. "Don't apologize."

"Emma." His voice matched the pain on his face.

Winds of rejection speared through me, but I wouldn't let him see me cry. I rose to my feet. Forced breaths made their way to my lungs with each backward step I took.

"It's fine. I'm gonna head home and try to beat this storm. You should go, too, before your guitar gets wet." And before I kept rambling and made an even greater fool of myself. I turned and almost sprinted out of the grass.

A *whack* crashed behind me, as if Riley'd hit something. "Emma, wait."

But I couldn't. Couldn't wait. Couldn't face him. Once my sneakers hit the sidewalk, I didn't stop running until the skies opened up, and the cold rain soaked deep enough to numb an ache it couldn't wash away.

## 20

## SHATTERED

AEROBICS COULDN'T HAVE ENDED SOON ENOUGH. The first one out of the gym, I whirled around the doorframe and peered across the hallway to the wall where Riley usually waited for me.

Why I would've expected him to be there, I had no idea. Of course he was avoiding me. I'd put him in the most awkward position imaginable and then ran away from him. Literally, ran away. The memory had grown even more humiliating with time.

Book bags and shoulder blades hedged me closer to the vacant wall. I curled against the bricks. Minutes lapsed. People swayed by in a blur of indecipherable conversations until they dwindled one by one, and the bustle of sneakers receded behind an echo of how irrational I'd been for waiting at all.

My fist scraped down the wall to my side. I'd promised myself. Vowed I'd never end up here like this—

alone in a corridor, waiting for someone who wasn't coming.

Except it wasn't just someone. It was Riley. As hardened as I wanted to be, I couldn't strong-arm away my feelings for him.

They followed me outside and ignited memories I could relive over and over again—my arms sliding around his neck on their own, my body forming to his, his heartbeat against mine. Everything about our kiss was perfect.

Until he'd apologized.

I cringed at what I must've looked like. I'd practically jumped him like some roadie teenager, for crying out loud. Had his looks of pain been pity for me because of how caught up I already was? Or had he kissed me expecting to feel more than he did?

Bitter air cut through me with the very thing I'd wanted to spare him from. Disappointment.

A familiar vise tightened around my chest. Cold granite spread over my heart until something inside stopped it from breaking. A warmth. A call. A love that rivaled every thought screaming for my acceptance. Caught in a war, I wanted to run but stopped short on the pathway at the sight of someone approaching.

Riley came to a standstill for the briefest moment. Lowering his head, he made slow but resolute strides toward me.

I tucked one side of my coat into the other and

prayed for a way to salvage our friendship. "Riley, I'm sorry for messing things up. I never should have—"

"Please don't. You haven't done anything wrong. I'm the one who shouldn't have kissed you. It wasn't fair. To either of us."

His words lodged shrapnel of rejection into previous battle scars before I could find a shield.

He stopped himself from reaching for me and clenched the back of his hair. "I can't do this anymore."

The chill in the air stung from every angle.

He inhaled deeply, broadened his shoulders, and faced me again. This time, his features matched the unyielding stone bench beside us. "I should have walked away a long time ago."

I stood against the wind. He couldn't give up on our friendship. "What about grace?" I whispered.

He stared at the concrete, his silence his answer.

"My life is better with you in it, Riley." Couldn't he see that? That he was the one who'd helped me find the courage to really live again?

Shards of the sunset splintered through the tree branches and tore across his face. "I'm sorry for letting you believe that."

His stoicism backed me against the lamppost, where the light exposed my tears.

Riley automatically brought me close then. The same level of emotion I'd fallen in love with filled his eyes as he slowly brought his fingers to the nape of my neck. I gripped his shirt, wanting to hold on—to him, to us. His chest rose in shallow movements, as if fighting to keep him in place.

The wind calmed. My heart settled. I lifted a hand to his cheek and searched his eyes with everything in mine —praying, pleading.

He drew in a breath at my touch, then seemed to will himself to step back and look at me with the conviction of a friend. "You're going to nail that interview tomorrow. You'll keep your scholarship, go on to get the kind of job you've been fighting for, and find the future your dad taught you to believe in. You deserve your dreams, Em." His gaze fell from mine. "All of them."

Everything in me wanted to tell him *he* was my dream, that I needed him to stay. But the detached look in his eyes told me it was too late—he'd already left.

He pressed a kiss to my cheek. "Goodbye, Emma."

His silhouette drifted past the light's dim glow and faded into the shadows. Night closed in a claw at a time until there was nothing left but the debris of hope strewn across a sidewalk as empty as I felt.

# WRECKAGE

In one of Jaycee's satiny blouses, a pencil skirt, and heels, I looked just like the other five girls waiting their turn to interview for the Business Analyst position at Clear Channel. Well, almost. Jaycee's skilled makeup work could only disguise so much of last night's wreckage.

I slid the pearl along my necklace. If this wasn't my last promising lead, and Mr. Oakly's deadline wasn't so close, I wouldn't have come. If I got the position, I'd be reminded of Riley every day. How he'd gone on a mission to find another internship opportunity for me. The way we'd rehearsed interview questions. That kiss.

My stomach tensed. Now, I wouldn't even be able to tell him how it went. The wound of losing his friendship seared all over again.

A girl two seats down from me swept her pin-straight blond hair over her shoulder and drew my focus back to the other candidates. The blonde's brown boots rubbed against a matching leather briefcase while she thumbed through a *Vogue* magazine like she was some executive's daughter without a single worry.

Miss Leopard-Print Heels beside her tapped a padfolio against her knee-length jacket, as if it was perfectly normal for all college students to afford cashmere.

If the girls weren't intimidating enough, the three male Express model lookalikes topped it off. Tweed blazers, meticulously trimmed beards, confident reflections they periodically examined in their smart phones. A tawny-haired guy in the corner stared at me while the words, "in the bag" rolled off his lips into the receiving end of his cell.

It was like someone had cast me into a twisted TV movie—*The Devil Wears Prada* meets *The Hunger Games*, where candidates were armed with iPads and eyelash curlers.

My snicker petered into a sigh. Riley had made it easy to believe I had a chance here. He'd made a lot easy to believe. Was any of it real?

The memory of him walking away last night pulsed each time Brunette Number Three drilled her nails over the chair arm. I clutched my manila folder. *You can do this. You have to do this.*

A girl with a teal belt around her nonexistent waist-line stood with her back holding open the door. "Miss Matthews," she read from a clipboard.

No one moved. The woman tugged her rimless glasses down her nose and glared across the waiting room. "Emma Matthews," she said again.

My chair agreed to release me, but my nerves weren't as obliging. Following one tentative step forward, I made it across the small room in Jaycee's heels without spraining an ankle. "Yes, ma'am."

Both salon-manicured eyebrows peaked with disapproval at my choice of salutation. She lowered her clipboard to her side. "Come with me."

Trotting behind her, I kept my folder against my chest. But the farther we walked down the glass-walled hallway, the more see-through I felt.

The afternoon sun filtered through the offices along the left-hand side of us. I breathed in the comfort it brought until the tips of my shoes bumped into the assistant's designer sling-backs.

She waited a moment before facing me, probably forcing down an expletive. "Do you have your résumé?"

I tapped my folder. "Yes, ma—"

Her sharp scowl cut off my now-confirmed-avoid-at-all-costs title. "Have that ready. Ms. Steele is accustomed to keeping a tight schedule."

*Ms. Steele? Seriously?* That's *her name?*

"Is something wrong?"

"I'm sorry, I thought I was meeting with..." I leafed through my folder for the paper Riley had given me with the contact info on it. "Mrs. Weberly."

Somehow, Mrs. Weberly sounded far more approachable than Ms. Steele.

While fanning her lashes, the assistant gripped the top of the clipboard and pinned the opposite end to her hip. "Ms. Steele's opinion is the only one that matters."

Her gaze marched up and down my profile. Something shifted in her expression. Pity? I must have looked worse off than I thought. I fluffed my hair out from behind my ears like it would help.

She put her hand on my shoulder. "Shoulders back. Always. She needs to see you're confident. No stuttering. If a question catches you off guard, you have exactly five seconds to recover. Understand?" With a quick near smile, she grabbed the chrome door handle. "And Miss Matthews? Leave off the ma'am reference. 'Ms. Steele' will do."

A burst of cool air from inside the office rushed over my flushed cheeks.

"Your two-fifteen, Ms. Steele." The assistant looked at me and jutted her head toward the empty seat.

Right. I eased my clenched fingers from my folder and cautiously approached the oversized, L-shaped desk.

Ms. Steele held out a collection of envelopes without prying her focus away from her computer screen. "Alyssa, these need to make it to the mailroom by two-thirty. Reschedule my four o'clock with Mr. Pruett to tomorrow. Tell Stan he had better have those briefings on my desk by the time these interviews are over. I have real work to do today. And cancel my dinner date. Appears I'll be eating in again."

When she looked up, her bangs swayed above thick liner accentuating the expectations in her eyes. "That'll be all, Alyssa," she said without releasing me from her silent assessment.

"Yes, Ms. Steele." Alyssa flitted away while scribbling ferociously on her clipboard.

The door closed and sucked all the air out with it. Though the pristine office looked nothing like Mr. Oakly's, it held the same wall-closing feeling I got anytime I sat opposite one of his scrutinizing glares.

Ms. Steele rubbed her pointer finger under her chin and tapped her shoe into her desk's clear paneling, probably counting the minutes I was wasting.

I smoothed out my skirt and took my seat. Keeping my shoulders back as instructed, I presented my résumé before she requested it.

She reclined in her sleek black chair. Her waistband was as high as her button-up dress shirt was low. "Business major at Reed," she read aloud.

"Yes, ma—" I cleared my throat in a quick recovery. "Ms. Steele."

Two seconds later, she set my résumé on her desk and arched her laced fingers above it. "Why are you interested in working at Clear Channel?"

I crossed one leg over the other, clasped my knee, and strove to recall the answers I'd rehearsed. My throat felt more parched than the artificial plant on her desk.

"I believe Clear Channel would provide an excellent opportunity to turn my academic preparation into practical experience. I've always admired media and the arts and can't think of a better scenario than getting to incorporate my business training with the entertainment industry."

Ms. Steele tugged open her front drawer, pulled out a swatch of blue fabric, and proceeded to clean her glasses while I delivered my prepared answers to each of her questions. She leaned over the single piece of parchment she'd used to size me up before I ever started rambling.

"And tell me, Miss Matthews, what do you have to offer this company that no one else in that waiting room has? What makes you unique?"

The words struck my eyes before bottoming out in my stomach. Every memory of not being enough trampled over the faint whisper in my spirit with the resounding answer I'd wasted the last five years trying to change.

What made me unique? Nothing.

My five-second recovery time lapsed. And even though my interview had probably ended the moment I'd walked through the door, I found Ms. Steele's gaze once again and offered all I had left to give. "I can't tell you if the other candidates' résumés are more impressive than mine, but I can assure you that I'm a hard worker, a quick learner. I'm determined to prove you wouldn't be making a mistake by hiring me. I—"

"That'll be all." She fluttered her hand toward the door as she had done with her assistant earlier.

It took me a moment to stand, to blink. The executive door shut behind me, severing my chance of securing the only internship lead I had left. My shoulders flinched, then sank. I should've beelined it out of there, but I couldn't move. In that narrow hallway, all I could do was wait for the cement to dry around the crumbled cinder block I had no choice but to piece back together around my heart.

## NUMB

THE CONCEPT of time lost its meaning, as if someone had shoved a blunt object into the spoke of a wheel to prevent it from turning. But maybe that's what it's supposed to feel like when you lose everything.

Jaycee knocked on the bathroom door. "You all right in there? You've been showering for almost an hour."

"I'll be out in a minute." I turned the knobs and watched my rationale for thinking a shower would've made a difference race down the drain. Cleaning hadn't helped. Prepping for classes had failed. Nothing lessened the blow of the last few weeks.

In my robe at the sink, I dragged a towel across the fog-coated mirror. A sliver of my reflection peeked through the condensation. I wiped the mirror. Again. And again. No matter how hard I tried, fragments of the person I'd tried to be bled into fragments of the person I'd feared becoming.

I caved to the floor in a heap beside my wet towel. A container of disinfectant wipes from under the sink rolled into my legs. Without a thought, I tore one out and didn't stop scrubbing every inch of the bathroom until my fingernails turned raw and the disinfectant fumes drove me into the hallway.

Hunched against the wall, I drew my legs close and stifled tears I refused to cry. *Don't be weak. Don't you dare give in to despair like Mom did.*

Someone touched my arm. The back of my head hit the wall.

"A little on edge?" Jaycee stood above me with her hand outstretched, but I didn't want help. I wanted to be alone.

I forced myself off the floor, escaped to the bedroom, and closed the door.

It swung right back open. Big surprise.

"I'm not in the mood, Jae." I yanked shirt after shirt out of my dresser in search of my favorite long-sleeved tee.

"Too bad." She advanced. "You may not want to talk, but you can at least listen. Look, I know you're upset about Riley and the internship. I get it."

I slammed the drawer. "No, you don't." I'd always admired Jaycee. Maybe even bordered on envying the way everything came together so easily for her. But I'd never been spitefully jealous of her. Until right then. "Please don't tell me you understand. I don't need to hear any platitudes right now, especially from you."

The fiery words smoldered with regret the second they left my mouth. The expression on my best friend's face didn't help.

I tugged my shirt over my head. "I'm sorry. It's just…" What excuse could I give?

"No, I'm glad you're angry. You can't keep your emotions buried, hoping they'll disappear if you ignore them. If you want to yell, we'll crank up the music so you can scream, and nobody will hear you. If you want to cry, I'll buy you a pallet of Kleenex from Costco. But I swear, if you keep moping around here or go on any more cleaning binges, I'm gonna have to take a step of intervention. Don't make me hide the Clorox wipes from you, because I'll do it."

We both cracked a grin.

She tilted her head, her voice softening. "What happened to strong, driven-Emma?"

"Maybe she was a lie like the rest of it." A cloak for the scared, insecure Emma—the one I'd been pretending didn't exist.

"Em." She crossed the room. "Just because it hurts doesn't mean it was a lie. I know the last thing you need is some flippant cliché about how time will heal, but I want you to promise me you won't give up." She tucked an arm around me and rested her head against mine. "I'm here to lean on, but you gotta keep standing."

"It's hard to stand when your legs are numb."

"You girls filming a soap opera in there?" Trevor yelled from down the hall. "It's time to roll."

"Hold your horses, will ya?" Jaycee shook her head, then dipped another grin my way. "See what fun you could be having? Come out with us tonight."

I gathered my wet hair in a band and plopped onto my bed. "No, thanks. You guys go."

It took a minute for her furrowed brow to relent. "Tomorrow, then. And no buts," she said before rounding the corner.

I smiled at her persistence. Honestly, I loved her for it —she and Trevor both. But once they were gone, a relentless replay of memories streamed across the bedroom door's flat white panels. I shut my eyes. The brokenness I'd been suppressing pierced through, like a shadow that had deepened after a momentary glimpse of light. My arms constricted around my knees in another failed barricade. The room's emptiness felt too raw, too near. I had to get out of there.

On the trail, the sound of gravel churning under my sneakers echoed the creek's steady flow. Everything was moving—always moving. Same as I was supposed to be doing. I hadn't stopped running for a reason. When you stop, you feel.

Windows in classroom buildings darkened the longer I walked. Little by little, benches lost their occupants, and the busyness of the day yielded to the stillness of night.

I wandered onto the deserted football field. Memories of being there with Riley piled onto the entire wreckage of the semester and drove me to my knees.

"Dad," I whispered, "I'm sorry I've let you down."

Shimmers of lamplight flickered over the creek, but clouds kept the feeling of his embrace hidden with the stars.

The voice of abandonment raged against my yearning for a father.

Wind soared through the treetops. Leaves stirred. Thunder sang. Noise clamored all around me until—just for a moment—the storm silenced, and all I could hear was the sound of one whisper calling to another.

Part of me wanted to shut it out, but it wouldn't let me. The tender calling splintered through my shield of anger until there was nothing separating me from the pursuit of a love I longed for and questioned at the same time.

"God." I gripped the tops of my thighs. "Please."

A single raindrop splattered onto the ground beside me. I drew in a breath but didn't have time to move before a sheet of rain struck the darkness. One by one, unrestrained tears drained from heaven, as if the Father wept for my heartache as His own.

A cold breeze groaned across the grass in place of words I couldn't find. My lashes fell. My strength faltered. And there in the middle of an empty field, on dew-soaked knees, I laid my heart before the One who had broken it the most.

I wanted to believe He hadn't left me. That He heard me, saw me. I wanted to trust His arms were safe enough to hold every piece of me that had come undone. And that somehow there was purpose, even in the broken-ness. I wanted to believe it. I *needed* to believe it. But unlike the raindrops disappearing into the creek without a ripple, the cost of hope in a fallen world always left behind a trace of its existence.

Pain.

It soaked into me with the rain. Cold and pervasive, it drove my knees deeper into the mud, and my heart farther from hope.

I waited but knew I couldn't stay in the storm. Sodden on the inside and out, I left my broken prayers on the field and started home.

The rain subsided by the time I reached the trail. Someone stepped onto the gravel from the shadows. A tight gasp pushed me backward until Trevor came into view. I lowered my hand from my chest and exhaled. "Trev, what are you doing here?"

The understanding pouring from his eyes eliminated the need for a response. I could've been looking at my brother.

My throat tightened. "Please, go and have a good time with Jae tonight. Don't worry about me."

I tried to pass him, but he wouldn't let me run away. Not from him, not from the pain. He caught my hand and held me close. "Em, it's okay."

I wrestled to pull away and pretend I didn't know what he was talking about. That his words weren't ripping through the caution tape holding my heart together.

He wrapped his strong arms around me, cradled my head between his shoulder and chest, and rested his hand over my hair. "It's going to be okay," he whispered again.

His tenderness broke my resolve. All at once, the tears I'd harbored spilled down my cheeks. It wasn't okay. Honestly, I didn't know if it ever would be. But as I clung to fistfuls of my friend's coat, Jaycee's words filtered to mind.

*Keep standing. Just. Keep. Standing.*

## 23

## DANCE

SOMEWHERE ALONG ONE continuous cycle of shuffling between classes, November colors had withered under December frosts. Two years in Oregon had prepared me for its winters. At least, I thought they had. But this year, the cold cut deeper.

A. J. materialized next to me on the sidewalk. "Hey, stranger." He flicked the book in my hand. "Heard you've been ditching your friends for the much more exhilarating companionship of your textbooks."

"Sorry, A. J., I'm not very good company right now. It's better if I keep to myself."

He set his hand over my forearm and drew us both to a stop. "Better for who?"

Beside us, a maple tree's leafless branches swayed in the silence waiting for answers I didn't want to get into. Not now, with his transparent expression seeing everything I couldn't hide. I rushed down the sidewalk without voicing a response.

"Heartaches heal, Emma," he called up to me. "But only if you let them."

I stopped. His words penetrated through the textbook clasped in my arms and joined the wind coursing through my coat straight to my vocal cords. "Some things aren't reparable."

A. J. caught up to me. "Just because someone doesn't know what he lost, doesn't mean it isn't worth keeping." He turned me around and lifted my chin. "You have a lot to offer, Em."

The honesty in the way he looked at me couldn't block out the memory of Ms. Steele's sharp eyes searching mine for a list of all I had to offer—a list that never came.

"You're wrong." I wiped my cheek with my sleeve. "It doesn't matter anyway. This is probably my last month here. I bombed my interview for the internship I was counting on."

"So. Move on to the next one."

I shrugged past his straight-faced pose. "Thanks, Captain Sensitivity."

He caught up to me again, laughing this time. "What were you expecting? A pity party? I think you've got that covered all by yourself."

"Wow. I'd offer you a shovel, but I doubt you can dig that hole you're standing in any deeper."

A. J. set my book on the ground, grabbed my hands,

and wiggled my arms like wet noodles at my sides. "C'mon, shake it off. I know rejection stings, but regret is worse. Trust me. Never hold back, remember?"

Yeah, look where that'd gotten me. Besides, it was too late.

"The fight's over. I can't meet my advisor's deadline."

"Why don't you talk to Dean Jeffries directly? Ask for an extension."

"I don't think that'll fly."

"You don't know if you don't try." A. J. angled his head, stroked his chin, and stared at me like a coach debating on whether to put me back in the ring. "You got some fight left in you, girl. I can see it."

"Oh, yeah? How's this?" I tugged his beanie over his eyes and shoved him off the sidewalk.

He hopped in front of me, undaunted. "Think we need to work on that. Why don't you hang out with me this afternoon?" He peered from side to side, bent forward, and lowered his voice. "I know a couple of guys we can sucker into a racquetball match. I've brushed up on my hustling skills since our last game. So, don't worry." He winked. "They'll never see it coming."

"You're never going to let me live that down, are you?"

"Uh-uh-uh. Careful. You don't want anybody to see that smile of yours. You might give them the impression you still remember how to be happy."

Where was a racquet when you needed it? "Cute, A. J."

"You know what you could use?" he persisted. "A night on the town."

I tripped over my book and landed on a stone bench with my legs dangling over the side.

"Case in point." He helped me to my feet. "Seriously, Eeyore, you need to get out from under this cloud and engage life again."

I picked up my book, wishing life came with an instruction manual. Or even better, a desensitization button, shock therapy—anything to keep life from hurting.

A. J. uncrossed his arms, and the playfulness in his voice gave way to an unexpected sobriety. "Life's meant to be lived, Em, not waded through like a zombie. You have friends who miss you."

His words landed to my gut. I pressed the book to my stomach again. "Guess I have been pretty detached lately."

He started to clap. "Congrats. You just won the understatement of the year award."

And there was the A. J. I knew.

"Funny." My coat scratched against his puffer vest as I skirted past him. "Don't you have a J. Crew photo shoot to go to or something?"

He raised a sassy brow. "Are you saying you think I look like a model?"

"You're impossible sometimes, you know that?"

"Guilty," he said with over-agreeing dimples. "But that's why you love me."

My eyes rolled in response to his witty charm. "You better be careful on this ice. That big head might topple you over onto that good-looking face of yours, and then where would your model career be?"

"Good-looking, huh?"

Oh, good grief.

"Bye, A. J." Waving behind me, I ambled around the corner of my apartment building.

"You think I'm attractive, Emma Matthews," he called. "Admit it."

He attracted my nerves. I'd give him that.

Smiling in spite of myself, I hustled out of the cold and up the stairs. A breeze snuck in with me and fanned a pink sticky note pinned to the bulletin board above the phone. *Mr. Oakly called*, it read. *Said it's urgent.* As opposed to the last two times he called? I shut the door and sighed. I had to face him sometime.

Jaycee bounced down the hallway with the energy of a toddler who'd gotten a hold of a dozen cookies. "Trev and I are going out tonight. But tomorrow, we're finishing decorating for Christmas. You and me. No excuses."

"Um... okay." I turned to Trevor in a silent plea for a little assistance.

He backed away, palms up in surrender. Coward.

Jaycee's two-tiered earrings jangled with the same sharp pitch in her eyes. "Don't look at me like that. We haven't had girl time in forever. There's an entire cheese-cake in the fridge waiting for us. And hazelnut hot chocolate. With whipped cream. Oh, *and* I already made a Christmas playlist." Her voice had jacked up three octaves by the time she stopped to breathe.

Trevor reentered with his thumbs hooked in his pockets. "Don't worry, Em. It'll be fun."

"Does that mean you're helping?"

"Ooh, sorry. No can do. Wouldn't want to deprive you two of precious bonding time," he said without missing a beat. "But tonight, I'm taking my girl dancing." He stole Jaycee from me, twirled her around, and lassoed her in for a kiss.

They were cute enough to be on their own stage. Sickening, but cute.

After another lingering kiss, Trevor spun her out of his arms and down the hall. "Meet you out front."

"Be ready in five."

I followed her into our room. "You know, when you two aren't making me gag, you're really kind of adorable."

"You taking lessons from A. J. on how to give a compliment?"

I plopped onto my bed. "No, really, I mean it. It's like you guys live in this real-life fairy tale."

"Why, because we're in love? That's not a fairy tale. It's part of the dance of everyday life."

Maybe for people like her. I twisted a loose thread from my comforter around my finger and wrestled with A. J.'s words.

*"Just because someone doesn't know what he lost, doesn't mean it isn't worth keeping."*

But how can your heart be worth keeping when those you give it to always leave it behind?

Jaycee tied her scarf into intricate artwork in front of the mirror. "Don't give up on love, and it won't give up on you."

I fell backward, the mattress springs moaning with doubt. "Yeah, I don't think it necessarily works that way, Jae."

A second after I threw my pillow over my face, the bed dipped beside me. She tugged the pillow away and looked at me with full-on best-friend sincerity. The kind that heard and felt exactly what I didn't have to say. "Em, listen to me. I know it's hard to see right now, but there's an incredible plan for your life. Love included. And you're being made ready for it through everything you face, even loneliness."

It wasn't contrived or a well-meaning platitude. It was a statement of conviction—one I wished were my own.

"You sure I can't skip this part of the plan?"

"Your dreams are coming, girl." She squeezed my hand, then flitted toward her dresser. "And they're gonna be worth every step it takes to get there."

Heat from the overhead vent blew the leaf on my desk into the picture of Dad and me. Dreams. Promises. Hope. Was it all an out-of-reach fairy tale?

Jaycee zipped up her boot. "I can stay home tonight if you need me to. Trev won't mind."

"Are you kidding? After his little warm-up performance earlier, he'd be devastated." I swiped a book off a stack on my desk. "I have my own date with a mystery novel. I'm good."

"You can always play some Christmas music." She stashed a tube of lip gloss in her clutch purse. "But that cheesecake better still be here when I get back."

"No promises," I yelled on my way to the living room.

I flipped on the Christmas lights and laughed. Two red and green totes hid the top of the coffee table. That couldn't be good. It was bad enough when we had only a dorm room to plaster with tacky Christmas decorations. Now we had an entire apartment to turn into an *Elf* scene. She'd already outdone last year in the living room alone. The multicolored tinsel topped it off. We were bound to win some kind of award.

Jaycee peeked around the wall while stroking a final touch of blush over her cheek. "You positive you want to stay in tonight?"

"I love you guys, but the prospect of being a third wheel? While dancing, no less? Yeah, not happening. You guys have fun. Show everyone up with those dance moves of yours."

"Psh, girl, we're gonna own that dance floor. Trev knows the deejay."

Of course he did.

Halfway through the front door, she stopped again.

In a mauve knit beanie, brown boots over her jeans, and a glittery scarf topping her sweater, she glowed with a beauty that made it easy to understand why Trevor's face lit up every time he looked at her.

"You're one hundred percent—?"

"Jae."

"Okay, okay. Leaving." Amazingly, she shut the door.

A sharp breeze whirled in uninvited. I shivered, grateful to put off dancing with winter, at least for the night.

The scent of chai lured me to the kitchen with the perfect invitation to enjoy a cozy evening in instead. I settled into my favorite chair, warmed my fingers around my mug, and tried to drink in Jaycee's assurance.

I opened my novel. Maybe I'd have better luck reading.

Then again, maybe not. The business card Miriam had given me tumbled out. I'd completely forgotten sticking it in there. I picked it up. *I wonder if—*

A knock at the door rippled across the room. I flinched so hard, tea streamed down my hands. Who'd be coming by at this hour? Slurping up the liquid from my palm, I crossed the kitchen and cracked the door halfway open.

I should have known.

## 24

### LETTING GO

A. J. STOOD SMACK in front of the door with his hands behind his back and a look growing more mischievous by the second. There went a quiet, uncomplicated night alone.

He peered around me at the novel teepeed open on the table. "Still having a hard time closing the chapter on the solitary confinement scene you've been stuck in, huh? I had a feeling this might call for some reinforcements."

He flung his arms out from behind his back, a DVD in one hand and a Gingerbread House kit in the other.

I crossed my arms over my hoodie and shook my head.

"Oh, c'mon. I know you can resist *my* dashing charm, but David Bowie?" He waved the DVD in front of me. "Even you can't say no to *Labyrinth*."

My tight lips yielded to a smile. "Okay, fine. You win."

"I'm sorry, I didn't catch that. Did you just say *I won?*"

I shook my head as I let go of the door. "Hilarious."

"Just trying to make sure I get to see your smile again. Memories don't do it justice."

Did he always have to hold that look in his eyes?

He inched closer. "There's the Rosy I've been missing."

I scuttled to the table in search of my mug and a chance for the heat to drain from my face. He didn't think...? I mean, he knew we were just friends, right? Even if Riley didn't want my heart, I'd left it with him.

Seemingly unfazed by my reaction, A. J. tossed his leather coat over a chair. "First things first." He picked up the corner of my novel with two fingers and let it dangle in the air like a piece of trash he didn't want to touch. "Let's dispose of this accomplice keeping you away from your friends."

"And you call *me* melodramatic? Give me that." I stuffed my rescued book under the seat cushion next to me and sipped my now-lukewarm tea.

A. J. swiped off his beanie, dropped into the nearest chair, and spun the Gingerbread House box in a circle on the tabletop. "Second step, remember how to be a kid again."

The box skidded across the table into my stomach. I lifted my mug and slurped tea from my fingers yet again. Glancing at the cover made it hard not to give in. "Okay, I'll do it. But only because the sooner we put it together, the sooner I get to see David Bowie."

"See, I knew he'd drive you crazy. It's the hair, isn't it?"

I threw his beanie at him. Whether or not I wanted to admit it, A. J. had a gift for making me laugh.

His attention bounced between the design on the box and the heap of miniature candy canes, gumdrops, and licorice strewn across the table. With his hair flattened from his beanie, he looked like a kid in a kindergarten class, trying to figure out how to put a puzzle together.

"You don't know how to do this, do you?"

"No idea." He held up two pieces of the giant cookie. "Between your *festive* decorations and these sugar-coated walls, I feel like someone vanquished me into a Candy Land board game."

"If it makes you feel better, I promise to come play basketball with you some time."

He blasted a look of disbelief my way. "Promise?"

I shrugged. "I sort of owe you a rematch, don't I?"

"You got that right. And no child's play there either. You're going down, sugar." He popped two gumdrops in his mouth.

I hurled one straight at his face. "Really, A. J.?"

"What?" He flung his hands out to either side of him. "We're going to eat it when we're all finished, right?"

"Just help me hold these pieces up while I layer on the icing."

Twenty minutes later, we both stepped back from the kitchen table with fingertips mortared in frosting and eyeballed our master creation. It was a little lopsided, and definitely skimpy on the gumdrops, but charming nonetheless. A. J. reached to break off a piece of cookie.

I smacked his hand. "Don't even think about it. We have to enjoy our hard work."

"Exactly." He reached again.

"You know what I mean."

"Okay, okay." He licked sugar off his thumb as he ducked into the living room. "But if you're gonna deprive me of candy, then you at least gotta sing along with David Bowie to make up for it. C'mon, we can do a duet. I'll sing the goblins' part. You rock the solo."

"Does anyone ever tell you how crazy you are?" I called from the pantry.

His husky bravado carried into the kitchen. "Only you."

I grabbed two bags of popcorn and flopped down on the opposite end of the couch from him. The night's dropping temperatures etched crystallized designs across the windows, but the bitter cold couldn't extend its arms inside. Not tonight. Tonight, I began to thaw from the inside out.

In my over-worn hoodie, fleece pants, and fuzzy socks, I tried not to spill my reheated cup of tea every time A. J. had me cracking up. As if watching a 1986 movie wasn't comical enough, he sent me past the snorting phase into the laugh-so-hard-no-sound-comes-out phase.

By the time the credits rolled, we'd torpedoed enough

popcorn missiles from both ends of the couch to turn the space between us into a bona fide battle zone.

Sitting beside him, with buttery kernels in my hair, I couldn't help thinking back to the night we'd first met. Since then, he'd broken every presumption I'd made about him.

Except one.

He turned out to be a good friend after all. One I needed more than I realized.

All packed up, he stalled at the front door, fumbling the DVD case around in his hands.

I nodded toward the kitchen table. "You can have a piece of the gingerbread now."

His face lit up in mock horror. "*Before* you have the chance to show our creation to Jaycee? Wouldn't dare." He patted his contented stomach. "Think I've had enough for tonight anyway. You enjoy it for a few days. Just be sure to save me a little for next time."

I poked him in the arm. "Are you covertly making an excuse to come and check on me?"

"Apparently, not very well." A self-conscious laugh colored his face a shade lighter than the candy canes as he shifted his beanie back and forth over his head.

"Are you… blushing?" I edged closer, the way he always did to me. "What's wrong, *Rosy*?" I teased.

For a second, he appeared even more flustered but then advanced right back. "Look at you, Miss Sass. See? I knew you had some fight left in you. Just needed a little prodding."

"Your specialty."

He shrugged. "We all have our gifts."

Not so sure I did, but at least I had friendships that kept me pressing forward when I lost my way. "You were right, you know. About my needing to move on. I'm just trying to figure out where to go from here."

His smoldering eyes backed me into a chair. "Sometimes, the only way to start is by letting go."

A knot raced up my throat. "What if I let go, and there's nothing left to hold on to?"

"Then you reach for a different dream."

I clutched the top of the chair. "I'm not sure I'm ready for that."

His brow furrowed, and so did my heart. Didn't he understand?

He smiled sadly. "Then the dream will be there when you *are* ready." He kissed my cheek. "Good night, Emma."

"A. J." I caught the door. "Thanks. For tonight. You've been a good friend to me."

He lingered over the threshold a minute longer, then turned with his head down. At the banister, he paused to glance up at me one more time before jogging down the stairs to the exit.

I closed the door, backed against it, and stared down the hall into a haze of thoughts. I still didn't know what lay ahead, but I knew it was time to engage life again. And as difficult as it would be, I knew where I had to start.

In our bedroom, I unburied my journal from a pile of

junk in my desk and sat on the edge of my bed. A crisp white page looked back at me, waiting for words I would've given anything to speak to the person who'd always instilled courage in me when I needed it the most.

*Dad, I'm trying to find where you're leading me. But no matter what I do, I'm left standing against a question that's never answered.*

*Why?*

*God could've healed you. He could've kept our family together as easily as He could've kept my internship from falling apart. How do I reconcile that with all you taught me to believe in? I don't understand why faith asks so much, and love costs more than we have. Both were supposed to get us through this, but we're still broken. All of us.*

*I've tried to pretend I'm not. I've tried to keep my promise to you, but I can't do this on my own anymore. Please help me find the strength to keep going, even when I can't see how.*

I traced my hand down the page, breathed out, and closed my eyes. No sound came. No movement stirred. Nothing changed. But with my journal cradled to my chest, I sensed a father's arms closing around mine. Alone in that tiny room, I pressed in to an embrace I wished could've been real and waited for the courage to embrace a truth I couldn't put off facing any longer.

Sometimes, holding on to dreams means learning to let them go.

MONDAY MORNING, I drove Jaycee's Fiat to Riley's apartment. Sunbeams stretched down a front door I couldn't bring myself to knock on. Between my unanswered calls and the empty space on the sidewalk he never showed up on anymore, I'd learned some doors were kept shut for a reason. I set the long overdue music box he'd lent me on the porch and walked away.

Trouble with loans? They expire.

This early in the day, the vacant streets made the drive to the woods shorter than usual. The car sputtered into the same spot in front of the same trail Riley and I used to come to together.

The forest still played its soothing song, but things had changed. Layers of brittle pine needles now hid the trail beneath them. A broader ceiling of sky poured through the barren treetops and eroded the quaintness I remembered.

The deeper I walked into the forest, the higher I tugged my scarf up my neck. Not that it mattered. Once I reached an Elm tree along the periphery of the clearing, memories of being there with Riley seared into me with the wind.

The feelings they stirred seeped through every layer I'd foolishly tried to pin over my heart. I braced a palm against the nearest boulder and gripped the folded-up page I'd written last night. Three breaths passed. Four. I needed to do this.

Inhaling deeply once more, I covered the note on the

ground with a small, flat stone. And in the middle of the place where dreams began, I let them go.

Straightening, I pulled a crinkled business card from my pocket and dialed a number I should've called a long time ago.

## 25

## STIRRED

AFTER TYING up all the loose ends that afternoon, I strode through Mr. Oakly's office door without stopping to announce my arrival.

"You may not be very good at returning messages, Miss Matthews, but you're certainly punctual." He evidently didn't need to lift his head to know it was me. "Two days ahead of the end of the semester, to be exact."

As if I'd forgotten his end-of-term deadline. I choked back the response I wanted to give, marched up to his desk, and set a crumpled piece of paper on top of the one he was hunched over.

He peered at me from above his frames and then down at the scribbled-over list of internships he'd given me at the beginning of the term. He took his glasses off. "Miss Matthews, I've been hard on you because I hate to see my students graduate without a plan to succeed in the marketplace."

"You don't have to worry about that. I found an internship with a guaranteed job lead. I start January fifteenth."

Mr. Oakly's chair creaked into a straightened position. He slid his glasses back on and held the piece of paper at reading distance. "Financial Analyst with Edwards Jones," he read.

Did he think Miriam was a better fit for the position?

Swallowing any sign of doubt, I kept my shoulders level with the bookshelf. "I already spoke with Dean Jeffries about what really happened at Xander and convinced him my history of academic excellence warranted some leeway on the deadline. He agreed to postpone my scholarship evaluation until the end of next semester to allow time for my internship supervisor to submit a performance review."

Mr. Oakly shifted in his chair, his scrutiny not wavering.

That made one of us.

I ordered my voice to remain steady. "So, I get to keep my scholarship for another semester, my mom gets a revised bill, and you get another prize student who ups her chances of landing a job after graduation. Am I missing anything?"

His lips twitched underneath his scruffy mustache. "Sounds like you've got it all worked out."

On paper, maybe, but in my heart?

I ignored the answer. It didn't matter. No more floundering. As long as I took Renee's advice on not hoping for more out of work than a paycheck this time, it'd be fine. More than fine. It'd be exactly as I'd expected it would be before Riley...

My shoulders drooped, my courage fading. "You can confirm this all with Dean Jeffries."

His suspenders stretched to the max as he rose. "I'm on my way to see the dean right now, as a matter of fact."

"I'll follow you out."

I stayed in step with him until we reached a bend in the hallway, where I veered toward the stairs. The door closed behind me. Once alone, my valiant display of confidence plummeted to the bottom of the vacant stairwell.

Truth was, an act only worked with an audience.

I plodded down the steps, pushed the exit open with my back, and kept my eyes away from the sun on my way to the campus center.

The desolate halls left no question that the majority of students had already wrapped up their final exams and headed home for winter break.

"What time should I pick you up tonight?" A. J. sailed around the corner like some kind of apparition.

I dropped my keys. "Do you always sneak up on people in empty hallways?"

"Only pretty, unsuspecting girls."

There was that infamous charm again. "I think I've been friends with you long enough to graduate from the unsuspecting crowd."

He scooped up my keys from the floor and dangled

them on his finger. "You thought I was talking about you?" The corner of his mouth peaked to the left.

"Give me those." I swiped the keys from him.

"You still haven't answered my question."

I unlocked my mailbox. "What are you talking about?"

He reclined sideways against the wall while I peered into my open mail slat. "I'm taking you out. A night on the town, remember?"

I peeked up without moving. "I don't think that's a good idea."

"Uh-uh, no arguments. Consider it an extra step of intervention. For good measure. It's just what you need." He jogged backward toward the exit. "Trust me."

"I don't know. I'd rather—"

"See you around six," he yelled on his way out.

"You're maddening sometimes, you know that?"

The empty corridor magnified the sound of his laughter, which seemed to follow me to my apartment like one of those musical greeting cards I could open whenever I needed it. Knowing him, whatever his plans were, at least they'd be fun.

Unless he thought...

My stomach dropped.

***

BETWEEN THE PROSPECT of A. J. thinking we were going on a date and the added distraction of packing for our three-week break, I'd crammed all thoughts about my meeting with Mr. Oakly into a distant suitcase in my mind by the time six o'clock neared. It was resolved anyway. I'd set out to move on, and I did. No more fretting.

My cell vibrated against the kitchen table with an incoming text. *Dress warmly for tonight.*

"Jae, do you know where A. J.'s taking me?"

She perched herself on the counter and stirred her coffee. "Nope, but he's pretty stoked to surprise you."

His escapades in the hallway earlier had made that much clear. "Why didn't he invite you and Trev to come with us?"

"My guess is he's trying to avoid the whole double date scene. He knows how bent out of shape you get whenever you think he's trying to hit on you."

"And taking me out alone clearly won't make it feel like a date. Totally see his logic there." I picked at a stain on the place mat. He knew how I felt about him, didn't he?

Jaycee waved her spoon at me. "Give the guy some credit for taking you out. You haven't exactly been Miss Sunshine lately."

"What's that supposed to mean? I'm... sunshiny." I wiggled up in my chair until my shoulders reached my defense level. So, I'd lost my way for a little bit. I got back in the fight. "You have driven-Emma back again. And hey, I haven't raided the cleaning closet in weeks." I laughed, but Jaycee's expression didn't budge.

I set my phone down and faced her head-on. "Everything's how it's supposed to be. My scholarship's secure. I've got the perfect internship gig. Everything's good. Full of sunshine. Pinky promise."

"Except for the little fact that you're not really living."

That stung. "Can you be a little harsher?"

"Joy, Em." She hopped off the counter. "I'm talking about joy. I know things with Riley left you questioning everything, but at least you were alive then. Like I've never seen you. I miss that."

I stood up. "I can't bring Riley back."

"It wasn't Riley. It was you."

Wrong. It was a dream I'd already surrendered. I couldn't handle unburying it now.

A. J. popped through the front door, looking like he'd downed a container of chocolate-covered coffee beans. "Ready?"

He gave me a whiplash up-and-down glance, which I gave him right back. He'd exchanged his usual Nikes for a pair of Docs, and his hoodie for a brown sweater zipped up to his closely shaven chin. This couldn't be good.

"Um, I think maybe I should stay home."

"Not a chance." He grabbed my hand and hauled me out the door to his Acura parked at the curb.

Why I thought he'd let me dodge another night out, I have no idea. I sank into the warm leather seat. Between the heat and the instrumental Christmas music humming from the stereo, the atmosphere brimmed with an invitation to unwind.

"All set?" he asked as I buckled my seat belt.

*Doubt it.* "Are you at least going to tell me where we're going now?"

"And ruin the fun of watching you try to figure it out?"

The tighter I pressed my lips together, the wider his expanded.

A half hour into our drive, stress crept back over my body, muscle by muscle. Regardless of whether A. J. thought this was a date, he deserved my honesty on where we stood. Even if it meant admitting I was broken. That the warning label over my heart that used to read, *Fragile* had been replaced with the even more telling label, *Damaged*.

"Wanna tell me what you're thinking about?"

From the way he asked, he already knew the answer. Still, I had to make sure. "I think we should talk."

His laughter overpowered the shakiness in my voice. "Really, Em, relax. Tonight's about having fun. No ulterior motives." He lifted three fingers in the air to salute his oath. "Scout's honor."

Sometimes, I didn't know how he mastered being charming and adorable at the same time. He made this harder than it already was.

I pushed up my sleeves and rotated the vent away. "I need to be sure you understand my heart isn't available to give away." The words spewed out in a nonstop breath. Nothing like shooting it to him straight. I clutched my seat belt and waited for his response.

He kept his focus on the windshield. "I know." The words stripped his voice to a quiet shell of his normal deep bravado.

The piano on the radio sounded much louder than it had a moment ago. A ball of threadbare emotions trekked up my throat.

"Why don't we forget everything else for a while? Live a little. Have a good time. And for the record, I'm just a good friend taking another good friend out for a night on the town. If it helps, try to picture me as Jaycee." He batted his eyes.

"Close resemblance." I cocked my chin. "For the record."

"I'm not pulling off the J. Crew model look today, huh?" His laughter tapered. "Honestly though, try not to think so much tonight, okay?"

"Okay, *Jaycee*."

"Hey, whatever works. But how 'bout you don't call me that when we're in public?"

I flashed him a replica of the grin he'd given me earlier. "And ruin the fun of watching you squirm?"

"Touché."

He had no idea how disarming he could be. The relief of making sure he knew how I felt released the last bit of tension holding me back from enjoying an evening with a friend.

"Okay," he said. "According to the directions, we should be able to park right about... here."

We turned one final street corner and found a small parking lot manned by a gentleman collecting five-dollar fees from inside a tiny booth. The signs had made it clear we were somewhere in downtown Portland, but I still wasn't sure where we were going.

With my hat over my ears, coat zipped up clear to my chin, and fingers slipped into my glove's fleece lining, I was ready.

A. J. took my bundled hand in his. "Come on, Eskimo Girl, this way."

The intersection on Morrison Street drew me to a stop in front of a Christmas village. Lighted strands of garland topped with red fabric bows hugged each lamppost, animated Christmas figurines moved gracefully to distant music, and icicle lights dangled from the awnings of most every shop.

"What do you think?" he asked.

I spun in a circle to take in each detail. "It's beautiful."

"Don't get too starry-eyed yet. There's still more to see."

When we reached the center of the decorated area, A. J. leaned into my shoulder. "The first night we met, you told me you liked every genre of music. I'm holding you to that."

"Now I'm really nervous."

He stretched his arm across my shoulders and steered me around the last corner. My hand flew to my mouth. It drifted down to my scarf and back up again. A small jazz band was warming up on top of a wooden platform raised a couple of feet above the ground.

"The band's going to be playing outside? Right here?"

His face beamed in the shimmering lights of an over-sized Christmas tree. "They probably won't play more than an hour tops, but it should be a nice complement to the atmosphere."

He unlatched a small gate leading to an enclosed patio with a handful of black wrought iron tables and chairs. "Shall we?"

The music added the perfect undertone to an already charming scene I would've sworn someone had taken straight out of a movie. Even the candlelight in the red-tinted votive holders danced along to the music.

A. J. must've caught me swaying. The shadow of his grin climbed across the table. "See what happens when you stop thinking so much." He extended a hand toward me. "Come on, Rosy. Let's dance."

My arm slid off the table. *Did he think that was a logical statement to make?*

Behind him, a few couples already sprinkled the pavement in front of the stage.

I pulled in my chair. "You, my friend, have lost your mind."

"And *you're* being a party pooper." With his arm still outstretched, he looked at me with eyes as deep and clear as the sky above us. "C'mon, Em, have a little faith in yourself. It's not going to kill you to let your hair down."

He shifted his weight to one side. "Okay, I admit, it might be a *little* awkward to picture me as Jaycee right now. So, how about you settle for having me as your stand-in best friend for the night?" Gloating over his inescapable negotiation, he lugged me up from my chair.

I dragged my feet. "I'm a terrible dancer. I'm going to embarrass us both."

"Don't worry, I'll lead." He led me out to the open area peppered with other couples and spun me around until I smiled.

"There she is. See? You can do it." He twirled me again.

My eyes squeezed shut as he swept me into a dancing frame.

"You're meant to live with your eyes wide open, Emma," he whispered. "If you always keep them closed, you'll miss the life right in front of you waiting to be lived."

I wasn't sure I knew how to live anymore, but I knew I'd be lost on my own. I rested my chin over my hand on his shoulder, words so much harder to grasp. "You don't have to stand in for Jaycee, you know. You're already a good friend."

He leaned back, dimples dipping. "For the record?"

My eyes rolled skyward. "Yeah, for the record."

"Good." He lowered my hands to my sides. "Wait here."

"Wait, what?" But he was already gone, leaving me in the middle of the crowd. Alone.

I rubbed my arms, the evening breeze taking A. J.'s place as my dance partner. A minute later, the music stopped. A spotlight streamed through the fog rising from the pavement and covered me in a blanket of light. I froze. What was he doing?

"Hi everyone," A. J. said from behind the microphone. "Sorry for the interruption. Since it's Christmas, my friend has a gift to share with all of you. She's still learning to recognize her talent, so how about we give her a little encouragement to welcome her to the stage."

Amidst a simultaneous release of claps and cheers, a middle-aged woman dressed in a full-length wool coat nudged me forward. "You can do it."

The ground slid under my feet all the way to the front of the stage, where A. J. pulled me onto the platform. He positioned me in front of the microphone and strapped a guitar over my body. The pick slipped out of my fingers.

"You got this," another woman from my fellow dancers-turned-audience hollered.

Across the floor, gaze after gaze fastened on me. My pulse raced until the memory of Riley's words settled over me. *"You don't even realize how you view the world, do you? Like an artist. You should trust that more."*

Trust. I filled my lungs with air, and my heart with his assurance, and let my fingers feel the strings. One chord. Another. Something flickered inside me. A taste of something I'd lost. *"Joy, Em. I'm talking about joy."* It filled my eyes, my hands, my mind—overwhelming me with a truth I couldn't stifle no matter how hard I tried. My heart wouldn't let me live without joy.

The gentleman playing the bass joined me, followed by the other band members jumping in one at a time. Before long, the couples resumed their dancing, and the scene returned to the way it had been a few minutes earlier. Except that I was on the stage, and A. J. was in the middle of the crowd. Smiling at me.

Applause filled the transition as the band eased into their regular set.

I took A. J.'s hand but deepened my glare with each step off the platform. "I can't believe you. Did you plan this?"

"Maybe."

"I think I might hate you."

He scrunched his lips and shook his head. "Not possible."

"Oh, yeah?"

"Yep." He twirled me back into a dancing hold. "I just helped you face one of your fears. Showed you how to live without regret. Believe in yourself. You know, those little things friends help each other do."

I swatted him. "The kind of friend who'll always be here to take care of me, right?"

A. J. pressed his cheek to my temple, his mouth just above my ear. "Always," he whispered. He set my hand on his chest and placed his fingers over mine.

My body tensed, my rigid pose the exact opposite of his patient laugh.

"Relax."

Easy for him to say. Yet something about his gentleness countered my resistance as usual. I swayed softly while listening to him sing to the instrumental music.

"Have yourself a merry little Christmas. Let your heart be light. From now on, our troubles will be out of sight..." He spun me one more time across the enchanted street corner and curled me close again. "Merry Christmas, Emma."

With my head on his shoulder, a well of emotion collected on the front of his coat. He and Trevor had been such good friends to me. In all honesty, Riley had, too, before I drove him away. Having faith in myself had never come easily for me. But maybe that's exactly why God had placed them in my life.

The unexpected thought drew my eyes to the stars, and my damaged heart a little closer to healing.

The sounds, the lights, the feeling of gliding to the music stayed with me the entire ride home. Even after A. J. parked, the warmth from the heater and the splendor of a treasured night nearly lulled me to sleep right there in his passenger seat.

"Need me to carry you inside?"

"I think I can manage." I unbuckled my seat belt. "I had fun tonight. Really. Can't believe I'm actually saying this, but thanks for pushing me to live a little. I needed it." I smiled warmly. "Good night, A. J."

I opened my door, but he caught my hand before I

could get out. He leaned over the console. "Emma, wait…"

The vulnerability in his eyes smoldered with the unspoken words etched in his torn expression. The frigid air outside crashed into the heat intensifying inside. Neither of us spoke. Neither moved.

The silence throbbed, stealing my voice. Even if it hadn't, I didn't know what to say. I dropped my gaze to my lap and opened my dry mouth, but nothing came out.

A. J.'s fingers drifted from mine and found the steering wheel again. Head down, he let out a breath. "Good night, Em."

My heart constricted at the disappointment in his voice. "Merry Christmas, A. J. Thank you. For everything." I hesitated a second longer, then jogged up to my apartment.

A. J.'s tires didn't pull away until I turned my key in the deadbolt. Somewhere between one door and the other, I'd lost the warmth he'd stirred tonight. Even my fleece pajamas couldn't stave off the chill.

I crawled into my flannel sheets, bundled the covers under my arms, and waited for sleep to take over.

Life was easier to live with my eyes closed.

It felt like I'd barely been asleep an hour when my phone rang from my desk. Flinching, I almost tore the sheet off the mattress. My alarm clock blinked into view. "And you complain about me calling late?"

"Nothing a little Starbucks can't cure," Austin said

with far too much animation for the late hour. "You're not up?"

"Considering it's the middle of the night, that would be a negative."

"Well, considering I'm on my way to pick you up, maybe you should reconsider."

My body folded in half. "What? You're driving through the night? Are you crazy?"

"I like to think of it as being sensible. There's less traffic on the roads now. And... I have a surprise for you."

"A surprise." One that couldn't wait until the morning? "Should I be excited or nervous?"

"That depends. Are you crazy or sensible?"

"I think we both know the answer to that one."

Austin laughed. "Glad you can finally admit it. But don't worry. It's just an early Christmas present. One you're gonna love," he said in a singsong voice.

I balled my pillow in my arms, waiting. "You're just gonna leave me hanging, aren't you?"

"I think we both know the answer to that one."

## 26

# FINGERPRINTS

FORTY-TWO MADISON STREET, my childhood home. Where I'd found my identity—and lost it.

Even in winter, the old Monterey style house clung to the briny air the same way nostalgia clung to the family pictures that'd been up forever. The oak floorboards in the hallway creaked in their usual places, and the grandfather clock in the living room chimed its routine song.

It didn't make sense for a place steeped in memories to feel unknown. But maybe it wasn't my childhood home that had changed. Maybe it was me.

At least there was still one place stringing together my connection with a past I almost no longer recognized.

With one tentative step forward, I crossed into Dad's study and outside the rules governing time and motion. His home office looked exactly as it had before he'd died. He left a part of himself here, memories I could feel. His mahogany desk framed in shafts of moonlight. His collection of weathered books lining the walls. His scent lingering in the worn desk chair he refused to part with. Everything was here, except the one thing I needed most. Him.

I picked up an old Polaroid of Dad and a little girl hidden in his burly arms—the girl he made me promise never to lose.

But he'd made promises he couldn't keep too.

He'd promised that little girl God was working out a plan for her life. That it was safe to view the world with a childlike faith and to love without restraint. But how could I cling to a faith that couldn't save him? Or believe in a purpose blocked by constant failure?

Tears blurred his guitar in the corner, where dust hid the well-worn fingerprints that had held on to joy until the very end. I didn't understand it. Despite his faith, he still suffered. Despite his love, he still lost. Yet not once had he stopped living. Not once had he forfeited the joy of playing or closed off his heart to the life closing it for him.

"Jaycee's right," I whispered. "I'm not really living. Not like you did. Riley reopened my heart, and I can't close it now, but it hurts, Dad. How do you keep playing when it hurts?" I sank into his empty chair, into the hollowness his protective arms used to fill, and tried to remember the sound of him playing. "Please, I can't lose your music too."

"Doesn't seem right, does it?" Austin stood in the

doorway, nodding toward the guitar. "How quiet it is in here."

I don't know how long he'd been there, or how much he'd heard. But right then, it didn't matter. He towed me up from the chair into a hug without needing to say more, and I held on until the wave of pain passed.

"Ready for that surprise?" he said after a moment longer. "C'mon."

I couldn't step foot into the kitchen without smiling at the lineup of childhood crafts mounted on the walls like decorative art pieces. Leave it to our mom to find a way of adding charm to a room that still resembled a 1970s' tribute to posterity.

Austin spun in front of Mom's high-back chair with two tickets fanned out in his hands.

I looked from him to Mom and back. "You got me tickets to the symphony?"

"Surprised?"

I flung my arms around him again. "I haven't been to the symphony since I was—"

"Sixteen. I remember. Pretty sure you didn't stop talking about it for a month straight."

"Yeah, well, it was a special night." The memory of Dad giving me my necklace that night soared to my eyes.

Austin's face creased as it had a moment ago in the study, but he recovered just as quickly. "We gotta have something fun to do over this break, right?"

I pushed him into the fridge when he ruffled the top of my hair. Rubbing his shoulder, he yelped more pitifully than the fifteen-year-old dishwasher crying to be put out of its misery. As if my small fist could possibly make a dent in his bicep.

"What makes you think I'm bringing *you*?"

He feigned a look of betrayal. "Oh, really? So, it's like that. Too cool to hang out with your brother?" He crouched in a wrestling stance. "Let's see how cool you are."

"Don't you dare, Aust." I swatted his arms away. "Mom—"

I barely got the words out before he had me off the ground with one swift hip flex.

Show-off.

"Austin James." Mom scooted back from the table and lowered her reading glasses. "You know how I feel about you two roughhousing like that."

Austin eased me down until my back touched the cold vinyl floor. "You better be thankful Mom was here." He winked as he ruffled my hair again.

He pulled that stunt on purpose, didn't he? Trying to distract me from the pain of missing Dad. We went through the same loss, but he'd always been the stronger one. Still was.

He snagged two rolls from a pan on the stovetop, and I folded my arms over the top of Mom's chair. There with family, something sparked—the hope of a world where pieces still fit together, and music never stopped playing.

Austin nudged me with his shoulder while we walked along Geary Street after the symphony. "So, what did you think?"

A city trolley dinged on its way past us. The murmur of passengers' conversations drew my focus up from the pavement, and my thoughts back to the present.

"It was just like I remembered. Thanks for bringing me."

He dipped his head toward mine. "So, then, you wanna tell me what's bothering you?"

A salty breeze blowing off the San Francisco Bay carried a faint sound of music from the downtown pier with an echo of what was missing in my life.

"Hearing the symphony again got me thinking. All those instruments. The perfect blend of music. It's moving and overwhelming all at once. You feel it inside you, you know? Like there's something in there calling you, but you don't know how to get to it."

"Slow down, Plato. We just came from a concert, not a theater audition."

I popped him in the bicep. "It's eerie how much you remind me of Trevor sometimes."

"Sorry. Wasn't ready to switch over to Emma-mode." He loosened up his neck, flexed his laced hands, and held out his arm for me to hold. "Ready now."

"I'm serious, Aust. You don't ever have questions about life? Like your place in it all?"

"Not when I have a melodramatic sister worrying enough for both of us."

I elbowed him in the ribs.

He rubbed his side, laughing. "Dang, girl. You got a permit for those elbows? They could be some deadly weapons."

"You're hopeless. You know that?" I strode ahead of him, but he caught up, hopped in front of me, and walked backward.

"I'm kidding." He pivoted to my side and circled his arm around mine. "Of course I have questions. Everyone does, but you can't keep comparing your life to some expectation of the way you think things are supposed to be, or you're gonna miss everything Dad tried to teach us."

"You don't think I'm trying?" I stared down the sidewalk. "Sometimes I feel like I'm in that symphony, straining so hard to play with broken strings. Everything's screaming for me to run off the stage. But it's like Dad's there, holding me in place, begging me to keep playing."

Waves lapped against the boats at the docks, and I could almost hear Dad whispering for me to trust him. I grabbed Austin's sleeve. "I can't do this anymore. I can't keep disappointing him. I'm not like you, Aust. I don't have your faith or your talent."

"Is that what you think?"

A party of five stumbled through the double doors of the restaurant behind us with the flush of too many drinks coloring their faces. A seafood-scented breeze caught my nose at the same time Austin caught my hand and prodded me down the sidewalk, away from the noise of the city's nightlife.

He climbed up on a metal bench and rested his elbows on his knees. "You remember when we used to beg Dad to play his guitar from the deck 'cause we thought the music lured lightning bugs to the backyard?"

The memory soothed and constricted at the same time. "We were so sure something magical happened when he played."

"Maybe it did." Austin shifted on the bench. "For the longest time, I wanted to play just like him. I'd practice for hours, but it never felt like enough. I couldn't get his sound down." He blew on his hands to keep them warm. "I got so angry one time, I actually chucked my guitar on the carpet. Of course, he had to be walking past my room right then."

He shook his head. "He picked it up, played one of the songs he must've heard me practicing, then handed it back and asked me to play the same song." A quiet laugh collected in white puffs against the cold air.

"I remember just staring at him. I mean, was he serious? He had to know he was about to prove my point on how different two renditions of the same song could sound. But then he gave me one of those looks."

I raised a brow. "You mean, like the one you gave me a few seconds ago?"

"Something like that," he said with another laugh.

"But instead of dishing out some speech, he placed one of my hands over the guitar and set the other over my chest. 'Music comes from here,' he said. 'It's supposed to sound different from mine. People are waiting for you to share your own song.'"

Austin stared at the sky, smiling as though sharing a private moment with Dad. "I don't know. Something about his reassurance that day gave me the courage to stop trying to be someone other than myself. To trust I had something to offer too."

He hopped off the bench and pulled me in front of him. "I'm not saying it's easy, but you gotta find that same trust. Going to Dad's alma mater... Following after him in business. You're not him. He never expected you to be." He placed my hand over my heart. "Your song's here, Em. It's always been here. Don't be afraid to share it. Even when you think it's not enough."

A gust of wind rustled a plastic bag inside a city receptacle across from us. The sound chafed against the silence, his words against my fears. I wanted to trust those promises and believe I had a song of my own. One that'd give me the faith to live with my eyes open and see meaning instead of emptiness.

"It doesn't seem fair to open myself to a world that took Dad away from us. If anyone should've been able to live his purpose, it was him."

Austin hugged me to his side and rested his chin over my head. "He did."

Minutes drifted into the sound of cars rumbling

across the bridge above us.

"We can't avoid pain and loss," he said slowly. "Dad knew that and chose to keep playing anyway."

"How?" The frayed question shook my voice. "How'd he do it, Aust?" I still didn't understand it.

"Other than a ridiculous amount of grace?" His soft smile waned. With his hands in his pockets, he raised his shoulders. "I know his faith sustained him. I know he chose joy over his circumstances every day. But honestly? I don't know how as much as why."

I shook my head. "Why?"

"Because he wants us to do the same."

The sincerity in his eyes stole any remaining chance I had of willing back my tears. "Now who sounds like Plato?" A fusion of admiration and gratefulness closed in with my brother's hug. "When did you become so wise?"

"When I had to start taking care of my baby sister."

I shoved him off the sidewalk.

He laughed, then jumped right back over the curb. He set his hand on my shoulder, all remnants of his joking put aside yet again. "Em, I just want to make sure you know you don't have to stand on your own. If you don't have the faith yet to believe it yourself, you can borrow mine until you do."

A lump welled up in my throat. The lights on the bridge shimmered in place of the stars the way my brother stood in place for our dad. I grabbed hold of his faith. And without fully understanding how, I sensed it was about to change everything.

# BORDERS

TWO MONTHS. How could we have been back at school for nearly two months already? The dates on the calendar had disappeared along the hectic schedules driving us from one demand to the next.

I would've disappeared in the nonstop motion, too, without my friends rescuing me each week. Yet even with their expert skills, time felt stilted. Stagnant.

I pried open the living room window. Instead of a breeze, a restlessness swept over me. Things were right on target with my internship. I'd been the exemplary intern, received noteworthy feedback. By all appearances, I should have been relieved. And I might've been if something more wasn't pursuing my heart.

Jaycee hightailed herself from room to room like the leader in some sort of in-house version of a Chinese fire drill. After spending the last month coordinating an outreach in downtown Portland with her tutoring club, she couldn't have been more anxious to see all the hard work pay off.

"Um, Jae, you might want to slow down and save some stamina for this afternoon. Don't kids usually require a lot of energy?" I pushed a kitchen chair out in time to intersect her whirlwind path.

She dropped into it and let out a deep sigh. "You're right. It'll all get done. It's just that we have a real chance to build some bridges today. And if it's not a success, I'll—"

"Stop worrying." I tossed her a tangerine from the fruit bowl on the table. "You're the queen of organizing. It's one of your greatest strengths. Everything will be perfect."

She dug into the fruit with her nails. "Thanks. For your support and for being willing to come with me on such short notice. Miriam hated having to cancel, but her boss wouldn't give her today off. Poor thing, working two jobs and going to school. I don't know how she does it."

Miriam must've needed that scholarship as much as I did. Maybe we were all just trying to get by.

I spun my own tangerine in my hands. "I'm glad I can help, but... you're not going to make me dress up in a clown suit or anything, are you?"

A mischievous Trevor-look paraded across her face.

"Jaycee."

"Relax. No dress up. Promise. You'll be hanging out with the kids, escorting them to the different stations in the park. You're gonna be amazed at how easy it is to love on these kiddos." Following a quick pat on my hand, she jetted from the table, leaving a collection of orange peels piled on her napkin.

"Jeez, Jae, did you chew before you wolfed that down?"

"No time," she hollered from the bathroom.

She picked me up on her way out the door after her twentieth tornado whirl through the apartment. Not that I could blame her for being anxious. Elementary education wasn't simply a degree. Just like this inner-city outreach wasn't simply a bullet to add to her résumé. She'd poured every ounce of herself into the chance to impart hope to kids most people overlooked.

To share in even a glimpse of that kind of drive, I might've considered wearing a clown suit.

Stretches of Interstate 5 passed under Jaycee's Fiat. I rolled down my window, thoughts swirling. The night of the symphony replayed in my mind as it had so many times since I'd been back. *"You can't keep comparing your life to some expectation of the way you think things are supposed to be, or you're gonna miss everything Dad tried to teach us."*

Expectations. Maybe it was time to uncover the palette I'd locked away and let the colors splash all over the canvas, regardless of how it turned out. No outlines. No paint-by-numbers instructions or model to copy. Just the candid expression that only happened outside walls of expectations.

I sifted through a CD case Trevor left in the back seat, put one in the player, and bobbed my brows at Jaycee. "How about a little entertainment for the ride?"

"Michael Jackson?" she said once the beat dropped. "Only you, Em."

"Yeah right. You and me, girl. We can start our own eighties' music fan group." I turned up the stereo and swung an air microphone at her.

She swung it back for the echo and shook her head. "What's gotten into you?"

"Nothing. I'm just tired of borders, I guess."

She faced me, blinked, and then waved out her window. "Aye! Aye! Aye! I got my best friend back!"

"Really?" I pulled her in before we wrecked. "Okay, I'm not tired of *all* borders."

"Some things aren't meant to have borders," she countered.

Like friendship.

The next twenty minutes passed in laughter and shower-worthy covers of Michael Jackson's greatest hits —moments to add to the stockpile of college memories I'd treasure forever.

When we finally arrived, the city park greeted us with high-pitched giggles buzzing from one station to the next.

Jaycee pointed to the corner, where tall college students in clown costumes were busy forming shapes out of long, skinny balloons. "I spared you."

"I owe you one." I zipped my coat up to my chin as we headed onto the grass.

"Miss Jaycee, you made it." An older gentleman wearing a brown beret and square glasses gave her a side hug.

"Sorry we're a little late," she said. "We hit some traffic. Oh, Trey, I want you to meet my roommate, Emma Matthews."

He shook my hand with both of his. "Miss Emma, thanks so much for coming out. You could be doing a lot of things with your Saturday, but I promise these kids are worth your time."

Jaycee pulled a clipboard from her bag. "Trey helped me put all this together. He runs a non-profit center downtown."

He shimmied a business card from his wallet and handed it to me. "We're always looking for an extra pair of hands. Come by any time. We'd love to have you."

"Thanks." I turned the card over. *Portland Center: Making an Impact a Life at a Time.*

Jaycee flipped through some pages. "Em, we're expecting at least fifty kids today. So, take your pick and—"

"Actually," Trey said, "I think she already has an admirer."

A little boy, no more than five years old, stood beside my leg, peering up with round eyes that were much too big for his slender face.

I squatted to his level. "Hey, little guy, what's your name?"

He buried his chin against the tattered collar of a Captain America sweatshirt. "Michael."

"Hi, Michael, my name's Miss Emma. Do you want to go with me over to the face painting station?"

He nodded with the speed of a cotton candy-fueled sugar rush, fine blond hair waving all around.

"Okay, let's go." I took his hand. Good thing he picked me out instead of leaving me to choose one among them all.

"Have fun," Trey called from behind us.

A red-haired girl with a butterfly drawn on her cheek swirled a paintbrush in a Dixie cup as we approached.

"Hi…" I squinted at her handwritten name tag. "Julie. This is Michael."

"Hey, buddy. What would you like me to draw for you?" she asked in an animated tone all the adults were using.

He shrugged and twisted the rubber tip of his worn sneaker in the dirt.

"Hmm." She scrunched her lips to one side, hand on her chin. "How about a *lion*?"

Two pronounced dimples bookended a precious smile of missing teeth.

A lion it was—complete with a pink nose and whiskers. I admired the finished artwork but didn't have the heart to tell him he could have passed for a kitten. "Ferocious," I said instead. "Where to next?"

Michael spun in a circle to survey the playground for our next destination, then waved toward the opposite side of the park. "There!"

I shielded the sunlight with my hand until a small band set up in the corner came into view. "You want to check out some music?" *My kind of kid.*

Arm swinging, he rocked an impressive air guitar move.

"Wow, look at you. Okay, music it is." I knelt down to him again. "How about a piggyback ride?"

He jumped with more exuberance about that one thing than I'd experienced for myself all month. On my back, he hugged my neck as if I were his long-time babysitter rather than a stranger.

A stinging sensation pricked behind my eyes without any warning. Did these children lack love and attention so much that the simplest show of interest in them was all it took to make a difference?

The park closed in on me from every angle, and the memory of Riley's words from that time we spray-painted together made the tears even harder to suppress. *"Most people see an abandoned, useless corner of the city. Same way they see the kids in this neighborhood. Even the way some of them see themselves. But here, something changes."*

Michael flapped his arms with gusto. "Let's fly. Let's fly."

I batted away the sudden rise of emotion, tucked my arms under his legs, and sprang from the ground in take-off. We zigzagged across the crowded field on a turbulent flight that ended in one final hop. "Thank you for riding Air Emma," I said in my best flight attendant impersonation.

He slid off, and I stayed bent over with my hands on my thighs to catch my breath.

Michael tugged my pant leg. "I think someone wants to talk to you."

"Emma?"

One word.

One voice.

One look.

Everything else faded except a sound I knew by heart.

"Riley? W... What are you doing here?" My voice faltered under the riptide pulling my equilibrium off balance.

"My buddy Steve asked me for a favor. Said his guitar player bailed on him last minute." He looked away and kneaded the back of his neck. "I didn't expect to run into you here."

Didn't *want* to see me here, from the looks of it. Had he missed me at all?

"Riley, show time," a guy yelled from the stage.

"That's my cue." Head down, he lingered a second longer. "It's good to see you, Emma."

Still without meeting my eyes, he jogged backward, turned, and mounted the stage.

*That's it? That's all he's going to say after all this time?* My body felt like liquid lead sinking into the ground.

"Miss Emma, it's starting." Michael led me to an

empty seat in front of the wooden stage. The back of my jeans met the cool folding chair in time for him to climb onto my lap.

As soon as the first strum on the electric guitar pulsed through the speakers, a mosh pit of kids up front erupted in a cheer for more. The drummer tapped his sticks together three times, and an explosion of music rippled across the field.

Riley didn't look at me while he played, not even once. The bass vibrating across the row of metal chairs joined the unanswered questions rattling against my rib cage. I had to get out of there.

Before I could move, Michael looked up at me with an adorable lion face I couldn't possibly abandon. I wrapped my arms around him and the tiny flicker of joy he represented, afraid it'd burn out completely if I let it go.

The more I tried to force my attention onto him instead of the band, the more memories from the night Riley left reopened a chapter I thought I'd closed. I'd let him go, moved on. It shouldn't have still hurt this much.

Clashing cymbals and amp feedback ended the band's set. Riley's focus flitted to me for the briefest second, and I knew it wasn't over. Not for me. I transferred Michael to the seat beside us. "I'll be right back."

Knelt by the stage, Riley lowered his head again when he saw me approaching. He snapped his guitar case brackets shut but didn't face me even after I said hello.

I buried my worn coat cuffs under my fingers. "Why are you doing this?"

"Doing what?" he said in a monotone response I couldn't make fit his voice.

"Why won't you look at me?"

He rose to his feet and shifted his gaze toward me then. I searched his eyes, frantic to find what I remembered. But instead of windows, I found walls. Impenetrable blue walls staring through me. I wanted to yell at him—shake him—anything to make him look at me the way he used to.

"I'm sorry, Emma. I have to go." Guitar case in hand, he turned and left me standing there, watching him walk away.

Again.

Michael's precious face intersected my line of sight to Riley's back. I had to let it go. For him. The short walk wasn't long enough to mask the pain. But for Michael, I'd pretend it was. "Did you enjoy the music?"

Another energetic nod followed little fingers grasping mine, and I held on to the only thing keeping me from re-shattering right there on the playground.

Jaycee bumped into us. "Hey, you two." She rubbed Michael's head. "Having fun?"

His leap in the air answered for both of us.

"Awesome." She brandished one of her teacher poses —head angled, arms crossed. "You're going to come back next time, right?"

He shrugged. "You gonna have cotton candy again?"

Jaycee couldn't hold in her laugh. "You bet."

The streetlights flicked on. "Jae, how do I connect him with his parents?"

Her blank stare motioned me over to the side out of Michael's hearing. "This isn't the kind of neighborhood where parents come at dusk to pick up their kids."

I had to be missing something. "They're just children."

She grabbed my shoulders, scooted me a little farther away, and shielded Michael behind us. "They're children who fend for themselves on the streets most of the time. Michael will walk to his house with some friends."

I peeked around her to his little five-year-old frame. With one leg crossed over the other, he stood there, unaware of the risks he faced and the odds against him. The park started to press in again. And right then, I knew—my heart was spoken for.

My arms locked around him in a hug I didn't want to release. "You take care of yourself. If anybody messes with you on your way home, you give them your best, most ferocious lion roar, okay?"

He threw his hands in the air and roared, and my heart broke a little more. But maybe part of finding your purpose is finding what makes your heart sing and weep at the same time.

With Michael's lion face fixed in my mind, I stared out the car window on the way home. Images blended together like watercolors fanned across an unending canvas. "I wonder if Michael has anyone to take care of him."

"So, that's what has you so deep in thought?" Jaycee said. "I thought maybe it was—"

"I can't." I stopped her before she could say Riley's name. "I can't think about him."

"O-kay." She dragged out the word in two dramatic syllables.

After my peek into that vault this afternoon, the door had to stay locked. There was only one thing from today I could risk investing my thoughts in.

"Do you think those kids have a chance of ever getting out of that neighborhood?"

"Honestly?" Jaycee said. "I think they get stuck in a generational cycle of poverty. They don't know any other future."

There had to be a way to break that cycle. My eyes didn't stray from the window. "Do you think Trey'd consider turning a volunteer position at the center into an internship?"

My midterm performance review from Edwards Jones should be enough to sustain my scholarship. I could talk to the dean about finishing the second half of my internship at a different site.

"Are you kidding? He'd be thrilled to work with you. Especially with your training in business. He's always looking for ways to equip the high schoolers with life skills. It'd be perfect... except you already have an internship."

A secure one, maybe, but not the right one. Sure, I liked business. But to use my training to do something I felt called to? I'd given up dreaming for that possibility altogether.

What if I could help kids like Michael push past their borders too? Show them they weren't abandoned, that they mattered and had a future?

All at once, every failure and disappointment that'd been fighting for dominance over my spirit surrendered to the whisper telling me none of it had been in vain. My internship at Xander, the way the afterschool program proposal had awakened a sense of purpose, the extensive research I'd done for that project. I thought it was all a mistake. But what if it wasn't? What if it was preparation for what was coming?

Vision ignited. Faith surged. It seemed so clear now and, for the first time, within reach. Tears stirred at the reminder of Austin's assurance. *"If you don't have the faith yet to believe it yourself, you can borrow mine until you do."*

"I think I finally found my own," I whispered against the window.

Jaycee's Fiat rolled up to the curb outside our apartment moments later. The second she shifted the car into park, A. J. lunged up from the stoop and barreled down the sidewalk straight for us. I'd barely unfastened my seat belt before he opened my door.

He clasped my shoulders and anxiously searched my eyes. "Em, please tell me you haven't…"

"Haven't what?" I stepped onto the curb. "A. J., what is going on?"

Jaycee's car door closed. I looked for her as she rounded the back bumper, hoping she could clue me in on what I was missing.

And then, I saw.

## UNHINGED

A FEW SPACES down from us, Riley stood beside his Civic. Waiting.

I headed for him without another thought, but A. J. stepped in front of me and obscured him from my view. "Please don't." His fingers slid from my shoulders down to my hands. "Don't let him hurt you again. You were just starting to…"

Starting to what? The torment in his eyes compressed around me with the answer I'd feared. He wanted more than friendship—something I couldn't give him.

"Em, don't go. Just… just stay. With me. Please."

Riley kept his head down. He'd probably come for closure, but it didn't matter. Despite why he'd come, I had to see him.

"I'm sorry, A. J. I have to go."

He didn't release my hand. "I'll wait for you."

He meant more than standing on this sidewalk until I came back. I could hear it in his voice. I waited for the tremor in my own to steady before I faced him again. "I told you my heart wasn't available," I whispered. "It still isn't. I... I'm sorry."

Chin falling, he let me go.

The early evening breeze quivered down the lining of my coat. I tightened both sides of my jacket across my body once I reached Riley.

He didn't look up. "I know I have no right to be here," he said, "but would you please walk with me? Just for a while?"

I stole a glance back at A. J. and Jaycee. My heart left me no option but to say yes.

We walked half the perimeter of the campus in deafening silence. More than I could bear.

"What are you doing here, Riley?"

He kept his gaze ahead of us, his voice soft. "I came because I want you to tell me the pain I saw in your eyes today hasn't been there this whole time." He stopped and reached for my arm. "Em, please. Tell me this hasn't all been for nothing."

"What do you mean, all for nothing?" I started to shake. "And how could you have seen what was in my eyes? You wouldn't even look at me. We haven't seen or talked to each other in months, and then today you acted like you couldn't get away from me fast enough. I understand if you don't want to be friends, but can you not even tolerate seeing me?"

Hand trembling, he released my arm. "I can't be close to you. Don't you see that?"

His words ripped through my paper-thin shield of fury. I spun toward the vacant football field before he saw the impact, but I couldn't shut out the ache of remembering his face after I'd told him I loved him. Of course he couldn't be near me. How could I expect him to pretend we could still be friends after knowing I wanted more?

I swallowed the pain of regret, wanting to free us both from its claws. "You're right. I'm sorry. I know it was disappointing enough not to feel anything when you kissed me. Then you had to deal with the guilt of seeing how much I *did* feel. I don't blame you for leaving." I turned slowly. "I'm sorry, Riley. For pushing you away and ruining our friendship."

Deepening shades of blue collided together in the sky and accentuated the torn look in Riley's eyes. "Do you honestly believe that?"

"You don't have to pretend anymore."

The look in his eyes backed me against the oak tree standing securely behind us. He came close enough to touch me but gripped the trunk on either side of me instead. I was afraid to turn away yet more afraid to stay still. My pulse thundered in my ears, every part of me aware of how much I still loved him.

"I felt *everything* when I kissed you, Em. Feelings I've never felt for anyone else." He raised a hand to my hair, barely touching it. "From the first day I saw you on campus, I knew there was something different about you. Something that kept drawing me to you even when I tried to fight it. You don't know how many times I told myself to walk away. And how many more times I wished I didn't have to." He shook his head. "You have no idea what kind of willpower it took not to pull you into my arms every time we were together."

"But you said…" My voice broke.

"That I couldn't do this anymore. Couldn't keep hurting you. I tried, Em. I swear I tried to be everything you were to me. I wanted to show you your dad was right about the song inside you. It's what made me fall back in love with music again. You opened my heart to things I thought I'd lost for good. I would've done anything to give you that same gift, but the more I tried, the worse I made things."

"Worse? What are you talking about? All you've ever done is help me—"

"Help? By pushing you to exhaustion on a project that backfired anyway? By losing control with your boss and costing you your internship? Which just happened to put your scholarship in jeopardy and almost drove your mom into a relapse—in case you forgot that part."

His forehead crumpled, the edge in his voice deflating. "You made it feel so easy to forget who I am and believe you were right about me, about us. But after Xander, I knew I had to leave as soon as I made up for costing you your internship. I didn't mean to kiss you and make saying goodbye harder on both of us."

The air was too thick to breathe, too thick to move. "Why didn't you tell me?"

"You would've asked me to stay." He pushed away from the tree. "Do you have any idea how hard it was to let you go that day? Even after I looked into your eyes, knowing I'd been selfish enough to let you give your heart to someone who can't control his own, I almost couldn't leave. That's what passion does to people, Emma. I've seen it. With my dad, our landlord, guys like your supervisor. How could I stay and let you settle for that?"

My heart sank into the bark behind me. Had his dad's words created such a distorted lens that he honestly believed he was anything like those men?

Dried leaves cracked under the footsteps drawing him close again. Crossing the barrier that had restrained him a moment ago, he lifted his hand to my cheek.

Heat sprawled across my skin and down my neck. *Breathe.* No measure of time could change the way his touch unhinged me.

His fingertips grazed my ear as he brushed back my hair. "I meant what I said. I'd do anything to love you the way you loved me. Even if it meant doing the hardest thing I've ever had to do."

I ordered myself to blink, to move—anything to prove I was awake, that I wasn't imagining all this.

"You deserve someone your dad would be proud of, Em." His hands fell to his sides. "Whether it's A. J. or someone else, I knew if I stepped out of the picture, you'd be free to—"

"Stop talking." I brought his lips to mine. Nothing else mattered.

He pulled back. "I can't. Don't you see—?"

"Don't *you* see?" I clasped his unshaven cheeks. "Look at me. I love how passionate you are. The way you *feel* the world instead of just seeing it. The way that expression comes through your music, your friendship. It's not a flaw. It's a gift. It's what connects you to people in ways others can't—what captivated me from the first time I saw you. The only thing that's hurt me is you not seeing it yourself."

I took his hand, traced each groove, each memory revived by his touch. "There has never been, there never will be, someone else. You. Are. My. Dream." My fingertips found the soft hairs at the base of his neck as I kissed him again.

His rigid composure melted into an embrace that returned mine with equal longing. Warmth spread to a place in my heart tailor-fitted for him alone.

He leaned back. A clash of desire and defeat etched his face in a war I understood all too well.

"I'm scared too," I said. "But we're not meant to stand on our own." It was one truth I'd finally learned.

He closed me in his arms, nullifying the distance that'd needlessly separated us all these months.

The last sliver of sunlight stretched over that

secluded part of campus the longer our conversation deepened under a sky caught between day and night.

One evening wasn't enough to answer every question or heal every hurt. I didn't expect it to. I was just grateful we had the rest of the semester to restore what we'd broken.

As long as he stayed this time.

A hint of nerves rumbled in my stomach on our walk back. I peered up the walkway in front of my apartment, relieved to find an empty sidewalk under the streetlamp.

Riley hunched against his car door, circled his arms around my waist, and took me in under the lamplight.

I untwined his hands from my back and brought them in front of us. "Will you stay? Just a little longer?"

He kissed my forehead. "For a little while."

It didn't surprise me to see Trevor and Jaycee sitting in the living room when we walked through the door, but my heart stopped at the wounded expression of someone else looking at Riley and me.

A. J. had waited after all.

## 29

# TIME

A. J. JETTED from the edge of his seat. He took one look at us hand in hand and flicked a derisive glare at Riley. "Gotta give it to ya, bro. You're better than I thought you were. What'd you do? Sing her a love ballad?" He zeroed in on my raw lips. "Then again, bet you didn't need any words at all, did you?"

Riley's knuckles whitened, but Trevor rose from the couch before things could turn ugly.

A. J. ripped his jacket off the chair and stopped beside me. "Looks like you don't need me to take care of you anymore."

I grabbed his arm. "A. J., I—"

"Don't bother. I'm out." The door's slam shuddered the walls.

Trevor stepped in front of me. "Leave it."

"I can't." I jogged after him. "A. J., wait."

He stopped halfway down the staircase without turning around. "I'm done waiting."

The cold banister gripped me in place as the exit door snapped behind him. I breathed in, then hustled down the flight of stairs and barreled outside. "Please don't leave like this."

He stood on the walkway like a stony blockade defying the wind in its path. All the words that'd been racing through my mind seconds before froze and then shattered when he finally turned.

"You deserve better than him, Em. Someone who'll never leave you." Each stride toward me drove my feet backward until my heels scraped the front of the concrete porch. He drew me near with one hand on my waist and the other moving to the back of my neck.

"You deserve someone who's in love with you." With eyes deeper than the cloudless sky, A. J. closed the remaining distance between us.

I searched for my breath, afraid of how close he was to me. "A. J.—"

The door flung open behind us.

"—don't."

Riley nearly lunged off the porch when A. J. didn't move. "She said back off." He shoved him away and looked at me over his shoulder. "You all right?"

A. J. charged back up the walkway. "I'm not the one who hurt her."

Riley didn't disagree. His shoulders fell. "I know." He exhaled deeply. "Forgiving me is her choice."

I held on to his arm, wishing they both knew there'd never been a choice to make.

"Last time I checked, Emma had a voice of her own." A. J.'s stare jumped from Riley to me. "Or did you let him steal that too?"

Trevor pushed through the door. "Walk away, bro."

"Stay out of this, Trev," A. J. said without budging his face from Riley's.

I braced A. J. again. "Please don't do this."

"Do what? Show how I really feel?" He glared at my hand on his arm. "Never hold back, remember? Can't live without a few regrets." His gaze flicked from Riley to me. "I've certainly taught you well."

The jab struck my eyes and scraped down my throat to the center of my chest. Everything inside begged me to look away and prevent him from seeing the impact of his blow. But all I could do was stand there, grasping for any hint of my friend behind those dark eyes.

A muscle running down his shoulder twitched as he faced the sky and swore under his breath. "Em..." He started forward again.

Riley moved to guard me, and, this time, A. J. lost restraint. His fist crashed into Riley's jaw with a noise so fierce, it resonated in my bones. He staggered backward and knocked me onto the stoop.

One glance at me on the ground was all it took. Riley lurched forward, rammed his shoulder into A. J.'s torso, and drove him down the sidewalk. A. J. thrust a knee into his stomach. A piercing groan struck the air as Riley folded in half.

My hand flew to my mouth. "Stop."

The jagged cry got lost in the sound of another punch. Riley swung a rib shot with his left hand and cut a right hook to A. J.'s jaw. Blood splattered onto the pavement.

I bolted to my feet. "Stop! Both of you."

Trevor wrestled A. J. off from behind but couldn't hold him.

I raced down the sidewalk. "Enough."

Their heartbeats pounded against my palms outstretched to either side of me. Faint lines of blood trickled from the corners of their mouths.

My hands strayed to my sides. Tears churning, I faced A. J. and prayed he'd meet my eyes. "Please," I whispered.

He looked at me then, hair flattened around an expression more wounded than any physical bruise. The hard lines on his forehead softened for the briefest moment. He swallowed, then jerked his tousled jacket back up his shoulders. And with his chest still heaving a dangerous level of adrenaline, he turned and walked away.

Gravity lodged me in place while the flicker from a damaged streetlight kept A. J. tangled in shadows ahead of me.

"Let him go. He's angry at me, not you," Riley said softly. "Give him some time."

What if some things were too damaged for time to heal?

Riley's face, bearing wounds of its own, called me to him. I knotted my hands around his waist, and he cradled me in a hold still trembling with the tension left in A. J.'s absence.

Trevor nodded to the street. "I'll go check on him."

He headed across the lawn while Jaycee held up an icepack from inside the doorway. Prepared as always.

We followed her inside. Underneath the bathroom light, I dabbed a cold washcloth over Riley's bruised jaw. He winced and set his hand over mine. "I'm sorry," he said. "For fighting with A. J. and hurting you. Again. He's right."

"Yeah, he is, but not about what you think." I rested against the sink's edge and twisted the washcloth. "He's right about regrets. When you left, they consumed me."

Riley winced again when he rose from the chair. "Em, you don't know how much I want to take back—"

"You didn't let me finish." I stared at the worn caulking between the floor's green tiles. "I have regrets, but A. J. helped me see I was wrong about what they were. I spent so long pretending to be brave, when, really, I was scared. Terrified that if I stopped running— if I slowed down long enough to let myself feel anything at all—I'd fall apart. It was easier to stay calloused. Closed off. So, I hid. In books, goals, apathy."

I lowered my head beneath his. "Until I met you."

The tendons on his neck pulled taut as he looked away.

I reached for his chin and turned him toward me. "You walked right through those walls like they weren't even there. Awakened things in me I thought were dead."

He removed my hand. "Things that ended up hurting you. You've been through enough pain already. The last thing you needed was someone you trusted pushing you into more."

"Actually, I think that's exactly what I needed. And stop blaming yourself for what happened at Xander." I curled my fingers around his. "You helped me see my dad was right. Life's a lot like being an artist. Even if it feels safer to guard my heart from disappointment, I can't silence what it was made for. It won't let me. There's gonna be pain."

I slid my arms around him. "But I'd rather risk the possibility of heartache than wade through life without experiencing what you've helped me feel."

I twisted toward the sink. "It took me falling apart to figure that out. Along with a few good kicks from people who care about me. A. J. being one of them." I set the coiled washcloth on the counter but couldn't face the mirror. Not after knowing how much I'd hurt him. "He was a good friend to me when I needed one."

"He loves you, Emma." Riley turned me around, his eyes soft and earnest. "Are you sure you're making the right choice?"

Did he still not understand?

"C'mere. I wanna show you something." From the doorway to my bedroom, I pointed to the pressed leaf that had never left my desk. "That choice was made for me a long time ago."

He crossed the room, ran his fingers along the grains of the picture frame next to the leaf, then lifted the laminated memory underneath the desk lamp. "I can't believe you kept this. After everything."

"I think part of opening my heart again meant finding the courage to let you go, but I never stopped loving you."

He set the leaf against the base of the lamp and left his head bowed so long, my pulse raced waiting for him to move again. Slowly, his eyes found mine.

No words. No space outside of the way a single look could make me feel. It intensified with each step bringing him closer to me. He smoothed a hand over my cheek. Then with equal tenderness, his lips pressed into mine. "I love you." He kissed my wrist. "More than I think I understand."

My fingers trailed down the threads of his shirt and entwined in the fabric along the hem. "Would you stay?"

His body tensed.

"Until I fall asleep?" I amended before his frown could turn into an audible objection.

"Just until you fall asleep."

He propped the pillows against the headboard. My body fit into the outline of his the closer I nestled. His heart thundered through his cotton henley onto my cheek until it gradually eased into a steady rhythm. It was like listening to a song written expressly for me. One I'd never tire of hearing.

As Riley sang softly, the sweet cadence lulled me deeper into the mattress. The emotional exhaustion of the day drained into the comforter curling around my sides. I'd be asleep in minutes, and he'd be gone. But for now, I burrowed tighter and soaked in the warmth of his arms.

"Where do we go from here?" he whispered.

I'd asked that same question so many times, always driven by fear, but something had changed. "We stay right here," I whispered back. This feeling, this moment —this was real. More intense than a memory and more enrapturing than a dream. I think that was what Austin had tried to tell me. That each moment, a day at a time, was where we painted our stories. A part of that canvas came to life in me over the last few days, and I knew exactly what I had to do in the morning before I added another brushstroke.

## 30

# RELEASE

In front of my advisor's office, I paused with my knuckles a centimeter from the door. *Don't lose your nerve now.*

"Come in, Miss Matthews." Mr. Oakly shifted some papers on his desk. "I have to admit, I'm surprised you called. I wouldn't normally be here this early, but it sounded urgent." He pointed to the chair in front of him. "Have a seat."

I hovered in the doorway. "Actually, I'm not staying. I only came to tell you I put in a request for Miriam Chen to take my place at Edwards Jones. She found the position first anyway. She just needed the right recommendation to get her in."

He blinked. Twice. "You what?"

I approached the chair and gripped its top edge. "I don't know what Miriam's GPA is, or if she's smarter than I am, but I've realized it's not a competition. It never has been. She deserves the same chance at finding her calling as I do."

I traced the seam along the chair's fabric. "I've decided to finish the second half of my internship at the Portland Center instead, starting this summer. I know it's not as prestigious as my Financial Analyst position, but it's where my heart is."

Mr. Oakly's fingers pitched a tent over his stomach as he stared at me from above the rims of his glasses. With his face mirroring the blank computer monitor, I couldn't tell whether he was hiding his shock or analyzing my motives.

A second later, his chair sprang forward, and he arched over his desk. "Let me get this straight. You're giving up everything you've spent the last three years working for? A respectable internship, guaranteed job security, a promising future—all to go work at some inner-city mission." He dropped his pen on the desk and hunched backward again.

"No, sir." I let go of the chair and of so many things I'd wasted time seeking. "I'm giving up trying to force myself into a mold of the way I thought things had to be. All the top grades, scholarship titles, and job securities mean nothing if there's no fulfillment in them. I don't want to spend my life trying to prove my merit. I want to spend it showing others they don't have to."

I paced across a carved-out path between stacks of dusty books. "I know the choice is risky. And yeah, to be honest, the thought of losing security scares the heck out of me." I stared at the burgundy tiles, talking more to myself than to him. "But I can't let fear keep my heart closed anymore. I have to choose to trust things are going to work out even when I can't see how, or I'm going to miss everything my heart was made for."

The tread on my sneakers gripped the carpet. My arms fell to my sides. Mr. Oakly's office was a far cry from my father's study. Yet right then, I would've sworn I was back home with Dad standing by my side. His faith ushered in a confidence like I'd never known.

"Things are going to work out," I said again. I didn't know how, but I didn't have to. For the first time— maybe ever—I trusted the One who'd been waiting for me to make the choice all along.

Leaving Mr. Oakly speechless in his desk chair, I walked out of his office and through unseen barriers that had always held me back. I soared down the hallway to the stairs, whirled around the banister, and didn't slow down until my feet hit the landing. In that empty stairwell, something stirred.

Freedom. Borderless freedom.

It welcomed me outside with a cherry blossom-scented breeze. Warm and bright, the sun doused the whole campus in colors of spring—colors I'd been missing.

A sense of newness followed me all the way to my apartment building until the scuff marks along the sidewalk drew me to a stop. Unbidden, the scene from last night tore right through the scene from Mr. Oakly's office and left a tumultuous realization in place of both.

I hadn't finished learning to walk by faith.

Trevor and Jaycee bounced through the door and met me on the walkway.

"How'd it go?" Jaycee asked.

"Um, kind of amazing, actually." I nudged a stick into the grass with my shoe. "I can't believe it's taken me this long to see what I'm supposed to do with my life."

Trevor patted my arm. "All part of the journey, Em."

"Thanks, Dr. Phil."

He puffed out his shirt. "I do what I can."

A couple of jocks strolled past us, tossing basketballs in the air. The stockier one hooked his arm above his head and pointed at Trevor. "'Sup, Andrews? Up for a little two-on-two?"

Trevor roped his arm around Jaycee's waist. "Sorry, boys, not today."

The taller one held the ball out with his palm. "A'ight, a'ight. We got you, bro. We'll hit up Bowers instead."

Last night closed in again. "How is he, Trev?"

"Don't know. He drove off before I made it to the parking lot. I waited up, but..." He squeezed my shoulder. "You know A. J. He's more of a hothead than I am."

"And that's saying something," Jaycee piped in. Trevor squished her to his side, squeezing all the air out of her laugh. She unlocked his arm from her back. "Don't worry, Em. If Ashlea has her way, A. J. will be forgetting all about his sorrows in no time."

"Ashlea?"

Trevor flipped his ball cap around. "Wow, and I thought A. J. was blind."

Jaycee smacked him in the gut. "She's been a little preoccupied, in case you haven't noticed." She tilted her head at me, lips to the side. "A. J. will work it off, cool down, and things will go back to normal."

"Doubt that. I'm not even sure what normal is anymore. So much has changed."

Jaycee pecked Trevor on the cheek and motioned toward the car. "Give us a sec, 'kay?"

When he headed down the sidewalk, she turned in front of me. "You need to give yourself some time to decompress. You had a pretty emotional day yesterday."

*"Congrats, you just won the understatement of the year award."* An inward wince immediately followed the memory of A. J.'s voice.

"Kinda hard to do that when I know how upset A. J. is." I craned my neck back. "I should've done things differently. Not depended on his friendship as much. Kept my distance."

She cocked her head. "Like he would've let you."

"Still should've tried."

"You were straightforward with him. He knew where you stood."

Just like I knew where he stood. Both of us wishing things were different, hoping we'd change the other's mind.

Another set of friends strolled by. Two guys, two girls, dressed like they were going on a hike.

"What if I've lost him for good?"

"He cares about you. When the emotions of it cool down, he'll remember that. I doubt he'd throw your friendship away any more than you would."

As I watched the group drift down the hill, my stomach clenched with the sense of something drifting out of reach.

What if Jaycee was wrong?

# TOMORROW

TIME REGAINED THE UPPER HAND. Another week. Another Friday night with the gang. Another absentee A. J.

I let go of the blinds. The creak of the bending vinyl echoed the lecture I gave myself for hoping he would have forgiven me by now.

Still, my throat almost closed completely by the time I made it from the living room window to the group huddled beside Trevor's car. Ashlea's glare mirrored the unspoken accusation her glossed lips struggled to hold back—A. J. wasn't there, and it was my fault.

My line of sight ricocheted from person to person until it stopped on Trevor. "Where is he?"

He glanced at Jaycee. "In the gym," he mumbled.

I turned but hesitated in front of Riley.

"It's okay." He nodded toward the sports center. "Go."

I reached up on my tiptoes to kiss him and started down the hill, away from my group of friends and toward someone whose friendship I had to find a way to repair.

The sound of a single basketball bouncing against the waxed floor shuddered across the gymnasium. Standing at the free throw line, A. J. looked at me for a split second before focusing on the net again. "What are you doing here, Emma?"

It sounded more like a complaint than a question. A string of rehearsed platitudes rang through my mind, but he deserved better.

"I promised you a game of basketball, remember?"

He made another foul shot. The snap against the backboard jutted into the edge in his voice. "It's Friday night. You should be out with your friends."

His exclusion of himself as my friend knocked the smile from my face. Behind the out-of-bounds line, I picked up the ball and clasped it in my arms. "I am," I whispered.

The evidence of his rigorous workout soaked through his shirt. A. J. snatched his water bottle up from the sideline, rubbed a towel over his face, and whipped it over his shoulder.

The sharp noise tightened my already-tense body. I squeezed the ball closer. "It's been two weeks. You can't give me the silent treatment forever."

He stared at the wall and squirted water in his mouth.

I grabbed his forearm. "A. J., please. Just talk to me."

He looked right at me then, eyes lifeless. "What do you want me to say?"

The pain in his words plunged through me. It's hard to trust things will work out when you're staring at the proof it's too late.

My voice grew faint. "I want you to tell me the truth. I want you to talk to me, please."

He wiped his face once more, chucked the wet towel on the floor, and wheeled away from me. Head down, he stopped midway to the locker room. "What can I say that you don't already know?"

His sneakers scuffed over the floor in a half-circle. A strain of anger and affection tore down his face. "Even when I knew your heart wasn't free to give away, I couldn't hold mine back." He faced the ceiling and laughed sadly. "Guess that's what happens when you live without regrets."

My courage drained to the floor with his balled-up towel. The gym blurred through tears filling in for everything I couldn't find the words to say.

As soon as A. J. came to me, I dropped the basketball and wrapped my arms around him. Each bounce waned one by one like a shot clock running out of time.

No matter how tightly I held on to him, we'd already forfeited the chance to keep things the way they were. Outside this moment—this timeless moment of love and friendship—stood the reality of choices made. Love and loss, friendship and brokenness, memories and regret.

He lowered his head close enough for his lips to touch the top of my ear. "You'll always hold a part of my heart," he whispered. "I'm not saying goodbye. Just give me some time."

My tears added to his sodden shirt. I held on, knowing what once was, and the hope of what might have been, would dissolve as soon as we let go. He kissed my cheek and crossed the gym.

"A. J.?" The tremor in my chest shot straight to my voice when he turned. "I'll wait for you."

Even if the words didn't mean what they had when he'd spoken them to me, his smile reassured me he understood. He disappeared into the locker room, and I dropped my face to my hands until the wave of regret subsided.

The streetlights blinked on while I walked up the hill toward my apartment. Riley rose from the stoop. He'd waited for me. I clutched my sides tighter.

"Everything worked out?" he asked.

I wasn't sure how to answer that question. I might not have fully lost A. J., but I'd hurt him.

"You're a good friend, you know."

I almost snorted. "Is that what you call it? I'm not so sure breaking a friend's heart bumps me into the *good* category."

Riley chuckled and threaded his fingers through my hair. "He's lucky to have a friend who cares about him as much as you do."

After the way he'd cared for me, A. J. deserved that much. But maybe it was too hard. For all of us. I dragged my Converse down the corner of the stoop. "You're not mad at me?"

"For caring about A. J.?" Shaking his head, Riley looked down. "I used to be afraid you'd realize he could love you better than I could." His arms circled around me. "But I'm starting to learn what it means to love. To trust." He rested his forehead against mine. "I'm not afraid anymore. Not after what you've taught me about grace."

Of all the things he could've said, he'd responded with the only thing filling his eyes. Selfless love. The kind I wasn't sure I'd earned.

The corners of his mouth sagged. "You still don't see."

"See what?"

"What I see." With my cheek in his hand, the tenderness in his touch poured into a kiss so soft I gripped his sleeve to keep from melting with it.

He leaned back just slightly, a smile re-emerging. "Tomorrow." He kissed my forehead and headed toward his car.

Did I miss something? "Tomorrow...?"

He shuffled backward down the sidewalk. "Tomorrow, I'm going to show you."

"Show me what?"

He kept his response hidden behind an unreadable grin.

I gripped the railing, a little afraid of what that meant.

# UNDONE

AMAZING how long a single night could feel. The reheated cup of tea Jaycee had made me earlier soothed and coaxed in perfect form until the clock took another stab at me. Twenty minutes left before Riley got there.

I fell face first onto my bed. Stupid nerves. I snagged my economics text from my desk and yanked off a highlighter cap with my teeth.

Jaycee flitted around the doorframe with a mug in hand. Hazelnut mocha fumes infiltrated our bedroom with enough strength to give me a secondhand caffeine buzz.

Five minutes later, I shoved my rainbow-highlighter-assaulted textbook off my lap and sprang for my dresser. I shifted sock after sock into a tight column in my top drawer. What did he have to show me? And why was he all mysterious about it? I shut my now-rearranged drawer, folded my arms over my dresser, and dropped my head onto them.

"Stop worrying," Jaycee said from her bed.

"You didn't see the look on his face before he left last night."

"You mean the one that announces to the world how hopelessly in love with you he is?"

"Funny, Jae." I leaned on my arms. "It's not that. It's just... I don't know. Something in his eyes. It makes me nervous."

Jaycee spied the half-vandalized book on my bed. "I couldn't tell."

I chucked a pair of socks at her, but it only made her laugh harder.

"You're not helping." I clipped on my necklace.

A perfect rendition of Trevor's devilish grin flaunted my way. "Are you sure? 'Cause I think a whole minute just passed without you noticing."

"All right, Trevor's mini-me. Just wait until the next time you're anxious about something."

"Out of love, Em. Always out of love."

"Mm-hmm."

"Relax. The guy adores you. What's the biggest thing he could do? Propose?"

My elbows slipped off the dresser. "You don't think..."

"Wow, be sure not to make that face when he's down on one knee. What's the panic all about? Thought he was *the one*."

"He is. But marriage?"

"Yeah, you know, that thing two people do when they want to spend their lives together."

Flashes of Mom in her comatose stage pushed me backward.

Jaycee's face softened as she crossed the room. As usual, she read between the lines. "I know it killed you to watch your mom suffer after losing your dad, but if you live in fear of all the bad things that *could* happen, you'll miss the good ones too."

I stared at the grains along the dresser and toyed with the knobs. I knew what she meant. As hard as it was to unravel the bad memories from the good ones, Mom wouldn't trade a single second of her marriage. I felt the same way about being with Riley. But the semester was almost over. He'd be moving on after graduation. What if love wasn't enough to keep us together?

A knock echoed down the hall with the sound that meant Riley and the possibility of what could happen were waiting on the other side of the front door.

My socks skimmed across the last five feet of the entryway. Swinging the door open, I didn't bother to untangle the rug bunched around my feet or the bottom of my shirt caught in the top of my belt.

Riley hovered in the doorway, head angled with that smile that had a way of trampling over every preceding thought. "Ready?" he asked.

His clear blue eyes fanned the butterfly wings already taking flight in my stomach.

Jaycee swooshed behind me. "The suspense is shooting off her like pop rocks. You don't hear that?"

If she weren't carrying a cup of coffee over the carpet, I would've hurled a shoe at her.

"Whatever you've got planned," she kept going. "Make sure it includes mellowing out that wound-up mind of hers."

"Wow, Jae, really?"

Riley laughed. "I'll see what I can do."

I shooed him into the hall and let the door swing behind me. My glare caught Jaycee's wink right before it closed. I was seriously going to have to limit the time she spent with Trevor before they morphed into the same person.

"Guess there's no point hiding it now." I trotted down the stairs after Riley. "You had me kinda stirred up. I didn't know wh—"

He caught me at the door, his lips confiscating the rest of my stammering. I reached for the doorframe behind me until he eased his mouth away from mine. "Unwinding yet?"

"Like that's helping." With his shirt balled in my fingers, I fought between wanting to shove him through the exit and wanting to pull him close again.

He must've felt it too. He placed one hand on the door handle and the other on the trim above my head. Currents hovered in the tiny space between us. "We should probably go," he said, voice raspy. But he leaned in instead of away and brought his hand to my face.

"Um, I think going requires us moving outside."

His grin hiked to the left. "I'm working up to that part." He kissed me once more, then finally pushed the door open like some kind of failsafe button.

Thank goodness for Oregon's cool spring air.

In the car, I buckled my seat belt and waited for my lungs to agree to work again. "So, you gonna tell me what you want to show me?"

He cranked the engine. "Actually, change of plans."

"What?" He couldn't be serious.

"That needs a little… tweaking. But it so happens I have something else to show you today."

"You're killing me, you know that?"

His mouth quirked. "Little adventure, remember?"

"The story of my life these days."

Someone tapped my window. I jumped and swung a glance from the window to Riley and back again. "Miriam?"

She waved me out of the car. "I don't want to hold you guys up, but I had to find you." The dark embroidery on her cardigan matched eyes as sweet and earnest as her voice. "Your recommendation for the internship at Edwards Jones… I don't know what to say."

"You don't have to say anything. You're the one who gave me the lead to begin with."

She shifted her backpack. "When I saw you that day outside Mr. Oakly's office, I could tell you thought I was trying to steal your scholarship, but I promise I wasn't. I didn't want it to be like that. I wanted to collaborate, not compete."

"I know. I'm sorry it took me so long to figure that out." I looked at Riley. "I can be a little slow sometimes."

She took my hand. "Can we start over?"

I squeezed back. "We already have."

Smiling, she looped her arm through her bag strap and continued down the hill. She stopped a few feet away, turned. "Thanks, Emma. For everything."

Behind me, Riley kissed the top of my shoulder. "And you wonder why I love you so much."

"Because you give me more credit than I deserve?"

He brought me around to meet an expression more consuming than his touch. "Because of what you give without even knowing it." He opened my car door. "One day, you'll see."

My earlier tension about what he had planned crept over my muscles again. But as the exit signs led us toward downtown Portland, I settled a little deeper into my seat. Maybe he simply wanted a day for the two of us away from any distractions.

This time, Riley parked in the Cultural District. Luscious café fragrances flowed along the riverside paths winding around fountains and sculptures. If we did nothing all day but amble together around the city, he'd have shown me enough.

A bustle of noise trailed the few blocks leading up to Pioneer Courtyard Square. The red-brick-lined courtyard lit up in a clamor of children's voices.

I stopped along the edge. "What's all this?"

"They're putting on a play today. I heard one of the leads is a real heart-stopper. C'mon." He folded my hand in the crook of his arm and led me forward.

A teenager wearing a black ball cap and a bass guitar strapped to his shoulder approached us. "'Sup, Riley."

Riley greeted him with a handshake-half-hug. "You're in the play?"

"Orchestra," he answered.

"Sweet." Riley rested his hand on my back. "Drew, this is Emma."

The teenager's gaze swept over me. "Hey, Mrs. Riley. He won't lyin' when he said how pretty you was." He took my hand and bent down to kiss it.

Riley waved him back. "All right. All right, stud."

"Hey, since there's no ring, I figure I got a chance, right?" Strutting with extra swag, he laughed as Riley ran him off.

I tilted my head. "Mrs. Riley, huh?"

His shoulders arched. "Didn't want to correct him. Besides, I kinda like the sound of it."

*Me too.* "He's one of the kids you jam with at that building you brought me to?"

"Yep, he's a killer bass player. Kid's got real talent." He curled me to his side. "C'mon, someone's waiting for us."

Waiting for us?

My new internship supervisor from the Portland Center waved from the third row of the stadium-style stairs. We slipped past a few people and took the seats he'd saved for us.

Trey clasped Riley's hand. "Right on time, my man."

"Thanks for the invite." Riley settled beside him.

I studied the pair of them. "Okay, I'm sorry. Am I missing something?"

Trey's throaty laugh bellowed into the sound of Riley's phone ringing. He stared at the screen. "Excuse me for a sec," he said without looking up. He walked out of hearing distance to take the call. Who was he talking to?

Trey nudged me in the arm and motioned to a group of kids waving at us from the border of the stage.

"Are they all from the center?" I asked.

"A lot of them. They're dying to meet you, by the way."

My heart did one of those flip-floppy things. "Really?"

"You kidding? Most of these youngins don't have many role models. All I had to do was tell them you gave up your other internship to come work with them, and they fell in love with you on the spot."

A lump swelled in my throat as I waved back to their adorable faces. "Hope I can give them the kind of love they deserve."

Trey took off his beret and set it beside him. "You already are, dear. Just by being here."

Riley's arm slid around my back. He kissed my temple. "Sorry 'bout that."

"Who was—?"

A burst of music blared through the standing speakers. Spotlights circled. The curtains opened and revealed a little boy dressed in a lion's costume with the same pink nose and whiskers I'd seen before. My hand soared to my mouth. I looked between Riley and Michael on the stage. I didn't think I'd see him again.

"Told you you had a way of touching a boy's heart, Emma." Riley's lips touched my ear. "Including mine."

I nestled into his side, still overwhelmed at times by the way he loved me.

After a priceless rendition of The Lion King I'd never forget, Trey led us into the mob of kids, each with a story to tell as unique as their costumes. They all jumped—literally—at the chance to give me a hug, starting with Michael. Surrounded, gratitude lit off inside me.

In the middle of the crowd, Riley held my cheeks with his hands and my heart with his eyes. He looked at me with every ounce of feeling I'd always fail to put into words. He swallowed. His brow wrinkled. "Em, there's something I need to tell you."

All outside noise subsided as the unease in his voice rippled straight down my body.

Something wet hit the tip of my nose. All at once, a steady patter of rain played percussion over the bricks. Squeals erupted from dozens of kids as the open courtyard turned into a frenzy of people scrambling to take cover.

Thankfully, the storm didn't follow us back to the

campus. Like the curtain on the stage, the clouds drew back long enough to permit the sun one final bow before ending the day.

We walked toward my apartment, a little soggy but still warmed on the inside. At least, until Riley's elusive forewarning sprang to mind again. He hadn't finished his thought on the drive back, and I was afraid to ask. Couldn't we forget everything else but right now?

His arm stiffened around my waist and secured me tighter to his side. It only took one glance up from the sidewalk to understand why.

## 33

## ALWAYS

A. J. STOOD at the curb in front of my apartment with his hands stuffed inside his hoodie pocket. My heels dug into the pavement, but Riley prodded us forward, his body tall and confident. Good thing one of us was.

A. J. stared at the sidewalk. His jaw flinched in and out, probably saying everything he didn't want to say out loud.

We stopped in front of him, and he looked Riley head-on. "I came to tell you no hard feelings." His cheeks swelled with air until it finally seeped out with a noisy groan. "Okay, that's not entirely true, but I'm working on it." He stubbed his Nike against an uprooted piece of concrete. "Her heart belongs to you. It always has."

His gaze drifted to me and lingered before returning to Riley. "Trev told me why you left. It took me a while to understand that you let her go because you love her. But now," he said, looking at me again, "I get it."

Without needing to say anything, Riley squeezed A. J.'s shoulder, nodded his understanding, and then joined the rest of our friends on the stoop, leaving A. J. and me alone.

A lengthy silence stood between us like a glass wall boxing us in place. With my hands clasped around my elbows, I rocked on the balls of my feet until I couldn't take it any longer. "A. J., I—"

"I know." He looked up then. "I'm sorry too. For a lot of things. For pushing when I shouldn't have. For being a jerk and making you cry." He inched toward me and rubbed his thumb across my cheek. "I told you I was just a friend helping another friend remember how to live again." His arm strayed to his side. "I'm sorry for lying to you and to myself."

"You were a good friend to me. I mean, you still are." If it wasn't too late. I stowed my hands in my front pockets and curled my lip under my teeth. We still had the summer, all of next year—time I didn't want to pass without his friendship.

A. J. took off his hat, ran his fingers through his hair, then slipped the cap on, and released a long exhale. "I'd like to think I could handle that. Being just your friend. I honestly don't know if I can, but…" He faced me again. "I'll try."

I raised my shoulders with hope. "Promise?"

His lips slid into the same grin that'd won me over from the beginning. He held three fingers in the air. "Scout's honor."

I grabbed his hand and wrapped his arm around me. For the slightest moment, things felt as they had always been.

Almost.

His arms stiffened into a guarded hug. The distance between us deepened the closer we were. It wasn't fair to wish for anything different. I knew that, but something inside still ached. This summer wouldn't be as easy as we wanted it to be. For any of us.

Ashlea appeared beside A. J. The minute I let him go, she looped her dainty hands around his forearm and led him up the sidewalk—away from me. How did I ever miss her signals? "C'mon, Becky rented a movie."

The sound of her voice drifted inside the apartment door. I smiled at the reminder that Ashlea's story wasn't over yet. None of ours was.

Though the rain had held off, the sky hadn't fully recovered from the storm. Riley pulled me close from behind and blocked out the chill. "How about we skip the movie and take a walk? Just you and me."

I turned around and looked up at him. His arms glided down my back, fitting around me like my favorite pullover. Soft, warm, comforting—a feeling I didn't want to let go of. Ever.

He pressed his forehead to mine. "What?"

"How do you know exactly what I need?"

He leaned back and traced his thumb over the skin around my eyes. "These tell me."

I brought his palm to my lips. "I love you."

As we walked, I held on to that love and to the hope of it being enough to get us through any circumstance.

We stopped at the sports field. Riley held on to two corners of a blanket as it expanded in the air and floated to the ground.

Stretched out on the layer of fleece, I curled up against the edge of his body and drank in the comfort of our favorite place on campus. Empty bleachers. Fir trees fanning against each other. A private view of the heavens.

Riley drew a pattern along my arm with his fingertip. "What are you thinking about?"

"This summer."

"You disappointed about not going home?"

"I'll miss seeing Mom and Austin." I scooted a little closer. "But my life's here."

"Then what's wrong?"

I twisted the knotted drawstrings on Riley's hoodie. "You're graduating. You'll be searching for a job, moving on. I'll be interning at the center. Jaycee will be prepping for student teaching. Everything will be different."

"Different isn't necessarily a bad thing."

I rolled onto my back and groaned. Now I had to add Riley to the Austin-Jaycee radio station. "You been talking to my brother?"

Riley propped himself up on his arm. The etchings of something unspoken creased his face. My stomach dropped as it had earlier when he'd mentioned something he wanted to tell me. Had he already gotten a job? Was it in another state?

He drew circles over the blanket with a blade of grass, stalling.

My conversation with Jaycee tore into me again. *"Thought he was the one."* I might as well have been trying to swallow a fistful of cotton balls. He *was* the one. The one I wanted to spend the rest of my life with. Every day. I couldn't lose him.

Riley kept his focus on the blanket. "During the time we were apart, I poured myself into my music. It was the only thing that kept me sane. The list of A&R reps you gave me sat on my piano for weeks. Every time I passed it, I heard your voice."

He fanned the blade into the grass and set his hand over mine. "You saw things in me I couldn't see. And because of that, I started to believe in myself. Knew it was time to stop focusing on my disappointment with the way things were and start having courage to dream about the way they could be. To really go for it, you know?" He tossed his head back. "They actually liked my demo, Em. They signed me."

A series of blinks came before any words. I cupped his cheek, feeling his happiness as my own. Of course they signed him. "I'm so proud of you. I knew they wouldn't overlook your talent."

"I wouldn't have risked dreaming if it hadn't been for you."

I lowered my hand from his face. "You keep giving

me more credit than I deserve."

"And you don't give yourself enough." He laughed softly. "You know, a girl once told me it's easier to believe in someone else than it is to believe in yourself. I think she might've known what she was talking about."

"Same as the guy who said we need someone in our lives to sing to us when we forget our song."

He kissed my forehead. "Always, Em."

*Always.* A promise I'd given up believing in. As earnestly as someone might mean it, how could someone promise *always* when time had the final say? I'd teased Riley about being famous and singing on stages across the states, but I hadn't thought about what that'd mean for us.

I snuggled my nose to his neck. "What's gonna happen? Now that you have a record deal?"

"To be honest, I don't know. Sounds like it's going to take some time to get all the details worked out." He scooted back. "I don't know how any of this is going to play out. Except that no matter what, it'll include you."

He brushed a strand of hair from my face and left his hand resting weightlessly behind my ear. I had to force in a breath when he looked at me that way. Same as his music, his love never needed any words.

I kissed his neck under his ear. Riley closed his eyes and sighed. The sound drew my lips across his cheek to meet his. Soft and tender, they drew me closer, deeper. The muscles running along his forearm pulsed against the small of my back. He interlocked his fingers with mine as the stubble on his chin sloped down my neckline to the top of my shoulder, his breath warm against my skin.

Every part of me teemed with heat. I sank my palm into the cool earth along the blanket when he found my lips again. I let go of his hand, gripped the back of his hair, and pressed in even closer.

His arms flexed to push himself away. He lunged to his feet. Alone on the blanket, I found my lungs again while I watched him pace across the grass. The evening's darkness couldn't hide the expansive motion lifting his chest with each breath. He still doubted his control, distrusted his passion. I could see it.

"It's okay."

"It's not okay," he said, his voice hoarse. "Being this close to you... The things you stir inside me." He exhaled. "I don't ever want to make you feel the way other guys have."

"You haven't."

Drawing in another deep breath, he returned to the blanket and encircled me with his arm. "You've entrusted your heart to me, Em. I promise to cherish that gift and honor your dad." He kissed the top of my head. "Always."

I wove my fingers through his and held him close.

The sky deepened further into a night made just for us. At least we had that much. Wrapped in Riley's arms and in his vow to protect my heart, I risked trusting another of Dad's promises. Some things were worth waiting for. *Please let our future together be one of them.*

## 34

## AMBUSHED

THE BLINDS beside my bed slapped into each other, and a full window-length of the sunrise ambushed my eyes. One forced blink at a time, Jaycee came into focus above me.

"Morning, Sleeping Beauty. I made you tea."

I had the faintest recollection of Riley tucking me into bed last night. Or maybe I'd dreamed it. If I had, it was definitely a dream worth going back to. I wedged against the wall. "Later," I mumbled into the pillow.

Jaycee lifted off the mattress. "Okay," she mumbled right back. "Guess I'll go tell Prince Charming to come back later."

I flung forward, the blood in my head catching up a minute later. I threw back the covers, launched out of bed, and tripped over the sneakers I must've kicked off sometime last night.

Jaycee's amusement followed one sweeping glance over the clothes I still had on from yesterday.

The clock blurred through the spider web of hair matted across my face. Six forty-five. What was he doing here this early? "How long has he been here?"

"Long enough to hear you snoring."

"Cute, Jae." I circled into the hallway.

She stopped me by the shoulders and redirected me toward the shower. "Trust me."

One peek in the mirror, and I didn't object.

Ten minutes in a room full of steam worked its magic. I threw on the clean shirt Jaycee left out for me, buttoned my jeans, and jogged down the hall with wet hair.

Seeing Riley across the living room caused every feeling from last night to wash over me again in a shower of its own. He wore fresh jeans and a dark blue henley, his hair a perfect mess. But it was the look on his face that made the skin on my neck burn under my cool hair.

He opened his mouth but withheld whatever he'd almost said.

Jaycee glided past me and set two suitcases down by the front door.

I held my arms out. "Going somewhere?"

Trevor's head popped up from the TV and flashed from me to Riley. "You haven't told her yet?"

"Told me what? What's going on?"

Trevor's obnoxious grin soared to new heights.

"Keeping a secret from Em? Takes guts, bro. Knew I liked you."

Riley glared at him. "Thanks, man, perfect introduction." Angling himself toward me, he brandished a smile in an attempt to dislodge Trevor's wrecking ball from his plans.

*Not going to happen.* "What secret, Riley?"

When he scrunched his lips together, I snatched a throw pillow from the couch and aimed it in his direction. "Tell me."

He lifted his palms in the air. "I was going to tell you after you were done getting ready."

I dropped beside him on the couch but kept my imaginary firearm locked and loaded. "I don't like surprises."

"I can see that." He disarmed me and tucked the pillow safely behind him.

"We're going on a vacation," Trevor blurted out with the intonation of a kid going to Disney World.

Jaycee elbowed him in the ribs.

He groaned. "What'd I say?"

Riley shook his head as he faced me again. "Well, not exactly a vacation. More like a weekend getaway."

"A getaway." I gripped the couch cover.

"Relax." His voice almost topped the microfiber's smoothness. "It's just a little road trip."

*A road trip?*

"That's all you're getting out of me," he said, apparently reading my mind. "A little surprise every now and then is good for you." He leaned in for a kiss.

I turned my head. Of course, that meant leaving my neck exposed along with the perfect opportunity for Riley to get the upper hand. It only took seconds for me to melt under his lips skimming my skin.

"You're cheating." I wrestled for the resolve to push him away from me.

"And *you're* still an adorable sore loser."

My arms resumed their stone-like position.

"Would it make you feel better to know you're really going to like where we're going?"

"We'll bring chai," Trevor said, coming to Riley's rescue.

Their two cajoling grins nearly garnered one out of me. Almost. It might've worked if I didn't get the feeling there was something more brewing here. A surprise was one thing. A gut-gnawing sense of gravity was another. Especially if it had to do with that thing Riley said needed tweaking.

"We can't just pick up and go on a road trip."

Jaycee scooted forward on the cushion. "Why not?"

I clambered up from the couch in search of some plausible excuse. Or at least a delay. I whirled around. "I haven't packed."

Jaycee pointed to the jumbo suitcases by the door. "Already done."

Okay, now I was really nervous.

"Shouldn't we be planning a graduation party for you? I mean, what about your parents?"

Riley reached me and interlaced his fingers with mine. "Graduation is just another day. There's no need to make a big deal out of it. And I didn't invite my parents."

"What?" I let go of his hands.

"Em, I'm not exactly close to my family. I doubt they'll mind missing it."

"I find that a little hard to believe."

"You don't know my dad."

"I don't have to. Family's family."

He stared at the baseboard. "Not all of us are as lucky as you in that department."

I grabbed his hand again, my heart aching for him and what he'd lost with his dad.

"Besides," he said, "our trip is going to be a perfect graduation present. I don't need anything else."

"Are you sure?"

He wrapped my arms around his back. "I'm positive. It's more than enough. And so is this."

Willpower conquered, I sighed in concession right before his lips warmed mine, every whim of protest devoured by his touch. Trevor cleared his throat while Jaycee flipped over a magazine page in her lap. But Riley didn't tear his gaze away from mine.

He fanned my hair off my shoulders and left his hand on my neck. "I still have something to show you, remember?"

*So that* is *what this is about.* If he needed a road trip to do that, it was more serious than I thought.

He nodded to the door. "C'mon. We've got a long drive ahead of us."

My stomach dropped a little more with each step down the staircase.

Jaycee heaved her monstrous suitcases into Riley's trunk. No telling what she'd packed for me.

In the passenger seat, I grabbed my seat belt and my last chance to protest. "What about Jake? We can't just leave your dog in your apartment by himself."

"My landlord's watching him. Trust me, they're gonna have a blast together. Not to mention Jake's a bit of a seat hog. It would've gotten a little cramped in the back if he'd come."

A laugh followed a visual of Jake climbing all over Trevor with his hot breath in his face. "Totally would've been worth it."

Jaycee bumped her knees into the back of my seat. "Girl, he would've been strapped in the front seat with you. These shoes are too expensive to be mauled by dog paws."

Riley and I exchanged a glance and cracked up. Trevor shoved a wad of gum in his mouth to keep from joining us. At least we had entertainment for the ride.

A few exits down the highway, I twisted to face all three of my companions at once. "You guys realize I'm going to figure out where we're going, right?" I pointed at a sign passing by. "I can read, you know."

"That's debatable," Trevor muttered.

I rolled my eyes at his unsolicited comment. "I'm just saying, it's not like you guys can blindfold me the whole way there or something."

Riley swayed his head. "Not the *whole* way."

"You can't be serious."

Evidently, he was. The last hour of our trip passed in units of sound rather than sights of the highway. The purr of the engine came to a halt.

Riley waved my hands away from the blindfold and scooted it back up my forehead. "Not quite yet."

My car door opened thirty seconds after his door closed. Holding my hand, he guided me up a series of stairs to a leveled platform, where he finally untied the fabric. "Okay," he said. "Open your eyes."

My arms fell limp at my sides.

This couldn't be real.

## 35

## UNVEILED

A REFLECTION of the evergreens behind us filled the oversized windows on the front of the house like a painting. I ran my hand along the intricate blend of wood and stone siding to make sure it was real. "How did you know how to find my uncle's lake house?"

Riley's sideways grin slid right into place. "I can't reveal all my secrets. Surprised?"

Dumbfounded was more like it. "It's unbelievable. I can't believe you thought to bring me here."

"I know this place holds a lot of memories. I wanted to make it special for you." He draped his arm down my back and drew me in front of him. "Which is why your mom and Austin will be here tomorrow."

"What?" How had he arranged all this? "I don't know what to say."

"Say you're ready for an amazing weekend." He

handed me a key and lifted both our bags from the ground.

I reached up to kiss him. "It's already amazing." Amazing how much this place looked just as it had seven years ago. And even more amazing how much it felt like home having Riley there with me.

The cedar interior engulfed us in a fragrant welcome. Trevor and Jaycee scurried past us in a beeline to the deck out back. Couldn't blame them. Nothing compared to the alpine vistas here.

Riley followed me down the hallway into one of the side rooms. The sight of the queen-size bed halted me mid-step. A twinge of heat prickled up my face.

He set my bag on the dresser while keeping his own in his hand and nodded behind me. "Trevor and I are staying across the hall." With a wink, he lugged his bag over his shoulder and crossed into the bedroom opposite ours.

Unpacking could wait. Though still and quiet, the house pulsed with memories. I wandered through every room, gliding my fingers over each piece of furniture.

Among a series of pictures garnishing the fireplace mantle, one caught my eye. I picked up the rugged wooden frame and blew off the dust collected on top of the glass.

A side ponytail and braces. Wow. I couldn't have been older than eleven or twelve. Austin's awkward middle school phase was as funny now as it was then. But nothing gripped me like Dad's face. It was just how I remembered him. Youthful. Vibrant. Chasing us around with endless energy all the way until he carried us to bed after we'd crashed in the middle of the living room or kitchen floor.

Old memories melded into new ones. Maybe there didn't have to be a tug-of-war between the two. Maybe my past and future were really just two colors on the same paintbrush—both adding to the mural Dad had seen all along.

I held the frame tight. Eyes closed, I could almost feel his arms around me the way he had them wrapped around us in the picture. Strong enough to wrestle with Austin, safe enough to protect me from my fears, and tender enough to reignite the look of first love on Mom's face, even after twenty-five years. Arms that had never left me.

Riley came up behind me and rubbed the tops of my shoulders. "He'd be very proud of you. Of the woman you've grown into and the way you've stayed his little girl."

I set the frame back in its place among the other memories, turned, and sank into words I was finally starting to believe.

"You know, I've spent all this time chasing after a way not to disappoint him. So sure I'd find his promises in a degree, a career, even in love like he and Mom had. But I think all he really wanted was for me to choose faith over fear."

I peered at the mantle again. My reflection blinked

back at me from the glass frame. "Guess you were right. Some things are easier to see from the outside looking in."

Riley's fingers slid into my hair behind my ear. "I'll never stop showing you."

Trevor and Jaycee barreled in through the sliding back door. "Two words," Trevor said, face beaming. "Jet skiing."

"Tomorrow, adrenaline junkie." Jaycee bent in half to stretch to her toes. "Hey, Em, will you take me for a hike around the neighborhood? I want to get a little workout in after being cramped in the car all day."

Riley offered an abbreviated version of the kiss they'd interrupted. "Have fun."

"Yeah, don't worry about us," Trevor called from the kitchen. "We'll make ourselves at home."

"That's what scares me." But one step outside made it hard to think of anything other than how much I loved it there. Jaycee sat on the steps and changed her shoes.

An hour later, I collapsed in the same spot. "Man, I forgot how steep those hills are."

Jaycee stretched out her hamstring. "It's good for the glutes."

I fanned my shirt away from the sweat rippling down my chest. "Yeah, well, my glutes might argue otherwise."

"You'll feel better after a shower. C'mon, I'll pick out some clothes for you to wear to dinner."

I stopped on the porch. "Are we going somewhere?"

"No, but we're on vacation. Every night is an excuse for a makeover."

"Ah, Jae, you know how I feel about you turning me into a dress-up doll."

"I prefer the word masterpiece." She batted her extra-long lashes. "Humor me. It's not gonna kill you."

"Fine."

She clapped her fingertips together and prodded me to the bathroom for a twenty-minute treatment of steam relaxation.

I pulled my hair loose from its band on my way to our room. Two steps inside, I stopped. A spaghetti-strap dress, coordinating accessories, and high heels stared at me from the bed. *You've got to be kidding me.* I lifted the dress up.

The effects of my shower therapy? Gone. Slid right out of my grasp with the satiny fabric gliding through my hands.

The girl really was trying to kill me. I shook my head while getting dressed. The things we did for friends.

Inside the kitchen doorway, my ankle bent sideways to the floor. Jaycee glanced up from a tray of fresh fruit. Regaining my balance, I sashayed on display.

Her whistle nearly drowned out the sound of my heels screeching across the tiles. She kissed her finger-tips like an Italian chef. "What did I tell ya? Masterpiece."

I glared at my spiky death traps. "I was thinking more along the lines of a train wreck."

"Oh, never mind about your shoes. You look

stunning."

More like half-naked, but who could disagree with the *What Not to Wear* queen? I slumped over the countertop and snagged an oversized strawberry. "Where are the guys?"

"Trevor ran up to the store, and Riley's out back waiting for you."

My last bite of fruit got lodged in my throat. "What do you mean, *waiting for me?*"

"Waiting, Em. As in, he's standing outside. Alone. Wishing you'd hurry up and go to him." She pushed me toward the dining room.

The back door glided smoothly on its tread at first, then jerked to a stop along with my entire body. Jaycee and I weren't out that long. How did the guys have time to transform the deck into a scene from a movie?

A light summer breeze flickered over wildflowers and candles dressing the patio table. Flames in the granite fire pit danced below cylindrical paper lanterns draped along the arbor's edge. In the center of it all, Riley stood, facing the lake.

He turned at the same time I stepped through the doorway. Another warm breeze skimmed across my shoulders in an invitation to join him.

I ran my fingers down the lapel of a suit that fit him flawlessly. "You look dashing."

He curled me close. "And you are absolutely breathtaking," he whispered just before his lips embraced mine.

I breathed in his Nautica cologne and hung on to his

lapel until my legs solidified again.

His hands glided down to my waist. "Dance with me."

Other than water lapping in the background, stillness hushed over the deck. I glanced at Riley's demo album lying on the table and scanned for any sign of speakers. "Here? There's no music."

His smile said otherwise. "There's always music."

I couldn't deny those eyes, let alone this enchanted dance floor. I tossed my heels to the side and let Riley guide me across the deck.

With my cheek settled over the melody of his heartbeat, time bowed with a smile as it extended me one more dance outside its reins. And before inertia set things back in motion, I fell in love a little more.

Riley kissed the backs of my fingers. "There's still one song I haven't played for you." He led me to a patio chair and retrieved his guitar from the corner behind the table.

"Am I your audience?" I asked, teasing as we used to.

"My audience of one, Emma." He rested his guitar over his leg propped up on the chair beside me. Similar to the way everything used to stop when Dad played, the entire lake paused to listen to Riley the moment his fingers caressed the strings. He began the same song he had on the day we first kissed.

"This song means more to me than any I've written. I want you to really listen to the lyrics. It's something I've been working on for quite a while. Since the day I first saw you."

Heat climbed my cheeks, but I couldn't unlock my gaze from his.

"It's called, 'Unveiled.'"

He said the title with such emotion, his voice gripped me before he sang the first word.

"Whose eyes are these, searching helplessly for joy?

"Eyes that stir a forgotten desire and unveil a hidden void?

"How do they awaken things, things I thought I'd lost?

"And revive my fragile hope in a love worth the cost?

"Why is it a mystery to me? Why does it have to be?

"I wonder if she sees what I see—this hidden treasure, whose eyes unveil me.

"If she could only see what I see."

Leaves rustled in the gentle breeze. The lanterns rocked beams of light across the grains of the deck and clothed Riley in a spotlight he was made for.

"Whose eyes are these, whose power I can't fight?

"In a crowded room, I search for only her eyes tonight.

"How do they see inside me, every defense shattered from the start?

"And find their way deeper into every part of my heart?"

Memories of watching him play that night at Nuts and Jolts blended into the picture of him in front of me now. Artistry clung to his fingers, every feature one with the music.

"Why are these eyes bound by doubt and insecurity, veiled behind a mask of fear, trapped in lies of forgery?

"How can I make her see her life's own tapestry, woven with layers of art and beauty?"

The chords rang with every bit of passion teeming in the way he looked at me.

"Why are these eyes unaware of the courage they've given me to believe in the person she's helped me to be?

"How can I make her see how every part of the journey is leading her closer to her dreams of expectancy?

"Why is it a mystery to me? Why does it have to be?

"Why doesn't she see what I see—this hidden treasure, whose eyes are veiled to me?

"If she could only see what I see."

The chair pressed into my back, his words into my soul. The emotion wrapping around me brimmed above my bottom lashes.

"Help me find a way. There's got to be a way.

"To unveil these blinded eyes, to see what I see looking back at me.

"I will be here waiting—until you find the faith to see —until you see what I see."

The ending to Riley's song resonated across the quiet deck.

He set his guitar aside and brushed his fingertips to my cheek. "Without even knowing it, you've given me the courage to look past the fears holding me back to risk a dream I'd given up on. You helped me see myself through your eyes and taught me what it means to walk by faith. Through doubts. Even failure."

He set my hand over my heart. "There's nothing missing. There never has been. *This* is who you are, Emma."

My body trembled with the earnestness in his words. A familiar grip tightened across my chest with the sound of my own voice echoing what I'd spoken to Riley months before. *"It's kind of sad, but the longer you give in to the label people place on you, the easier it is to believe."*

Whose eyes had I been looking through?

As if hearing my friends and family for the first time, the words they'd spoken over me whispered to my heart, stripping away labels until one final voice broke through. *"Being an artist isn't as much about mastering technique as it is risking the cost of opening your heart to the song you're meant to share."*

Dad had never doubted I'd discover that song. I'd been the one afraid—afraid of what it would sound like, afraid it wouldn't be good enough. But sitting here now, with all my vulnerabilities exposed, my heart erupted with an assurance it'd taken my entire journey to learn. Even broken strings have a song worth sharing.

Riley ran his hand down my hair and onto my cheek. "I'm in love with you, Emma. More than I thought was possible. There never has been and never will be anyone for me but you," he said, repeating words I'd spoken to him many nights before.

"From the day I first saw you on campus, you've

opened my eyes to a world filled with hope. You've taught me to believe in a love worth waiting for. A love I want to spend the rest of my life sharing with you."

Bending to one knee, he lifted up a tiny box with an emerald-shaped sapphire ring seated inside. "Emma— I'm a tea kind of girl—Matthews, will you do me the honor of marrying me?"

Underneath the glow of the stars and the light of Dad's promises, I looked into Riley's eyes and saw a future I no longer needed borrowed faith to believe in. His words were more than an invitation to *ever after*. More than simply a feeling. They extended beyond the borders defined by movies or fairy tales into something that exceeded what I ever thought, hoped, or dreamed love could be. Something I longed for and feared at the same time.

The sight of Riley's demo on the table reignited a tremor in my heart during a moment in which it had no right to exist—unbidden and unjustified, yet equally inescapable. Thoughts of where his record deal would take him swept in. My throat turned to sandpaper. My pulse drummed with an irrepressible sense of urgency until Riley's eyes found mine again.

His faith anchored me. My heart steadied. Every noise quieted except the one song I trusted. Standing there before the promise of always, I prayed for the courage to remain unshaken and spoke the single word that was about to change everything.

"Yes."

# ACKNOWLEDGMENTS

Dave, without your faith in me, this book would still be an unrealized dream. Thank you for your unswerving support, for all those Saturdays you gave me space to write, and for reminding me it was going to be okay in those moments when I doubted it the most.

Jessica, where would Emma and Riley be without your brilliant editorial insights? Thanks for brainstorming with me, pushing me to hone my craft, and encouraging me in the trade. You're amazing.

Erynn, you're a joy to work with. Thank you for your sharp eye, patient instruction, editorial feedback, and those *Princess Bride* comments that kept me smiling.

Shaela, I can't thank you enough for designing such a stunning cover that captures the story and genre perfectly.

Rachel, thanks for enduring the earliest versions of my manuscripts. Your tears, comments, and edits have sown into these stories and into a friendship I'm blessed to have.

Katie—girl, what a ride! Thanks for walking with me through the trenches of so many bottom-of-the-bell-curve days and for all those much-needed Starbucks dates and faith-building prayers.

Nora, there was hardly a day I worked on this series without thinking back to our shenanigans in college. Fairly certain I wouldn't have survived that season without you. Thanks for teaching me what friendship truly means. It's been a source of inspiration for this story and for my life.

Beth, thanks for your feedback on the story, for squealing with me in excitement like we were thirteen again, and for being one of your kid sister's biggest fans.

Mom and Dad, there aren't enough words to thank you for calling forth the gifts you saw in me, for cultivating a love for writing, and for cheering me along a seemingly endless journey.

All my earliest blog followers, Facebook fans, and launch team members, your support and encouragement have kept me going in more ways than you know. I hope this book will be a blessing to you in return.